SCENT OF TERROR

A CHRISTIAN ROMANTIC SUSPENSE

SULLIVAN K9 SEARCH AND RESCUE
BOOK 8

LAURA SCOTT

1

Bailey Adams cast an apprehensive glance over her shoulder as she approached her SUV. The man in the black coat and black cowboy hat still lingered behind her. He hadn't gotten too close, but this was the fourth time she'd seen him in the past two days. Feeling grim, she was forced to admit he was following her.

Why, she had no idea, but she suspected it was related to her husband's death seven months ago. Clark had died in a terrible car crash. One she had not believed was an accident. For weeks, she'd hounded the Cody police to investigate further, but to no avail. They'd repeatedly explained that without evidence of foul play, there was no reason to declare his death suspicious.

Over time, she'd convinced herself they were

right. Now she wasn't sure. She wrenched open her driver's side door and slid—or rather wedged—her pregnant belly in behind the wheel. She tossed her purse onto the seat beside her. After clicking her seat belt into place, she started the engine and put the car in reverse to back out of the parking spot.

The sooner she got away from Black Hat, as she secretly called him, the better.

Bailey gripped the steering wheel tightly as she drove through the recently plowed streets of Cody. They'd gotten an early November snowfall last night, but only about three inches. Could have been worse, as winter was fast approaching. She was grateful for her four-wheel drive to get her to and from work. The small house she'd moved into after the death of her husband, Clark, was on the other side of town from City Hall, where she worked as a receptionist. She loved her cottage, but the fact that it was located in a less populated part of the city meant the plows didn't get there as fast.

When she'd first moved in six months ago, she'd loved the isolation of the place. Now with Black Hat following her around town, she wished she'd chosen something more centrally located. A house with close neighbors rather than beautiful riverside views.

Her coworker, Stacy White, had tried to set Bailey up with her older brother, Todd White.

Bailey hadn't been interested, despite how Todd tended to pop in to see her while she was working. He seemed like a nice enough guy, but the last thing she needed was a relationship. Not when she had a baby on the way.

Still, having a man around would have been nice now that she'd noticed Black Hat following her.

A quick glance at her rearview mirror revealed a black truck keeping pace behind her. The color and model of the vehicle didn't mean much; most people in the area drove trucks or SUVs. And black was hardly an unusual color.

Yet she couldn't help but wonder if Black Hat was behind the wheel of that black truck.

Her thumb hovered over the phone button on her steering wheel. Her older brother, Miles, was in Alaska working the pipeline but had instructed her to call his best friend Trevor Sullivan if she needed anything. Calling the police seemed like overkill. Not only had they thought her paranoid about Clark's so-called accidental death, but Black Hat hadn't committed any crimes against her. Calling his behavior stalking was a stretch. Still, she couldn't quell the feeling of unease.

Maybe it was time to play the best friend card.

The black truck stayed resolutely behind her. Not getting closer, but not taking any turns either. Did he intend to follow her the whole way home?

She swallowed hard and pressed the green phone button. She said, "Call Trevor Sullivan."

After a beat, she heard ringing on the other end of the connection. When a deep husky male voice answered, she let out a silent sigh of relief. "Bailey? Is everything all right?"

"Sorry to bother you, but I think a guy wearing a black hat has been following me." Saying the words out loud made her situation feel all too real. "I mean, it could be my imagination, but I've seen him four times in two days. He wears the same black coat and black cowboy hat. He's never approached me or anything, but he's creeping me out. And now there's a black truck behind me."

"Where are you now?" Trevor asked.

"Heading home." Again, saying the words made her realize that was a stupid move. The last thing she needed was to be in her small cottage alone with this guy possibly following her.

"Don't go home, turn around, and head south toward the ranch." There was a note of steel in Trevor's tone. "I'm jumping in my car now and will meet you halfway."

"Okay." She subtly slowed her speed without hitting her brake. Then she quickly executed a right-hand turn, hoping to catch the driver behind her off guard. The main thoroughfare through town was just a couple of blocks away. She hit the gas, anxious to reach it.

Looking in her rearview mirror, she realized the black truck was no longer behind her. She blew out a sigh, half tempted to turn around to go home. Her feet ached, and she was hungry for dinner.

Yet she had seen the same man four times.

"Trevor? I, uh, may have overreacted." Pregnancy hormones were wreaking havoc with her emotions. "I thought there was a black truck behind me, but now it's gone."

"That's okay. I would still like you to avoid going home." Trevor's calm voice soothed her frayed nerves. "I don't want to risk the guy you saw earlier there waiting for you. Do you remember where the ranch is located?"

"I think so." She'd only been to the Sullivan K9 Search and Rescue Ranch once, and that was before she was married, but she knew the property wasn't too far off Highway 120. "I'm sorry to be a pain. I'm sure you have better things to do than to meet me."

"Nothing at all," Trevor assured her. "I've been meaning to reach out to you anyway. Miles made me promise."

She grimaced, knowing Trevor would honor his friendship with her brother, even if it meant babysitting a hysterical pregnant woman. "I'm fine. Just a little freaked out over Black Hat."

"Black Hat?" Trevor echoed. "Is that your name for him?"

"Yes." She relaxed now that the black truck was no longer behind her. "Maybe he's a friend of Clark's."

"Maybe." Trevor's tone was noncommittal.

She wished she'd moved out of the house she'd shared with Clark sooner, but she hadn't. After he'd died sliding off the highway and down a ravine, she'd felt guilty for being relieved she wouldn't have to divorce him. What kind of wife thought about things like that?

A week after his death, she discovered she was pregnant and felt guilty over her unkind thoughts all over again. For all his faults, she knew Clark would have been thrilled about the baby. A daughter. She'd learned from an ultrasound that she was having a baby girl.

She shoved those memories away with an effort. This wasn't the time to ruminate over her past mistakes. "I guess I can let you go," she said, breaking the silence. "I feel foolish for bothering you."

"I told you it's fine. I'm looking forward to meeting up with you. We'll grab dinner. Where are you now?" Trevor asked.

"Um, I'm heading south on Highway 120." She forced herself to sound cheerful. "It's getting dark, but thankfully, there isn't much traffic on this road."

"Yeah, that's good. I'm on the highway too." If Trevor was annoyed by the idle chitchat, he didn't let on. "We'll probably meet in about fifteen minutes or so."

"Great. I should let you go."

"I don't mind staying connected," Trevor said. "Tell me how you're feeling. Any problems with your pregnancy?"

"Nope, everything is going well. Doctor says I'm healthy as a horse. I'll see you soon, Trevor." Her thumb hovered over the end call button when she noticed a dark vehicle coming up fast behind her. "Wait! I think he's behind me!"

"Are you sure?"

"Yes! A big black truck—" She couldn't finish, as the vehicle behind her abruptly rammed into her. She caught a brief glimpse of the man's face behind the wheel. Then her head jerked, her teeth snapping together from the force of the collision. Her thumb must have ended the connection because she couldn't hear Trevor. Bailey lost her grip on the steering wheel, and the SUV swerved hard to the right. Her purse flew onto the floor. She caught a glimpse of a steep ravine and desperately tried to grab a hold of the wheel, wrenching it with all her strength to the left to avoid the edge.

The truck behind her rammed into her again. Even though she'd half expected it, the impact jarred her enough that she couldn't keep the SUV on the road. With a silent cry, she watched in horror as her car tumbled over the edge of the ravine, crashing into the valley below.

Her last conscious thought was that she'd been right all along. Her husband's death was no accident. It had happened just like this.

And whatever Clark had gotten himself into, she and her baby were in danger now too.

~

"BAILEY? BAILEY, ARE YOU OKAY?" Trevor planted his foot on the gas, increasing his speed. Bailey's last comment about the big black truck worried him.

Waves of guilt washed over him. He shouldn't have asked her to meet up with him on what was mostly a deserted stretch of highway. He should have told her to drive directly to the police station and to wait for him there.

His lapse in judgment may have gotten her into trouble.

"Bailey? Are you there?" When there was still no response, he belatedly realized she'd ended the call. He tried her again. This time, her phone rang multiple times until her voice mail kicked in. He ended the call without bothering to leave a message.

Was Bailey hurt? Or worse? And what about her baby?

Feeling desperate, Trevor pushed his speed even more on the rural highway. He needed to catch up with her.

Archie, his red fox English lab, was in the back crate area. The K9 had his head up and his ears pricked forward, no doubt keying in on the underlying panic in his voice. He spoke to the dog out of habit. "We're going to find her, and she's going to be okay. Right, boy?"

Archie's tail thumped against the bottom of the crate.

Talking to Archie didn't diminish the fear churning in his gut. He peered through the dark, trying to see her silver SUV. But the road before him was empty.

It didn't make any sense that he didn't see her car in the distance. Even at night, her headlights would be easy to spot. How much time had passed since they'd spoken? Five minutes? Ten?

He continued driving as fast as possible. But as mile after mile whizzed by, his sense of dread grew.

Glancing at the clock, he realized he should have caught up with her by now. So why couldn't he see her car? Had she pulled off to the side of the road for some reason? Maybe because she was feeling sick? His oldest sister, Maya, had suffered morning sickness that had lasted all day early in her pregnancy.

What did he know about pregnant women? Just the little he'd absorbed from his sisters' pregnancies. And what he'd been taught in his EMT training.

After a full five minutes went by without seeing her vehicle, he wondered if he'd passed her. Maybe she'd pulled off on one of the two-track roads. Yet even as that thought crossed his mind, he dismissed it. Bailey had wanted to meet him. Even if she wasn't feeling well, she would have stayed on the main highway.

After trying her phone again, he slowed and pulled over. He'd walk along the side of the highway to see if he could find her.

Archie was looking at him as if ready to play the search game. Too bad he didn't have anything belonging to Bailey.

Wait a minute, he did! Trevor leaned across the seat to rummage in the glove box. There was a red scarf in there that he'd kept meaning to return to her. To be honest, he'd had it for a couple of years, after her last visit to the ranch. It was a year before she'd gotten married. Though he knew he should have returned it, he'd simply carried it around in his SUV.

Despite the length of time he'd had the scarf, he

was convinced Archie would be able to home in on Bailey's scent. Their K9s could differentiate between two hundred and three hundred million scents. And Archie had been near Bailey last month.

Trevor pushed out of the driver's side and released the back hatch. Archie jumped down, tail wagging with anticipation. Trevor filled a collapsible bowl with water and offered it to his K9. While his dog drank, he pulled out the backpack and shrugged into it, struggling to arrange the straps over his winter coat. Then he grabbed his first aid kit too. He didn't work as an EMT anymore, but he'd taken on the role of medic during their SAR missions.

Archie finished his water, then looked up at him, waiting for his command.

"Are you ready, boy?" He didn't bother with a bag, simply holding the scarf near Archie's snout. His K9 sniffed it for a long minute, then his tail wagged with excitement. "This is Bailey. You know Bailey, don't you? Search! Search Bailey!"

Archie whirled away and lifted his nose to the air. There was a westerly breeze that Trevor hoped would work in their favor. If Bailey had gone off the road, the wind should have carried her scent toward them, rather than away. Unless, of course, she'd crossed the road and went off on the other side. Swallowing hard, he waited for his K9. After a few seconds, Archie trotted down the road, then veered over to sniff along the west side of the road.

Trevor followed, feeling sick to his stomach. The road had been plowed recently, so he alternated between looking for tire tracks heading off the road and watching Archie. As they made their way down the highway, Trevor lifted his heart in prayer.

Please, Lord Jesus, keep Bailey and her baby safe in Your care!

The prayer didn't take the edge off his fear as he'd hoped. He couldn't bear the thought of anything bad happening to Bailey and her baby. Not just because he'd promised his best friend to look out for her while he was in Alaska.

Because he'd always cared for her. Despite Miles making it clear she was way off-limits.

Archie moved quickly along the side of the road, his nose working eagerly. Trevor scanned the area, searching for signs of Bailey's car. When he saw the indentation of tire tracks going over the edge of the road, his heart sank.

No! Please, Lord, no!

He rushed forward even as Archie was already picking his way down the ravine. Seeing the silver SUV lying upside down confirmed his worst fears.

Trevor slipped and slid down the steep slope, following Archie. His K9 reached the vehicle first, sniffed intently at the driver's side door, then sat and barked.

"Good boy!" He had to force enthusiasm into his tone at his K9's alert and didn't waste time pulling the stuffed otter from his backpack. Their K9s viewed searching as a game that resulted in a reward for a job well done. But his concern for Bailey and her baby overrode everything else.

When Trevor reached the bottom of the ravine, he dropped to his knees to peer into the driver's side window. Bailey was hanging upside down with her seat belt holding her in place. He quickly shrugged out of his pack and found a knife. He half crawled through the broken window. Using his body as a cushion, he cut the straps. Bailey slumped against him without making a sound.

Was she dead? He gently eased her off him, turning her so that she was lying on her back. Normally, it wasn't a good idea to move an injured person, but he didn't have a choice. He pressed his fingers along the side of her neck, searching for a pulse. When he felt her faint heartbeat, he silently thanked God, then reached for his phone.

He should have called 911 right away. He raked his gaze over Bailey's still form as he waited for the dispatcher to answer. Bailey had a cut along the side of her temple, and he suspected there would be bruises to follow from the implosion of the airbags.

He could only pray the airbags had protected her and her baby.

"This is Trevor Sullivan. I'm at the bottom of a ravine with Bailey Adams. She was in a car wreck and is pregnant. Um, maybe seven months along? She's alive, but I need an ambulance here right away!"

"Where exactly is your location?" the dispatcher asked.

"We're on Highway 120 roughly fifteen miles outside of Cody. Please hurry. She's unconscious, and I don't know if her baby is okay."

"I've dispatched a squad and ambulance to your location. Please stay on the line."

"I can't. I need to provide first aid. Just send help." He ended the call, stuffed his phone away, and then crawled back out of the car. He glanced around for a level spot on the ground. He couldn't fully examine Bailey until he got her out of the wreck.

He bent again and ran his fingers along her neck and shoulders. Reaching in, he slipped his hands beneath her back and pulled her through the window, inch by slow inch. He supported her head as much as possible. Her puffy winter coat was snug against her rounded belly, and he couldn't stop thinking about the fate of her baby.

When he had her head and shoulders free, he

repositioned his grip and pulled her the rest of the way out of the wreck. He continued dragging her across the ground to the flat part of the ravine, then grabbed his first aid kit. With the light gone other than what the moon provided, there wasn't a moment to waste.

First, he used his penlight to examine Bailey's pupils. They were equal but a little sluggish to react, indicating she'd sustained a mild head injury. From there, he checked her pulse and blood pressure; both were elevated, which wasn't a surprise. He ran his hands over her extremities but didn't detect an obvious fracture or open injuries.

Lastly, he unzipped her coat and examined her pregnant abdomen. He swallowed hard when he saw the darkening bruise along the lower portion of her belly. Likely from the seat belt. Was it enough to have harmed the baby? He didn't know.

He placed the diaphragm of his stethoscope on her belly, listening intently. Archie stayed close to his side, as if sensing the seriousness of the situation. He didn't hear anything for a long minute, but then he felt the baby kick.

Thank you, God!

He blew out a sigh of relief while continuing to listen. He finally heard what he thought was the rapid beat of the baby's heart. At least, by his count, the rate was faster than Bailey's. It wasn't always easy to tell if he was hearing the mother's heartbeat or the baby's. He pulled the edges of the coat together and zipped it to keep her warm. Then he rummaged in his backpack for a foil blanket. They were thin enough to carry, and the shiny part of the blanket helped reflect the sun to keep a person warm even in the winter.

Unfortunately, there wasn't any sun to help him now.

When he'd done all that he could to mitigate whatever injuries she'd sustained, he took her hand in his. "Bailey? Can you hear me?"

Her eyelids fluttered, but she didn't say anything. Was her head injury worse than he'd thought? He released her to reach for the penlight. Her pupils looked the same as before, but he understood head injuries could evolve over time. Bleeding into the brain could be slow, and sometimes, it took a while to manifest as signs and symptoms.

The only way to know for sure would be to get a CT scan of her head. Something the hospital would do once they'd arrived. Same thing in regard to her pregnancy. Internal bleeding could also take time to impact her baby.

Time was of the essence, but there wasn't anything he could do until the ambulance arrived.

He couldn't see the road from the bottom of the

ravine. Somehow, Bailey had gone over the edge of the road at the steepest part of the culvert.

Then he remembered what she'd said about the black truck. Had the driver pushed her off the road? Had the black-hat guy done this?

"Bailey, you're going to be okay." His training instructor had emphasized the importance of talking to patients. That even if they appeared unconscious, it was possible they could still hear. "Your baby seems fine, and the ambulance is on the way."

Archie pressed his nose against Bailey's cheek.

"You're a good boy, Arch." His voice was low and thick with emotion. A few minutes later, he heard the faint wail of sirens. He leaned over Bailey, stroking her hair from her face. "Do you hear that, Bailey? The ambulance will be here very soon."

Her eyelids fluttered again, and this time her eyes opened. She stared up at him in confusion. "What—happened?"

"You were in a car crash." He searched her gaze. "Do you remember the black truck? Can you tell me if the truck hit you?"

"Truck?" Her brow furrowed, and she looked around at the culvert. "I'm hurt?"

"You're doing okay, but the ambulance will be here soon. We'll take you to the hospital where they can make sure you don't have any internal bleeding." He placed his hand on her belly. "I felt your baby kick, though, so I think you're doing okay."

"Really?" She winced as she lifted her hands and placed them on her abdomen.

"Yes, I felt the baby kick. Are you having a boy or a girl?" He remembered Miles saying something about a baby girl but had mentioned that she'd need a follow-up ultrasound to be sure. To his shame, Trevor hadn't asked about the baby's gender during their last conversation.

"Oh, I feel the baby moving." Her eyelids drifted closed. "Tired . . ."

Head injuries could cause sleepiness. "Bailey, open your eyes for me. I want to check your pupils again."

Her eyes opened, and again, she stared at him in confusion. "You know me?"

That took him aback. "Yes, of course. You're Bailey Adams, Miles's little sister."

She didn't say anything for a long moment. "Bailey," she finally repeated.

His concerns about her head injury ratcheted up several notches. He used his penlight to examine her pupils. He took his time lest he miss something.

They looked the same as before. Which was good and bad. Why was she so confused?

"I hear sirens," Bailey murmured.

"Yes, help will be here soon." Archie pressed his

nose against her belly, and she looked at the dog with a soft smile.

"What's your dog's name?"

Huh? He frowned. "Archie. You remember my K9, Archie, don't you?"

A flash of annoyance crossed her features. "How would I know your dog when I don't know you?"

The tiny hairs on the back of his neck lifted in alarm. "I'm Trevor Sullivan. Your brother's best friend. You've known me for years. Since we were kids."

At that, her eyes widened. "I don't understand. What's wrong with me?"

He slowly shook his head. "Don't stress. You've been through a traumatic event. You'll remember everything soon." He'd wanted to reassure her, but deep down, he wasn't convinced. He had heard of patients suffering temporary amnesia but had never experienced the phenomenon.

Until now.

2

———————

She struggled to hold her emotions in check as the EMTs lifted her onto the gurney. But deep down, she was terrified. Her sore muscles were beginning to make themselves known; she felt as if she'd been pounded by a gorilla. The EMTs had put a neck brace on her, so she couldn't see much of her car other than the wheels, which were pointing at the sky.

How had she ended up in a car crash? And why couldn't she remember anything? The nice-looking guy, Trevor, had called her Bailey. She had to admit the name sounded right.

He'd also claimed she'd known him for years. Years! So why couldn't she remember? Splaying her hands over her stomach, she fought to remain calm.

She was pregnant and equally terrified of losing her baby.

"I'll get your stuff out of the SUV and follow the ambulance to the hospital." Trevor's concerned expression made her fear she was hurt worse than he'd let on. "You're in good hands. Just try to relax."

She held his gaze for a long moment, wishing he would ride with her. But then she remembered his dog. "Okay. Thank you."

"I'll be there soon. You won't be alone for long." Trevor flashed a reassuring smile as the two EMTs carried her up the steep slope to the waiting ambulance. Staring up at the sky, she tried to do as Trevor suggested. She drew deep breaths, regulating the beat of her heart. Stress was bad for the baby. How she knew that, she had no idea.

Once she was in the ambulance, she tolerated the monitor being attached to her chest along with the IV they placed in her arm. "Are you in pain?" the EMT asked.

"I don't want anything for pain. Not when it may impact the baby."

The EMT nodded. "Okay, but if the pain gets too bad, you need to let me know."

That wasn't happening, so she didn't bother to respond. The pain was tolerable. The strange sense of urgency wasn't. She couldn't shake the sense there was something important she needed to do.

What was it? Why couldn't she remember?

The ambulance trip to the hospital seemed slow. She could feel the ambulance moving, though, so she assumed it was just that she was anxious to get there. Her main priority was to make sure her baby was okay. That she wouldn't deliver her baby prematurely.

She closed her eyes, taking another slow deep breath. The EMT was monitoring her closely, and she hoped that meant her baby was stable too.

From the moment she arrived in the emergency department, though, she was surrounded by medical professionals. Many greeted her by name, and she felt bad she couldn't respond in kind.

"My baby." She kept her hands on her belly as if that alone would be enough to protect her daughter. "Please make sure my baby isn't hurt."

"We will, don't worry." A nurse by the name of Emily smiled reassuringly. "Your vitals are stable, and we'll get a fetal heart monitor strapped to your abdomen soon."

"Thank you." Bailey had to close her eyes against the harsh overhead lights. Her head throbbed, more painful than the rest of her body. The light made her headache ten thousand times worse.

More wires were attached to her body, including

the promised fetal heart monitor. She tried to turn her head, but the neck collar held her back. She was tempted to rip it away so she could see her baby's heartbeat for herself, but instead, she tried to remain calm. Hopefully once they took X-rays, she wouldn't need it anymore.

"I'm an EMT, and I need to see her. I promised!" A deep male voice reached her ears.

"I know Trevor, he's my brother-in-law. Give him a minute, okay?" The female voice sounded like Emily's.

Bailey realized that not being able to remember forced her to use additional senses to navigate her surroundings. She frowned, then relaxed when she saw Trevor's face leaning over her. When he took her hand, she gripped it tightly, feeling as if he were a buoy in a turbulent sea.

"Hey, Bailey, I wanted you to know I'm here. I have your purse and phone from the car."

"I'm glad." She stared up at him for a long moment. Again, she felt there was something important she needed to tell him. "Thank you."

"Excuse me, I need to take some blood." One of the nurses nudged Trevor aside. He squeezed her hand, then released her to give the medical staff room to work.

Bailey closed her eyes again, barely feeling the

pinprick of the needle. She was oddly comforted by Trevor's presence. He seemed concerned about her and so incredibly kind.

Too bad she couldn't remember him.

"We need to get a CT scan," a male voice said. "I know she's pregnant, but that's a risk we'll need to take."

Bailey's eyes shot open. Risk? She didn't want to do anything that would risk her baby. "No. Please don't."

An older man's face filled her field of vision. "Ms. Adams, we need to make sure you don't have any internal bleeding. That would be far more harmful to the baby than the scan itself. We've estimated you're thirty weeks along, which means the baby is pretty much developed by now. And just to be sure, I've checked with the OB doctor on call. He's agreed with our plan."

Tears filled her eyes. "I don't want anything to harm my baby."

"I know, but trust me, this is important, or we wouldn't do it."

She reluctantly nodded. He had a point about the bleeding. She couldn't lose any blood as that would absolutely have a negative impact on the baby. Moments later, she was rolling through the hallways to the radiology department for a CT scan.

She hadn't wanted them to remove the fetal monitor, but Emily assured her the baby's heartbeat was stable and that the OB doctor on call was on the way in from home to examine her. Both comments brought a measure of comfort.

The scan seemed to take forever. Forced to stay still, she concentrated on taking slow breaths to calm herself. Her head pounded with every beat of her heart. The table beneath her moved slowly through the scanner, and despite her discomfort, she was grateful to have this level of medical technology available to her.

That thought made her wonder if she had medical insurance. Surely she had a job? She strained to remember, but that only made her headache worse. After a few minutes, she gave up. Whatever job she had, it seemed logical she'd be granted a couple of days off after being in a car crash.

"Good news," Emily greeted her when she returned to the ER from radiology. "Your neck and spine have been cleared. We can get rid of that neck collar now."

"I'm so glad." The moment the collar was removed, she turned to look at her surroundings. To her surprise, Trevor and his beautiful K9 were in the corner of the room. Trevor was seated in a chair, with his dog . . . What had he said the dog's name was? Archie. Archie was stretched out at his feet near what looked like a purse.

Trevor smiled when he saw her glancing over.

"What about internal bleeding?" She studied Emily's compassionate face. "Have I been cleared that way too?"

"The doctor is reading your scan now. The spinal cord was one of our primary concerns. With internal bleeding a close second," Emily hastily added. "Your vitals are stable, so that's a really good sign."

Satisfied, Bailey closed her eyes and tried to relax. There weren't as many medical staff hovering around her bedside any longer. Apparently, the worst was over.

Well, except for the fact that there was a giant black hole where her memory should have been. The need to sleep hit hard.

Maybe once she'd gotten some rest, her memory would return.

TREVOR HAD STAYED out of the way as promised, but it wasn't easy to sit there doing nothing while the medical team worked on Bailey. He reached down to stroke Archie's fur. He was glad Emily Ross, his brother-in-law Doug Bridge's sister, was on duty tonight. Emily and Owen spent a lot of time on the Sullivan K9 Search and Rescue Ranch with their K9 in training, a chocolate lab named Bear. The puppy was growing by leaps and bounds, a born SAR dog. Bear loved playing the search game. Of course, Trevor was partial to his Archie, but really, all the K9s on their ranch were amazing.

The rapid yet steady beat of the baby's heart on the monitor was also reassuring. He silently thanked God for keeping Bailey and her baby safe. The bad car wreck reminded him of the crash that had killed Bailey's husband, Clark. He'd attended the guy's funeral seven months ago.

The parallel crashes bothered him, especially when Bailey had mentioned the black truck was behind her. Trevor was torn between staying to support Bailey as promised and returning to the scene of the crash to search for evidence.

Not that he was a cop, like his sister Maya and his two brothers-in-law, Doug Bridges and Griffin Flannery who were federal agents. When the cops had arrived with the ambulance at the scene, Trevor had mentioned the conversation he'd had with Bailey to Cody police officer Heath Anderson. Heath had promised to inform his boss, Sergeant Howell, about the suspicious circumstances of the crash. The Sullivan family had a great relationship with the Cody police department, especially since

Doug had uncovered a crooked cop back in January. In addition, most of the local police departments referred citizens with missing family members or friends to the Sullivan ranch. Their business had boomed over the past year. So much so that they were anxiously awaiting Owen and Emily's addition to the team. When Bear was ready, they'd be placed in rotation.

Trevor debated calling Doug or Griff about his concerns regarding the crash, then decided against it. There wasn't anything either of them could do now. He had to trust the Cody crime scene techs would do a good job of examining Bailey's SUV. He really needed to call her brother Miles but hesitated to do that until the OB doctor had examined Bailey.

He'd rather call Miles with good news, on the heels of the bad news of the crash. With Alaska being two hours earlier than their current time, he didn't have to rush to make the call.

"Ms. Adams?" A man in his mid-fifties entered the room. The way the guy glanced first at the fetal monitor, confirmed his thought that he was the OB doc on call. He then turned his attention to Bailey. "I'm Dr. Dailey. I understand you were in a car crash?"

"Yes." Bailey's voice was soft. She turned to look at the doctor through narrowed eyes. Trevor realized the light was making her head hurt and jumped up to turn it off. There was enough ambient light from the other rooms to see clearly. Bailey flashed a grateful smile. "Thank you, my head hurts."

Dr. Dailey glanced at Trevor, then back at Bailey. "I've taken a moment to review your chart. Your scans are clear, no signs of internal bleeding, which is great news. And from what I'm seeing here, your baby's heartbeat appears stable. Maybe a tad higher than normal, but that could be related to your anxiety."

"I'm trying to stay calm." Bailey's brow furrowed with concern. "It's not easy, but I'm doing my best."

"Oh, I know you are. It's not your fault. Once the adrenaline wears off, I'm sure your baby's heart rate will return to normal." Dr. Dailey removed a stethoscope from around his neck and listened to Bailey's heart and lungs. Then he moved the diaphragm to her abdomen. He listened for a while, glancing at the fetal monitor, then nodded and straightened. Draping the stethoscope around his neck, he gently palpated her abdomen. "Let me know if anything hurts."

"It doesn't." Then she winced. "Except for that area. It's tender where the seatbelt was."

"I noticed a bruise forming on her lower abdomen, where the seat belt had been." Trevor stood to join the conversation. "I'm hoping that won't cause any issues for her or the baby."

Dr. Dailey smiled. "Yes, I can imagine there will be bumps and bruises from the crash. The good news is that the baby is well cushioned with amniotic fluid. Your wife and baby will be just fine." Before Trevor could correct his assumption, the doctor turned to Bailey. "I want you to let me or your regular OB doctor know if you experience any sharp pain or bleeding, especially over the next few days. That could be an indication the placenta is pulling away from the uterine wall. If that happens, you need to get to the hospital as soon as possible. It's critical we deliver the baby immediately."

Bailey's wide eyes darted to Trevor's. Trevor nodded in understanding. An abruption of the placenta was an emergent condition covered in his EMT training. "We will absolutely get back here if there's any change in her condition."

"Good." Dr. Dailey took a step back. "I consider your condition to be stable. Just be sure to pay attention to any new signs or symptoms."

"Does she need to stay on bed rest?" Trevor asked.

Dr. Dailey looked thoughtful. "Not necessarily, but don't do anything crazy like run a marathon or do jumping jacks. Take it easy for a few days and I'm sure you'll be fine."

"Thank you." Bailey's eyes still held a note of alarm. "I don't run or do jumping jacks, so that shouldn't be a problem."

Dr. Dailey smiled and patted her hand. "You should follow up with your own OB doctor in a few days."

"We'll make sure of that," Trevor agreed. At this point, it was easier to play along that they were a couple. He didn't intend to leave Bailey's side. "Thanks for coming in."

"Not a problem." Dr. Dailey turned and retreated from the room. Since Bailey still looked upset, he went over to take her hand. Archie stood, stretched, and came to stand beside him.

"You're going to be okay, Bailey. I'm trained as an EMT and know what to look for. You just need to do your part by paying attention to what your body is telling you. If there's any change at all, you need to let me know."

"Okay. But what about my memory?" Her blue eyes were full of anguish. "When will that return to normal?"

"I'm not sure." He frowned and glanced out to where Emily was chatting with Dr. Dailey. "I'll ask for a neurosurgery consult. They're the experts in treating concussion and amnesia." He couldn't fault the staff for making Bailey's physical condition and that of her baby a priority. Now that life-threatening injuries had been ruled out, he was anxious to understand what the treatment recommendation would be for her memory loss.

If there even was a treatment option.

"Trevor?" Bailey's hand tightened on his. "Where's my husband?"

His gaze sharpened on hers. "You remember Clark?"

"No, but I assume I'm married." She splayed her hands over her abdomen. "I wouldn't be pregnant if I wasn't."

She sounded sure, which again proved her basic personality hadn't changed. "He died about seven months ago."

"Oh. So that's why I'm not wearing a ring." She frowned, then asked, "What happens if they discharge me? I don't even know where I live."

"I do. And don't worry, Archie and I will be staying with you for the next few days." He glanced down at Archie, glad he always kept an overnight bag, along with extra food for his K9, in his SUV. "We won't leave you alone."

"I appreciate that. I can't lie, I'm afraid to be alone." She grimaced and shifted positions on the gurney. "I don't even know where I work to call in sick tomorrow."

"I'll help you with that." He pulled out his

phone. "I need to call your brother to let him know you're okay."

"I have a brother?" Her voice rose in agitation.

"Yes, Miles. He's two years older than you are." He cupped her hand between his. "Remember, I told you I was good friends with your brother at the scene of the accident. That's how I know you."

"That's right. You did say that. But I feel like I should know my own brother." Her distress tugged at his heart.

"Take it easy, try not to stress. Remember what Dr. Dailey said."

"I know, I know." As if to prove it, Bailey took a slow deep breath. "Go ahead and call him."

He held her hand for a long moment before releasing it. He took a step back, almost tripping over Archie. "Stay, boy." He dug his phone out of his pocket, then thought better of making that call in front of Bailey. "Actually, I need to take Archie outside. He may need to get busy."

"Okay." A small smile tugged at the corner of her mouth. "He's so pretty."

"That he is." He knew Bailey had always loved Archie, and seeing her react the same way now was heartening. "Come, Archie."

He headed out of the emergency department, stopping briefly by Emily. "Bailey still has amnesia. I assume you're getting a neurosurgery consult for her?"

"Yes, Dr. Kline is on the way." Emily frowned. "I have never cared for a patient with amnesia. It's rare."

"I know, me either." He grimaced and gestured to Archie. "I'm taking him outside to feed him and to make a few calls. I'll be back soon."

"Okay." Emily leaned over to pat Archie. "Seeing him makes me miss Bear."

"Bear is in good hands with Owen." Trevor continued through the department until he was outside. He led Archie to his SUV and opened the back. He opened the container of dog food and filled a collapsible bowl. Then he made Archie sit. His dog stared up at him, waiting for the signal. It was part of their training that the dogs only ate when their handler allowed them to. "Go get it, boy."

Archie pounced on the dish like he was starving. Out of all the K9s on the ranch, Archie ate the fastest. It was almost comical how the dog attacked his food as if it might disappear if he didn't gulp it down fast enough. Normally, Trevor used a dish with grooves in it to force Archie to slow down. But he hadn't packed it.

"Easy, boy." He bent to pat the dog. Archie looked up at him for a moment, then went back to scarfing down his food. When he'd finished, Trevor led him to a grassy area so his K9 could get busy. With his dog cared for, he pulled out his phone. Miles answered on the first ring.

"Hey, Trev, what's up?"

"I'm calling because Bailey was in a car crash. She's okay," he hastily added. "Her scans are clear; she has no internal bleeding or fractures. The OB doc was here to see her as well. He examined her and has deemed her baby is fine."

"That's good to hear, thanks for letting me know the good news. But what happened?" Miles asked. "Bailey is such a careful driver. She wouldn't risk driving on slippery roads without a good reason."

Trevor stared out into the darkness, trying to decide how much to tell his friend. He didn't want Miles to worry, especially since he was so far away. He didn't want to bring up the fact that Bailey may have been rammed off the road or that she was still suffering from amnesia. "I'm not sure, but I will stay with her for the next few days. Thankfully, our SAR calls have slowed down a bit, so it won't be a problem."

"Do you think I need to quit my job and fly home?" Miles asked.

"No, that's not necessary." He hoped and prayed he wasn't lying. The fact was that having Miles there wouldn't help much. Trevor could watch over Bailey, and he could enlist the help of his family to figure out what was going on as far as the mysterious black truck. He knew Miles needed to keep this job and risked losing a large bonus if he didn't fulfill his contract. "I promise I'll stay close. If her condition changes, I'll call you."

"Yeah, okay." Miles sounded mollified. "Thanks, Trev. I owe you one."

"No worries. Besides, you'd do the same for me."

That made Miles laugh. "As if I'd have to with your eight siblings tripping over themselves to watch over you. I guess that's one of the benefits of having a large family."

Since that was true, he couldn't argue. "One quick question, though. What do you know about Clark's death?"

"What do you mean?" Miles sounded surprised. "The cops deemed it an accident."

"That's what I thought." He would have pressed for more but didn't want to raise Miles's suspicions. "Just checking. I'll be in touch again tomorrow."

"Thanks, Trev. Tell Bailey I love her."

"Will do." Trevor ended the call, then went over to clean up after Archie. He couldn't help but wonder if Bailey's husband's death was connected to her recent crash. Without Bailey's memory, though, finding a link would be difficult.

But not impossible. Once she was discharged,

he'd take her home. Maybe he'd uncover some clues there that would help.

He sent a quick text to Doug and Griff, asking if they could dig into Clark Miller's background when they had time. Bailey had taken back her maiden name after losing Clark. He was on his way back into the hospital when Griff called.

"What's going on?" Griff asked.

Trevor sighed and quickly provided the scant details he had. "I know it's not much, but I'm concerned about Bailey. First, she saw some guy following her, called him Black Hat because he wore all black, including a black cowboy hat. Then she sees a black truck behind her and ends up upside down at the bottom of a culvert."

"Yeah, that does sound suspicious. I'll see what I can dig up. Keep your phone on." With that, Griff ended the call.

Satisfied he'd done what he could for the moment, Trevor called Archie over and headed inside. His K9 eagerly followed. True to her word, Emily had contacted the neurosurgeon who was at Bailey's bedside when he came in.

"I'd suggest putting yourself in familiar places," the doc was saying. "Most patients remember on their own. If yours hasn't returned in a few days, you should return to the hospital so we can do another scan."

"Thanks, doctor." Bailey's lips smiled, but her gaze remained concerned. She apparently wasn't thrilled with his response.

"You may want to see a psychiatrist," he added. "Stress accompanied with trauma can prevent memories from returning. It's almost as if your mind doesn't really want to remember and has put a block in place to prevent that from happening."

"But I do want to remember." Bailey's voice rose. "I feel like I need to remember. That there's something important that I need to remember."

"Easy," Trevor warned. He found her comment interesting and wondered if her mind was protecting some secret. "Maybe you're pushing too hard."

The neurosurgeon eyed him for a moment, then nodded. "That's true. The more you relax, the more likely you'll remember."

Bailey didn't say anything more, but her expression spoke volumes. As the doctor left, Emily returned.

"Okay, I have your discharge orders," she said cheerfully. "You're to take it easy, which includes staying off work for at least three days, and return to the hospital if you have any changes in your condition."

"I understand." Bailey still didn't look satisfied.

Then her expression softened. "Thanks for everything."

"You're welcome. I'll leave you in Trevor's capable hands." Emily bent over to remove the cardiac leads from Bailey's chest and the fetal monitor from around her abdomen. He turned away to give her privacy, bending to give his K9 some attention.

When Bailey was dressed in her clothes and ready to go, he grabbed her purse and escorted her outside. His SUV was parked close to the building. When she was settled in and Archie was in the back, he slid in behind the wheel and started the engine.

"How far away do I live?" she asked, as he pulled out of the parking lot.

"Not too far." For a moment, he considered taking her to a hotel. Then he remembered the doctor's suggestion that she be in familiar surroundings. "I know the way."

She fell silent, as if the events of the evening were catching up with her. He glanced at her often as he drove. When he pulled up to her small house, she looked at it with interest.

"I live here?"

"Yep." He tried not to be disappointed that she didn't remember it. He opened the back hatch for Archie, then went around to help her out. She dug in her purse and pulled out a key ring.

When they reached the front door, he put the

key in the lock, then froze. The door hadn't been locked. Asking Bailey if she remembered locking it wouldn't help, but he quickly put his hand out to stop her from coming too close. "Stay back."

"Why?" She sounded cranky. He stepped in front of her and pushed the door open.

The house had been tossed. Her belongings were turned over, broken or searched. It was confirmation for what he'd already suspected. Bailey's going off the road was no accident.

Someone had tried to kill her.

3

____

Irritable, Bailey was about to push past Trevor, when he turned and grabbed her arm. "We need to get out of here."

"Why?" When he moved out of the way, she glimpsed the mess. Although *mess* was too mild of a term for the mass destruction she saw in the house behind him. She'd hoped to remember where she lived, but she didn't. The place didn't feel like home.

Especially now. Her blood ran cold as realization sank deep. This wasn't the work of troubled teens. There was something bigger going on here. "I don't understand. Who did this? And why?"

"I wish I knew. We'll call the police on the way." Trevor tugged on her arm. Archie sniffed around the doorway with interest. "Please, Bailey, get in the car."

"I'm supposed to surround myself with familiar things." Even as she uttered the protest, she knew it was fruitless. Whatever familiar items she might have had were probably gone. Or destroyed beyond recognition. She reluctantly turned and walked back down to the SUV. Trevor opened the passenger door for her.

"Stay here and call 911. I'm taking Archie inside." He shut the door and turned away. She heard him say, "Come, Archie."

She suddenly wondered if she had a room set up for the baby. It would seem like a normal thing to do. Had the person who'd trashed her home ruined the nursery as well? Useless tears pricked her eyes. She blinked them back with an effort.

Pulling out her phone, she dialed 911. The dispatcher answered almost right away. "What's your emergency?"

"There's been a break-in at my home." Bailey stared at the doorway where Trevor and Archie had gone. "I need the police to come right away."

"What's your address?"

"Um." Good question. She had no idea, then she recalled Trevor turning onto Windmill Lane. "My name is Bailey Adams. I live at the end of Windmill Lane."

There was a long pause. She heard the clicking

of a keyboard in the background. "I have you at 207 Windmill Lane. Is that correct?"

How should she know? But, of course, she didn't say that. Better to go along with whatever information this woman had on file. "Yes, please have the police respond as soon as possible."

"I've dispatched a unit to your location. Are you safe?"

Bailey almost barked out a laugh. She didn't even know her own name, much less if she was safe. Again, she strove to remain calm. Resting one hand on her belly, she continued watching the front door. "I'm with Trevor and his K9, Archie."

"That's good. Officer Riley will be there soon."

"Thanks." Bailey ended the call and lowered the phone. Her head hurt, her muscles ached, and her home had been trashed. She couldn't imagine this day could get any worse.

The nagging feeling that she had something important to do wouldn't leave her alone. It was like a constant buzzing in the back of her mind. Her empty memory mind.

When the front door swung open revealing Trevor and Archie, she sighed in relief. There was something in Trevor's hand as he strode toward the SUV. He opened the back hatch for his K9, then opened her door.

"I found this." He handed her a photograph. "The frame was broken and taken apart, so I just have the picture."

"Thank you." She stared at the image of two people standing side by side. A taller man had his arm wrapped around her shoulders. He must be her brother, Miles.

Trevor waited a beat, then closed her door and ran to the other side to get in behind the wheel. He glanced at her as he started the engine. "Do you recognize him?"

"No." She desperately wished she did. What kind of person can't remember their own sibling?

"That's okay." Trevor reached over to touch her hand. "Don't push it."

Easy for him to say. He wasn't the one living with a black void in his mind. Swallowing her frustration, she sighed. "I called the police. They should be here soon."

"Good." Trevor backed out of the driveway, then pulled over to the side of the road. Hearing the wail of sirens, she turned to see the red and blue flashing lights coming down Windmill Lane.

"The dispatcher asked for my address." Her voice hitched, and she steadied it with an effort. "I couldn't even tell her the house number."

Trevor winced. "I'm sorry. I should have made the call."

She tapped the photo. "Is this why you went back inside?"

He nodded. "That and I wanted Archie to sniff around the place. He's a great tracker. I'm hoping that he'll alert us if he catches the scent of the bad guy."

The idea of a K9 doing that intrigued her. "He can really isolate one scent like that?"

"Absolutely." Trevor had to raise his voice to be heard over the sirens. The Cody police cruiser pulled into the driveway. "Sit tight. I'll be back." Trevor slid out of the car, leaving the engine running.

Bailey was suddenly annoyed at how Trevor was taking charge here. This was her house, wasn't it? Just because she didn't remember it didn't mean she shouldn't be involved in what had happened.

Releasing her seatbelt, she pushed out of the passenger seat to join Trevor and Officer Riley.

"I don't know the time frame when this may have happened," Trevor was saying. "Bailey works a nine-to-five job at City Hall as a receptionist."

She did? That was helpful to know.

"I spoke to Bailey while she was heading home, that's when she mentioned thinking someone was following her. I convinced her to turn around to meet me on the highway instead. That's when she ended up in the culvert. This damage could have happened anytime between nine in the morning and now. Although I didn't see anything suspicious when we drove up, so I suspect he's long gone."

"Is anything missing?" Officer Riley asked.

Bailey closed her eyes, wishing for the zillionth time that she could remember.

"I'm afraid we won't know that for a while," Trevor said cryptically. "I can say the TV is still inside, so whoever did this didn't bother to steal it. There could be other items missing. I'm not sure. My priority is to take Bailey someplace safe."

Officer Riley's gaze dropped to her pregnant belly. "Of course. That makes sense. We'll take the report and board up the house until you can get a chance to look around."

"Thanks, Jeff." Trevor took her hand, a gesture she found comforting. Her earlier annoyance faded. Trevor was doing his best to support her. Maybe it was only because he was her brother's friend, but she had to admit she was glad she wasn't navigating this mess alone. "We'll let you know if there's anything has been taken."

"Thanks. Where will you be staying in the meantime?" Jeff Riley asked.

"I'm not sure." Trevor's evasive answer surprised her. "Call the ranch if you need to reach us."

The ranch? Bailey glanced at Trevor in surprise. She hadn't realized he lived on a ranch.

Or rather, she hadn't *remembered* he lived on a ranch.

She was suddenly struck by a wave of sheer exhaustion. Her body craved sleep. But then her baby somersaulted in her womb, making her smile. She might need rest, but the baby was active.

A prelude to what her life would be like once the baby was born.

A fresh wave of terror washed over her. What if her memory hadn't returned by then? What if she would have to navigate her new life as a single mother without knowing the people around her? How on earth would she manage?

"Bailey?" Trevor still held her hand and must have sensed her tension. "Are you okay?"

With Officer Riley there, she forced a nod. "Yes. Of course."

Trevor's expression indicated he knew she was lying, but he didn't say anything. Instead, he turned toward the SUV. "Let's get out of here."

She followed him back to the SUV. Archie was still in the back, his dark eyes watching them. He was unusually quiet for a dog, she thought as she set her purse down and buckled in. Normal dogs barked at strangers.

Trevor didn't say anything until they were back in downtown Cody. "We'll stay at the Elk Lodge, if that's okay with you."

"Um, sure. But I'm not sure if I have enough money to pay for a room." She had no idea what her financial situation was, other than her home was cute but not extravagant.

"I'll take care of it. Don't worry about that." He frowned, then added, "I want you to relax, Bailey. To rest your mind as much as possible. Maybe once you get a good night's sleep, your memories will return."

"I hope so." She tried to sound positive, but it wasn't easy. Swallowing hard, she knew she needed to take his advice.

Stress wasn't good for her or the baby.

The Elk Lodge was nice, with its warm welcoming blaze in the massive stone fireplace taking up one whole wall in the lobby. She was surprised when Trevor asked for a suite. And that the clerk didn't bat an eye when she saw Archie standing beside them.

The suite seemed like an extravagance, but she bit back a protest. It was nice of Trevor to make arrangements that offered her privacy. Not that any man would be interested in a pregnant woman. She felt like a whale and wished she had a change of clothes as she followed Trevor and Archie down the hall to a room on the first floor.

"You take the bedroom. It has its own bathroom." Trevor nodded toward the doorway leading to a separate room. "Archie and I will stay out here."

"Thanks." She quickly ducked into the room, eager to make use of the bathroom. The fluids the hospital had given her had worked their way through her system. When she returned, she saw Trevor standing near the window, looking outside. He turned to face her, and his smile made her heart do a crazy thump. Why was she noticing how attractive he was? She had much bigger issues to worry about.

"Are you hungry?" he asked. "We can order room service."

"I could eat. My stomach feels a bit queasy." She sank onto the sofa. "I didn't know you lived on a ranch. In fact, I don't know anything about you."

Trevor nodded. "Let's order food, then I'll fill you in."

She scanned the menu. "Grilled cheese sounds good."

"Great." He rose and placed their order. Then he crossed over to sit beside her. Archie was stretched out on the floor in front of the door like a furry sentinel. "I'm the second youngest of nine kids. We lost our parents six years ago in a plane crash and have turned their former upscale dude ranch into a mission of doing search and rescue for the community."

"Nine kids!" She couldn't imagine.

"Yeah, I know." He grinned. "Maya is the oldest, she's married to Doug Bridges who works for the DEA, and they're expecting their first baby around Christmas. My brother Chase is second oldest, he and his wife, Wynona, have a son, Eli, and they're expecting after the first of the year. Jessica is next, she's married to charter pilot Logan, and she is also expecting."

She placed a hand on her belly, thinking she'd be in good company with his sisters.

"My brother Shane is fourth in line; he's married to Libby. My sister Alexis is married to Griffin Flannery; he's an FBI agent."

Bailey found that interesting. Maybe that was why Trevor carried a gun and seemed to think and act like a cop.

"My twin brothers, Joel and Justin, are next. Joel just married Trina, and they have a son, Ben, which is really Trina's nephew they adopted. And Justin married Raine two weeks ago."

"Everyone's married but you?"

"Me and my younger sister Kendra are still single. We're starting to feel a bit left out," he said dryly. "I must admit, I've come to love my new in-laws. For years, we've dedicated our lives to serving the community, which has been amazing. But it's also nice to see the Sullivan family expanding. I believe our parents are smiling down from us in heaven."

That was a nice image. Then she remembered her nurse. "How does Emily fit in?"

"Oh yeah, I almost forgot about Emily and Owen. Emily is Doug's sister. She and Owen have a chocolate lab puppy named Bear and are training him as a SAR K9. Owen does construction and has been helping with updating the cabins at the ranch as our family expands."

It was a lot of names, considering she couldn't remember her own. "I hope there's not a quiz."

"Nope. I'm only telling you about my family because I want you to feel comfortable with me." Trevor's gaze turned somber. "I will never hurt you, Bailey. And I promise to protect you and your baby."

Tears pricked her eyes. "Thank you." Pregnancy hormones or a delayed reaction from her amnesia —either way, she was grateful for Trevor's support.

And she wished more than anything she could remember him.

ARCHIE JUMPED up to stare at the door seconds before he heard a knock. His K9 let out two staccato barks, but since it wasn't his alert, Trevor wasn't worried. Still, he took a moment to use the peephole, before opening the door.

"Room service?" The young man held a tray.

"I'll take it." Trevor set their meals aside, pulled cash from his wallet, and tipped him. "Thanks."

"Have a good night." The kid pocketed the cash and left without looking back. Trevor glanced at Archie who'd already lost interest in the delivery boy.

"Smells good," Bailey said, struggling to get up from the sofa. He would have offered her a hand, but she managed on her own. "I hope the grilled cheese settles my stomach."

He nodded as he uncovered the dishes. His burger was huge compared to her grilled cheese. He took a seat beside her and reached for her hand. "I'd like to say grace."

"Oh, ah, okay." Bailey looked adorably flustered. "I guess I didn't remember that," she quipped.

He gently squeezed her hand, then bowed his head. "Lord Jesus, we thank You for keeping Bailey and her baby safe in Your care. We ask You to bless this food and to continue to cover us with Your strength and protection. Amen."

"Amen," Bailey murmured. She glanced over at him. "I feel bad that I forgot to pray."

He hesitated, unsure how to respond. He'd always prayed before meals, that was something ingrained in the Sullivan family since they were little kids. But he knew Miles and Bailey weren't raised as believers. "I don't think you need to feel bad for having a head injury. Just know that God is watching over you and your baby. If you need extra support, I hope you lean on Him in prayer."

"Thanks. I will." She seemed to accept his advice in stride. Maybe she'd feel differently once her memory returned. "I find it comforting to know God is watching over us."

"He is. And I'll pray for you too."

She flushed. "Um, thanks. I'm not sure I remember how to pray."

He wasn't sure she ever had but decided this wasn't the time to mention it. "Just talk to Him with your heart. He'll know what you need."

"What I need most is my memory." She took another bite of her grilled cheese. They ate in silence for a few minutes.

Trevor wished he'd asked more questions while they'd been on the phone earlier that evening. She'd mentioned Black Hat, thinking the guy was following her. Then she also talked about the black truck. But that was all, she hadn't mentioned anything else. He wondered what she'd thought about her husband's death. Miles claimed the police had ruled it an accident.

Yet now that she'd been forced off the road, he

found that difficult to believe. Unfortunately, he'd kept his distance when Bailey and Clark were married, mostly because he'd never liked the guy. Not that Clark had ever been rude or mean to him. Or to Bailey, as far as he knew. There was just something about the guy that bugged him.

If he were honest, he was secretly annoyed Miles had warned Trevor away from his sister back when they were in high school. As if Trevor wasn't good enough. Then a few years later, Miles had seemed to think Clark was the perfect guy for her. Sure, the guy co-owned the Sweet Water Pub and Grill, and he seemed to have plenty of money, but so what? That fact alone didn't make him a good husband.

Miles hadn't appreciated the faith Trevor and his family had been raised with. Faith in God and believing that Jesus died for their sins was more important than money. Which he knew was easy for him to say, especially now. He knew Miles and Bailey had been raised by a father who drank too much and couldn't hold a job. They'd grown up poor, which had colored their attitude toward life.

He and his siblings hadn't known how wealthy their parents were until they'd died, leaving millions of dollars in a trust. Maya and Chase had decided it was best if nobody knew the details about their financial situation to keep money grabbers at bay. The rest of the siblings had agreed with the plan.

Using Maya's expertise as a K9 cop, they'd eagerly trained their respective dogs to be experts at search and rescue. Maya had brought a professional trainer to the ranch to work with them. They'd cross-trained their dogs to search for gold, which was gunpowder and gun oil, as well as for people. Only Alexis's K9 was trained to find cadavers, and she'd used Denali in disaster sites across the country.

The fee for their service was a bag of dog food. Some people wondered how they managed to support the ranch, but often those they'd rescued had overcompensated by donating several bags of dog food.

In Doug's case, he'd donated eighty-one bags, which was still their top donation. Not to mention a joke among the family.

Would Miles have approved of Trevor dating his sister if he'd known about their trust? Maybe, but Trevor thought that was a stupid reason to approve or disapprove of a relationship. He'd grown up seeing how much his parents had loved each other and knew he'd never settle for anything less than what they had.

"I'm going to get some sleep." Bailey's voice interrupted his tumultuous thoughts. "Good night."

"Good night. I'm here if you need anything." He stood as she picked up her purse and walked to the bedroom. When she softly closed the door behind her, he glanced down at Archie. "We're going to guard her, boy. Okay?"

Archie thumped his tail on the floor in agreement.

He set their tray of dirty dishes out in the hall-way, then realized he needed to take Archie out. He glanced at her closed door. It wouldn't take Archie long, so he didn't disturb her. Sleep was probably the best thing for her.

Would Bailey's memory return in the morning? He prayed it would.

"Come, Archie." He made sure he had the key, then stepped into the hall. Archie trotted beside him as they walked to the side exit. Trevor glanced through the glass door before going outside.

"Get busy, Arch." They used that term to tell their dogs to do their thing. Another training tip from Maya.

Each of their dogs were amazing when it came to SAR missions, and it was rare for them to fail in finding their victim.

When Archie finished, Trevor held the door open for him. He turned to scan the area, narrowing his eyes when a car engine started up. In the dark, he couldn't tell what kind of vehicle it was, other than the headlights were square and set up high enough that they could belong to a truck.

Lots of Wyoming residents drove trucks, so that

fact alone wasn't cause for concern. Yet Trevor stood there for a moment, waiting for the truck to slowly roll past. It was a dark vehicle, but again, impossible to say for sure what color. Black, dark gray, gunmetal gray, or even a dark blue or green.

He was being paranoid. There was no way for the driver of the truck who'd rammed into Bailey to know where they were staying.

"Let's go, Arch." He led the dog back down the hall to their suite. Using his key, he entered the room, then double-locked the door behind him.

Then he made sure the curtains covered the window and shut off the inside lights. He stood to the side of the window, watching through a crack in the curtains to make sure the dark truck didn't return.

It didn't. He let out a sigh and stretched out on the sofa. There was no point in opening the sofa bed. He doubted he'd be getting much sleep.

"Lie down, Archie." He waited for his K9 to stretch out along the sofa. "Good boy. Guard."

Labs weren't known to be attack dogs, but it wasn't that long ago that his brother Joel's K9, a black lab named Royal, had alerted on a bad guy's scent, growling a warning when the guy was in the area. He firmly believed Archie would do the same thing.

He pulled his weapon from its holster and

placed it on the end table beside him. His brother Chase made them do target practice every few months to keep their skills sharp. He'd never been put in a position to use his weapon, but recently while helping his brother Justin on a case, he'd come close.

And he wouldn't have hesitated to use deadly force if needed.

The same way he wouldn't hesitate now.

He must have slept for a few hours because Archie's growling woke him from a sound sleep. Trevor bolted upright, going from sleepy to wide awake in seconds. He grabbed his handgun and slid into his shoes. A quick glance confirmed Bailey's bedroom door was still closed.

Archie was staring at the door, his hackles up. Not a good sign.

Moving silently, Trevor crossed to the door to peer into the hallway. He couldn't see anyone out there but knew the person could be standing off to the side, out of view.

Archie continued to growl. But then his K9 abruptly turned his head and stared at Bailey's door.

"What is it?" He was torn between the possible threat outside their room and whatever had caught Archie's attention in the suite.

Bailey's scream had him bolting toward the door. Archie barked and growled as he flung the door open. A man was half in and half out of the window.

Trevor leveled his weapon at the stranger who was dressed in black. No cowboy hat this time, though. "Stop or I'll shoot!"

Rather than stopping, the guy ducked out of the window and disappeared. Trevor spared Bailey a quick glance, noting she was in the bathroom doorway as he ran forward. "Get him, Arch!"

Archie leaped through the open window. Trevor had to fold himself in half to get through, but then he sprinted after his K9. He hadn't seen a weapon in the guy's hand, but that didn't mean he wasn't armed.

Most people in Wyoming carried a weapon.

As if reading his thoughts, the crack of gunfire rang out. He ducked and jutted to the side, seeking refuge behind a small tree.

"Archie, come!" He didn't want his dog to be in the line of fire.

His K9 whirled and returned to his side. The rumble of a car engine made him realize the guy was about to get away. "Stay, Archie." With that, he darted out from behind the tree and ran forward, trying to get a glimpse of the license plate.

But it was too late. The big black truck was already careening around a corner. He stared after it for a long second, before turning to jog back to his

K9. Was it the same one he'd noticed earlier? He didn't know. Yet being found at the hotel wasn't good.

He needed to get Bailey off-grid. From this point forward, he wouldn't trust anyone outside his family.

Not until he understood exactly what was going on.

4

———

Bailey hurried to the window, peering out as Trevor had followed Archie in chasing the stranger who'd tried to come into her room. Her body trembled with fear and anger. Who was that man? And why had he climbed through her window?

She'd been taking one of her frequent trips to the bathroom, courtesy of the baby sitting on her bladder, when she'd heard a faint noise. When she'd opened the bathroom door, she froze when she saw the man straddling the window. Thankfully, Trevor had burst into the room with Archie, scaring him off.

As she stood shivering, she realized the window had been cut away. She hadn't heard him doing that from inside the bathroom.

Did she know him? She hadn't been able to see his face, as he'd been ducking under the window when she'd stepped out of the bathroom. Despite sleeping deeply between bouts of getting up to pee, she was frustrated that there was nothing but a swirling mist where her memory should be.

Her stomach clenched with fear. She'd rested for almost five hours, but that still hadn't helped. What if she never remembered her life before the accident?

Archie and Trevor didn't come back right away, and she frowned when she saw the dog sniffing around the ground. What was he looking for? After a few minutes, the K9 sat and barked. Trevor bent, picked something off the ground with his gloved hand, then praised the dog.

The pair quickly returned to the hotel. Seeing them approach, she asked, "What did he find?"

"Shell casing." Trevor raked his gaze over her. "Are you okay?"

Not even close, but she nodded. She was impressed that Archie had been able to find the shell casing. "He's gone?"

"Yep. Took off in a dark truck." He gestured to the hotel. "Put on your shoes and grab your coat and purse. I'll bring Archie in through the side door to get my backpack, but then we're leaving."

The directive shouldn't have taken her by surprise. Of course, they couldn't stay, especially since her window was gone. "Okay."

His expression softened for a moment, and he looked as if he might say something more, then he turned and hurried around the building. She slipped her shoes on and reached for her purse. It was on the other side of the bed from the window. She paused, wondering if the intruder had planned to grab it. It didn't seem logical this was about a robbery. Putting a hand to her still-throbbing temple, she stepped into the main suite. When Trevor couldn't get in, she crossed over to undo the deadbolt lock.

"Thanks." He scowled. "I'm sorry. I never anticipated he'd try to get in through a window. Looks like he used a glass cutter for access."

"I saw that." She tried to calm her racing heart. "How did he know we were here?"

Trevor shook his head and bent to grab his backpack. "I don't know. Are you ready?"

"Yes, but shouldn't we call the police?" She shrugged into her coat and glanced back at her room. "You have that shell casing, right? And they can't give this suite to anyone else with the window missing."

"Yeah, we'll call them. They can come and dust for prints, although I noticed the guy was wearing gloves. No matter what, we're not staying here to wait for them." He turned toward the door. "Stay close, Bailey. You remember where the SUV is parked?" When she nodded, he turned to head down the hall. "Come, Archie."

The K9 trotted alongside Trevor. She followed, trying to visualize the man's features in her mind. But he remained a faceless threat.

With a click of Trevor's key fob, the lights flashed and the rear hatch opened for Archie. The dog eagerly jumped into the crate area. She hurried to the passenger-side door, glancing furtively over her shoulder. The intruder was long gone, but she couldn't seem to help herself. She had the odd sensation that she'd been looking over her shoulder a lot.

Trevor stashed his backpack in the rear seat, then slid in behind the wheel.

Once they were out on the road, she saw red and blue flashing lights. It seemed she was seeing them a lot too. "Did you call the police?"

"No, but I'm sure someone else reported the gunfire." He glanced at her. "We'll follow up with Sergeant Howell when we've found a new place to stay."

"And where is that?" She didn't like not knowing things. Or rather, not remembering things. "Have I met Sergeant Howell?"

"I don't know if you have or not, but we haven't

seen him since this started." He reached over to touch her arm. She appreciated the connection, especially since she felt as if she were drowning in quicksand. "I know him through my siblings. He's a decent guy and a good cop. He'll understand we couldn't stay because I needed to get you to safety. And I'm not sure where we're going yet. I need to call my sister Kendra in an hour or two. She's the expert in finding places where we can stay off-grid."

"Okay." There was no point in stressing over locals she couldn't remember. Bad enough that she couldn't recall her own brother. The photograph Trevor had rescued from her house was still tucked in the side pocket of her passenger-side door. She pulled it out to look at it again.

There were some similarities in their facial features, but his hair was blond compared to her dark-brown tresses. She'd examined her own reflection in the mirror with the same result. Like she was looking at a stranger.

With a sigh, she slipped the picture back into the side pocket. It was no use. She still didn't remember him.

The police sirens were louder now as the cruiser sped past them to reach the hotel. She pulled out her phone, realizing that less than 30 percent of her battery life was left. She picked up her purse, but there wasn't a spare charger in there.

"Something wrong?" Trevor asked.

"Just looking for a phone charger." She dropped her purse on the floorboard. "I guess it doesn't matter. I can't remember anyone to call."

"Hey, we're going to get through this." He took her hand again. She gripped it tightly, knowing it wasn't smart to be so dependent on him. But what choice did she have? Her car was totaled, and her house had been wrecked.

She was pregnant and on her own, except for Trevor's unwavering support.

"I don't know how I'd manage without you." Tears filled her eyes again, so she looked away. "I'm sorry. I wish I could remember you."

"Don't worry about that. Better for you to rest your mind. I'll figure out a place for us to stay and keep you safe."

She knew he would, and that almost made her want to cry more. Was she always so emotional? Or were pregnancy hormones responsible? She didn't know.

When a phone rang, she jolted. Trevor gave her hand a reassuring squeeze, then released it to push the talk button. "This is Trevor."

"It's Tom Howell. I just heard about the report of gunfire at the Elk Lodge, and Bailey Adams's recent car crash along with the break-in at her house.

That's three events in a matter of hours. What's going on?"

"Hey, Tom. I'm sorry your guys woke you at four thirty in the morning for this." Trevor's tone indicated he'd assumed the sergeant would have been called earlier.

"Yeah, I'm not happy they waited until now either. But I especially don't like knowing a pregnant woman is in danger." Bailey thought the sergeant sounded annoyed. "I am glad she's with you, Trevor."

"Me too. I intend to keep her safe," Trevor said.

"Do you have any suspects?" Howell asked.

"I wish." Bailey felt Trevor's gaze on her. "A man cut through the glass of the window in the Elk Lodge. We caught him trying to climb in. When Archie and I took off after him, he fired a gun to hold us back. That's the report of gunfire you heard. I would have returned fire, but he was already in his truck and driving away. Archie found a shell casing, so I have that for you. But I'm fairly certain the guy was wearing gloves, so I don't know that you'll get prints."

"Good news on the shell casing. Do you have a description of the perp or the truck?" Sergeant Howell asked.

Again, Trevor glanced at her. She shook her head, then spoke up. "Sergeant Howell, this is Bailey. I only caught a glimpse of him. All I can say is that he was dressed in black. No cowboy hat that I remember."

"I didn't see a cowboy hat either," Trevor agreed. "And the truck was dark in color. Bailey noticed a black truck behind her prior to the crash, so I believe it's the same one, but I couldn't get the make or model or license plate number."

"Great," Howell muttered. "That doesn't narrow it down much."

"I know. But I was thinking you should check the video at the gas station close to the Elk Lodge. That may provide a glimpse of this guy."

"I will. I wanted to talk to you and Bailey first."

"Understandable. But, Tom, I'd like you to share that video with me when you get it," Trevor said.

There was a pause, then he said, "I will. Are you going to give it to your FBI brother-in-law?"

"Yep." She had to admire Trevor's bluntness. "No offense, Tom, but the more cops digging into this, the better. As you said, we have a pregnant woman in danger. Besides, I'm starting to think Bailey's husband's death wasn't an accident."

She turned to stare at him. Accident? He hadn't mentioned Clark died in an accident. For some odd reason, she'd assumed he'd passed away from cancer.

Wasn't that how most people died?

"I know Bailey asked us to review Clark's fatal car crash several times, but honestly, we never found anything to suggest foul play." Howell's tone was defensive. "I wouldn't lie about that."

Fatal car crash? She gripped the armrest, feeling dizzy. Why hadn't Trevor told her that important detail? Her husband had died of a car crash, and now she'd been in one too.

Was she in danger because of him?

WITH A WINCE, Trevor realized he should have told Bailey the information he'd learned about her husband's death. She wasn't the only one with memory issues. He kept forgetting she didn't know anything about her past.

Including the fact that she'd apparently gone to the police about her husband's fatal car crash.

"Tom, would you be willing to share your investigation into Clark's death with me?" He knew he was asking for the impossible. The police wouldn't share their investigations with the public. "You said yourself it was deemed an accident."

"If I don't, are you going to sic Griff on me?" Howell asked.

"Probably." He didn't see any reason to lie. "Bailey's life is on the line here. I don't think standing on protocol is the smart way to go. As I said before, we need all hands on deck."

There was a long pause as Tom considered that. Then the older man sighed. "Fine. I'll share the file. But if you learn anything more about the guy in a black hat, or the black truck, or anything else, I need you to let me know. And I'll need that shell casing too."

"I promise. And the same goes." Trevor was glad the Cody police got along well with the Sullivans. "Thank you."

"Yeah, yeah," Tom groused. "I'll be in touch."

When Howell ended the call, he turned to Bailey. "I guess I owe you an apology."

"Yes." Her voice was taut. "You should have mentioned my husband may have been murdered."

He couldn't blame her for being upset. "I'm sorry. But you heard Sergeant Howell. Your husband's death was ruled an accident. They didn't find any evidence of murder."

"So I'm supposed to believe my car crash was an accident too?"

"No, that's not what I said." He reached for her hand. She tugged it away. "I think your car crash was an intentional act. But thinking isn't proving. And without your memory to tell me what happened on the highway last evening, there's no way to know for sure."

She laced her fingers over her pregnant belly. "Is there anything else I need to know? Was Clark a criminal or something?"

"No. He co-owned the Sweet Water Pub and Grill." He glanced over. "Does that sound familiar?"

She shook her head and bit her lip. "I wish it did. I must have eaten there if my husband owned the place. I'm surprised. Based on my small house, I wouldn't have thought we'd have a lot of money."

"He had investors from what I understand." Trevor wished he'd paid more attention to the things Miles had told him about Clark. "I don't know all the details, except for the fact that you purchased the house you're living in now after he died."

"So I don't have a lot of money?" She frowned, clearly trying to make sense of things. "Shouldn't I have gotten part of the pub?"

"I'm not sure how Clark's will was set up." That was something Trevor could dig into, though, first thing in the morning. He didn't like the idea of Bailey scraping by for money. Maybe the pub's financial situation contributed to Clark's death. Although he'd have thought Tom would have ruled that out in his investigation. With a mental shake, he focused back on the present. "You work at City Hall as a receptionist, so you may be able to get the public records on the pub in the morning."

"Okay." She sighed. "I guess that's better than sitting around doing nothing."

He'd have to figure out a way that she could get to City Hall and back without Black Hat knowing it. Bailey had mentioned seeing the guy four times in two days. He assumed at least one of those times was when she was leaving work.

"I feel like we're driving in a circle," Bailey said after a moment. "Didn't we pass that storefront earlier?"

"Yeah, we are. I'm doubling back to make sure that nobody comes up behind us." He was surprised she'd noticed. "We can't get a rental property until later this morning, so staying on the road seems our best option. As soon as it's closer to six, I'll call my sister Kendra. She's been helping with getting rental properties for us when needed."

"I'm surprised you'd stay in rental properties when doing search and rescue missions."

"We've found ourselves in some dicey situations recently." He didn't want to get into the crimes he and his siblings had helped solve over the past year. Although he found it rather ironic, he was the one on the run from danger now. The month of October had been quiet, so he'd assumed the worst was over. Technically, Bailey was the one in trouble, but there's no way he'd let her deal with this on her own.

Even if her memory was fully intact, he'd stick to her like superglue.

"Is there anything else I need to know?" Bailey asked, interrupting his thoughts. "Were Clark and I happily married?"

"As far as I know, yes. And I know your brother really liked Clark."

She frowned at that but didn't ask anything more. He was glad she hadn't sought his opinion of the guy. Not that it was relevant.

His personal feelings weren't important. Finding Black Hat or the black truck were all that mattered. Once the police had their suspect in custody, they'd understand exactly how Bailey's crash and her husband's death were connected.

Or so he hoped.

He kept an eye on the rearview mirror as he took the long way around town. He had instinctively headed to the far side of the city. A few months ago, his brother Joel had stayed in a cabin that was on the northwest side of Cody. It was the opposite end from where Bailey lived, and while he'd rather head all the way to Greybull or some other city, he thought it better to stay close. For one thing, he still had the shell casing. For another, he really wanted to see the paperwork for the Sweet Water Pub.

Would Kendra be able to secure that cabin in the woods again? When Joel had been there back in

August, a bomb had gone off under his SUV, causing damage to the front of dwelling. The Sullivans had paid for the repairs, so he knew it was back up and running as a rental property.

His younger sister would balk at being used as the ranch secretary, but the truth was that they all protected Kendra from the harsher side of life. As if losing her parents when she was barely nineteen hadn't forced her to grow up fast. It had. She'd insisted on training her K9, Smoky, to perform SAR missions, but they'd always managed to make sure she took on the easier searches. Partially because a year ago in November, she'd suffered a bad fall and sustained several fractures.

They'd all been forced to grow up fast, he silently admitted. He'd been an EMT for two years and had been training as a firefighter when their parents had died. He'd quit school and moved back to the ranch without a second thought. Maya and Chase had moved back, keeping the family together. He'd admired them for what they'd done.

The shared tragedy had drawn them closer together. Far more than if they hadn't gone through the loss.

Was that a part of God's plan? His siblings would say it was. At the same time, it was difficult to imagine why Bailey being in danger was part of the Lord's master plan.

"The streets are so empty," Bailey said. "It feels like we're the only one on the road."

"Yeah." He glanced at the rearview mirror again. Archie was stretched out with his eyes closed. "Traffic will pick up soon."

"Your idea of checking gas station video was great," Bailey said. "I hope the police get it first thing."

"They will." He had learned a lot about police work over the years they'd been doing search and rescue. Especially in the past ten months when his siblings had been drawn into danger. He glanced at his fuel gauge. "Speaking of gas stations, I need to fill up."

Bailey reached down for her purse and rummaged through it.

"Don't." He put a hand on her arm. "I have plenty of cash."

She grimaced and opened her wallet. "I guess that's a good thing because I only have ten dollars."

He frowned, wondering what had happened to Clark's portion of the Sweet Water Pub and Grill, but he didn't voice his concern. He pulled into the next gas station and killed the engine.

"I need to use the restroom," Bailey murmured. "Especially if we're not going to be stopping at another hotel anytime soon."

The closest motel to their current location was

the Wild Bill Motel, which was known to rent rooms by the hour. It was no place he'd go by himself, much less with Bailey. He glanced around the empty lot. The gas station was open, and when he glanced at his watch, he realized they'd been driving around for almost an hour.

Time flies when you're having fun.

He escorted Bailey inside the gas station, partially to keep her close, but also to pay the attendant in cash. The scent of freshly brewed coffee made his mouth water.

"Here, I'm filling up outside." He slid fifty dollars across the counter. "I'd love some coffee, too, when I get back."

"Okay." The clerk was young, maybe eighteen or nineteen. He yawned widely as Trevor turned to head back outside.

The cold November wind hit him square in the face. He hadn't paid much attention to the freezing temps, too concerned with getting Bailey to safety. He opened the back hatch for Archie, letting the dog stretch for a bit.

"Get busy."

Archie looked at him, then went over to pee on a bush.

Trevor smiled. "Good boy."

Archie wagged his tail and came bounding back.

The look in his K9's dark eyes asked if they were going to be playing the search game.

"Not now, boy." He bent to pet the dog's thick fur. "You did your good deed for the day, remember?"

When he finished with the gas, he headed back inside, bringing Archie with him. He poured himself a large coffee and carried it to the clerk. When Bailey joined him, he gestured toward the coffee station. "I'm not sure if you can have caffeine, but there's tea and hot chocolate if you're interested."

"Thanks. Hot chocolate sounds good." She turned to help herself.

Through the glass window, Trevor frowned when he saw a black pickup truck roll past. He moved quickly to Bailey's side. "I need you to go back toward the restrooms. Come, Archie."

"What's going on?" She stopped filling her cup.

"I just saw a dark truck." He tugged her toward the restrooms. "Stay here with Archie. I'm going to try to get a closer look."

"Okay." Bailey's eyes were wide with fear, and she reached down to rest her hand on Archie's head.

He quickly turned and headed back out to the convenience store. The clerk was scrolling on his phone rather than paying attention to his surroundings.

Scanning the parking lot outside, he didn't see

any sign of the black truck. Had he overreacted? His gut was telling him no.

Then he saw it. The black truck pulled into the gas station parking lot. Trevor reached over to grab the clerk's wrist. "Call 911."

"Huh?" The kid looked confused. Then the truck's driver's side window opened, revealing the muzzle of a gun.

The guy behind the wheel opened fire, shattering the glass windows of the gas station. Trevor ducked low, using the counter for protection. Then he pulled his weapon and prayed.

5

Bailey had been hovering in the hallway outside the restroom when she heard the crack of gunfire and corresponding shattering glass. She instinctively ducked into the closest restroom, pulling Archie with her. She locked the door and huddled in the corner, her heart pounding. She hated knowing Trevor was out there facing the gunfire alone, but she didn't dare risk her unborn child by venturing out there to find him.

Why was this happening? Who was shooting at them? With shaky hands, she pulled her phone from her purse and dialed 911. The battery signal on her phone was low, and she hoped there was enough juice for the call to go through. Thankfully, the dispatcher quickly answered. "What's your emergency?"

"I—we're in a gas station, and someone's shooting at us!" She tried to remember exactly where they were. "I think we're on the northwest side of town. It's the Gas and Go station. I don't know the address!"

"I know where the Gas and Go station is and will dispatch officers to your location." Her calm tone was reassuring. "Are you safe?"

Not even close. Bailey wondered if she'd ever feel safe again. "I'm hiding in the bathroom. Just please hurry!"

"Officers will be there soon. Please stay on the line."

"My phone battery is low." She decided there was no point in wasting what little battery power she had left, so she disconnected the call. Stuffing the phone back into her purse, she strained to listen. Oddly, there was nothing but silence.

Her heart lodged in her throat. Did that mean Trevor and the gas station clerk were both dead?

The sudden pounding of a fist on the bathroom door made her jump. Black Hat?

"Bailey? It's Trevor!"

Archie wagged his tail, clearly recognizing Trevor's voice. She let out a sigh of relief, opened the door, and nearly fell into his arms. "Trevor? You're okay?"

"Yeah, but we need to get out of here." He held her close for a long moment. His grim expression was not reassuring. "The black truck took off, but we can't stick around."

"I—okay. The police are on the way." She reluctantly pulled out of his arms. "Where are we going?"

"I don't know." He took her hand. "I grabbed my backpack from the SUV, but we need to head out on foot."

She swallowed hard but didn't protest. It seemed odd to her that he didn't want to drive, but then again, the gunman had found them there. By tracking his SUV? That seemed like something out of a movie.

Yet seeing the broken windows and shattered glass on the floor of the gas station indicated their situation was all too real. And precarious. The clerk was sitting on the floor with his back to the counter, a dazed expression on his face.

"The police are coming," Trevor called to him. "Stay down until they get here."

The clerk nodded, clearly in shock. She felt bad for the young man, but since there was nothing she could do for him, she turned and followed Trevor outside. The cold November wind stole her breath, making her shiver.

Archie didn't seem to notice as he trotted alongside them. His nose was up as he sniffed the air with interest. Obviously, dogs explored their surroundings with their noses, not their eyes.

"We're going to find a place to call my sister Kendra," Trevor murmured.

"Okay." She glanced over her shoulder at the gas station. "What about your SUV?"

"I'll have someone from the ranch tow it back later." He grimaced. "We just got our replacement SUV after my brother's vehicle was destroyed by a bomb and now this."

She gaped. "A bomb?"

"Yeah. Don't worry, that was a few months ago. I shouldn't have mentioned it. It's just that our K9 SUVs are specially made with safety features for our dogs. Knowing mine has been shot up makes me mad." He paused at the street behind the gas station and looked both ways before leading her across to the other side. "We need to find a restaurant where we can wait for Kendra without being noticed."

She sighed, stepping carefully on the slick streets. Without her memory, she was no help in finding a place. There was nothing more terrifying than not being able to remember anything. Her life before the crash, her brother, even her dead husband.

Nothing.

With another shiver, she followed Trevor through several back streets. None of which were familiar. At least, he seemed to know where he was going. Moving in the darkness should have made her feel safe, but it didn't. In her opinion, they were more conspicuous walking around town like this. Two people and a dog didn't exactly blend in. Especially since most people didn't walk their dogs at this early hour of the morning in winter.

"Looks like we'll have to go a little farther." Trevor glanced at her. "Can you manage?"

"Sure." It wasn't as if she had a choice. The cold temperature was starting to make her shiver, but she didn't complain.

They walked for what seemed like an hour, but was barely fifteen minutes, when Trevor's grip on her hand tightened. "I think that's the Sunny Side Up Café on the next block." Trevor tightened his grip on her hand. "You're doing great, Bailey. We'll be warm soon."

She appreciated his kind words, considering she was a liability in their attempt to escape. He and Archie could have gone faster without her.

Then again, they wouldn't be running from a gunman in the first place if not for her.

This guy was after her. Why, she had no idea.

Would she know more if she had her memory? The doctor had mentioned a traumatic event likely accompanied her amnesia. Maybe she had known something horrible prior to the crash that had caused her mind to shut down.

Whatever it was, she needed her mind to open back up and soon. Before they were all killed.

Welcoming lights beckoned from inside the Sunny Side Up Café. Trevor glanced up and down the street before opening the door for her. Archie walked in with them. There were plenty of open seats, but Trevor chose the booth farthest from the door. He shrugged out of his backpack.

"Lie down, Archie." Trevor took the seat that was facing the door, setting the pack beside him. Archie crawled beneath the table and let out a sigh. It seemed to her as if the dog had been there before.

"I'm surprised they don't mind Archie being here."

"The Sullivan K9s are well known in the area." He shrugged and handed her a plastic menu. "You never did get your hot chocolate."

"That's the least of my worries. I hope that clerk is okay." It felt wrong to be sitting here in a warm café while he was talking to the police. "Shouldn't we have stayed to talk to the officers too?"

"We'll do that soon. For now, it's better we stay safe." Trevor pulled out his phone, but their server came over with a pot of coffee before he could make a call. "Coffee for me would be great. Bailey, do you want hot chocolate?"

"Yes, please." She smiled at the woman whose name tag identified her as Doris. "Thank you."

"Sure thing." Doris filled Trevor's coffee, then carried the second mug back to the kitchen. She returned a few minutes later with a mug of hot chocolate. "Are you ready to order?"

"Two eggs over easy with toast and fruit, please." She tucked the menu away.

"I'll have the ham and cheese omelet with toast and breakfast potatoes." Trevor gestured to his mug. "Please keep the coffee coming."

Doris laughed. "Will do."

The moment Doris hustled off, Trevor stood. "I'll be back in a minute."

As he stepped away from the table to make his call, she sipped her hot chocolate. Archie shifted beneath the table. She awkwardly leaned down to stroke his soft fur. Her belly barely fit behind the table of their booth. She sighed and tried not to stress. There was no doubt in her mind Trevor Sullivan would do everything possible to keep her safe. But she worried that their best might not be good enough.

It seemed as if this unknown gunman had the advantage. That this guy, whoever he was, knew her. And likely knew Trevor Sullivan too. He must be a local resident. If that was the case, she didn't understand why the police wouldn't know his identity. How many bad guys could there be in a town this size? She made a mental note to ask Trevor about stopping at the police department after breakfast.

Her baby kicked, and she rested a hand on her belly. Feeling her unborn child moving about only reinforced her resolve. They would get through this. Somehow, some way, they would figure out what was going on.

Before it was too late.

~

TREVOR WAS grateful Kendra answered on the first ring. "Trev? What's going on?"

"I need help. You remember Miles's sister, Bailey?"

"Of course." Kendra yawned. "Why?"

"She's in trouble. Some guy is trying to kill her. I had to leave my SUV at the Gas and Go station; we're in the Sunny Side Up Café now. How soon can you and one of the other siblings get here? I need a replacement SUV and a rental house."

"I can be there in forty-five minutes or less." He heard a door opening and closing, indicating his sister had put her K9 Smoky, an Alaskan malamute, outside. "I'll send a request for the cabin Joel used, but they're not likely to respond until business hours."

"That works. But you need one of the other sibs to come too, Kendra. I'll use your vehicle, but you'll need a ride back to the ranch."

"I'm sure Joel won't mind tagging along. What else do you need?"

"Extra supplies for Archie. I have my backpack, but I only have enough dog food for a couple of meals." He kicked himself for not being better prepared. "I also need an extra vest for Archie and snow booties, in case we need to go into search mode. The temperatures have been dropping, and he doesn't have the furry coat your Smoky does."

"Sounds good. I'll hit the road as soon as possible." Kendra paused, then added, "Are you planning to call Chase?"

He groaned. "Yeah, I'll call him." Their oldest brother tended to be overprotective, especially of him and Kendra, the two youngest. Chase probably wouldn't like it that he'd asked Kendra for help, but driving out with extra supplies wasn't the same thing as being in the middle of danger. "Just get here soon, okay?"

"Soon," she repeated, then ended the call. He debated texting his brother now but then decided to wait. He'd call Chase once they were settled at the cabin. That way he could reassure his brother they were fine.

Or as fine as they could be under the circumstances. Black Hat showing up at the gas station was concerning. He couldn't imagine how the guy had found them there.

Had the guy been cruising the streets and just happened to spot his K9 SUV? Chase had gotten rid of the stenciling on their vehicles months ago since that had made it too easy for bad guys to recognize them. Yet anyone who knew the Sullivans would see the crate area in the back of their vehicles and assume it belonged to them.

He needed to do better in protecting her. Starting with his original plan of keeping her off-grid.

He strode back to the booth. "Bailey, we need to ditch your phone."

"Huh?" She stared at him in shock. "Why?"

"We can't take the risk your phone is being tracked somehow." He supposed the same could be said for his, but he couldn't give his up yet. Not until Kendra and Joel arrived. They'd work on getting disposable phones later, once the stores were open. "Please. I wouldn't ask if it wasn't important."

She dug in her purse, pulled out the phone, and handed it to him. "It's almost out of battery. And I have no idea who to call anyway."

He felt bad and considered having her scroll through her contact list to see if any of the names sounded familiar. Yet that might just make her more depressed about her memory loss. He powered the phone off and set it aside. They'd toss it in the garbage on their way out.

Taking a large sip of his coffee, he kept an eye on the front door. He hoped they'd gone far enough from the gas station that the gunman wouldn't think to look for them there.

But he couldn't afford to discount the possibility that this guy might find them through a process of elimination. The café had a back door through the kitchen. He'd get Bailey out that way if needed. Yet there was no hiding the fact that in her condition she wouldn't get far on foot.

No, he needed wheels and fast.

Doris brought their breakfasts. Then she refilled his cup. "Anything else?"

"No thank you." Bailey's smile didn't reach her eyes.

"I'm fine too." When Doris left, he reached across the table for Bailey's hand. "Let's say grace."

"Okay." She didn't look surprised as she had before. He was encouraged that she could remember they'd done this last evening.

"Lord Jesus, we ask You to bless this food. And we also ask You to keep us safe in Your care. Amen."

"And Lord, will You please restore my memory soon? Amen," Bailey added.

He smiled at her additional prayer. "Amen."

She held his hand for a long second before releasing it and reaching for her fork. He dug into his meal too. He glanced under the table at Archie, who appeared content. His K9 would need breakfast but could wait for Kendra to get there.

As they ate, he tried to come up with a plan of how to get to the bottom of this mess. He wanted to know more about Clark's ownership in the Sweet Water Pub and Grill but couldn't be sure that was related to the gunman.

Yet what other explanation was there? Clark had died in a car crash, and Bailey had been in one too. Now someone had gone through her house and shot up a gas station, along with his SUV.

In his mind, it made sense to start with Bailey's deceased husband and his business.

"I think we need to talk to the police." Bailey nibbled a piece of toast. "It seems to me they should know the local residents well enough to find this guy."

She had a point. Yet he also knew the police had ruled Clark's death an accident. They'd already spoken on the phone with Sergeant Tom Howell. Maybe talking to the guy in person would help. "Okay, we can head there when we're finished."

"I feel bad dragging you into danger." Her voice was soft. "But I also don't know what I'd do without you."

"Hey, I'm glad to be here. I would never want you to face this alone." He held her gaze. "I know you don't remember me, but I have always cared about you, Bailey. So please don't worry about a thing."

Her smile was a tad pathetic. "That's sweet of you, Trevor."

He hid a wince. It was something she would say to someone she cared about like a brother, which was fine. He wasn't looking for anything more.

Yet deep down, he knew he needed to guard his heart. It would be far too easy to fall for Bailey. Once her memory returned, she'd probably remember how much she loved her husband, Clark.

And how she was grieving over losing him.

Yeah, he needed to keep a friendly vibe between them.

His phone rang, interrupting his thoughts. Seeing Kendra's name on the screen, he quickly answered. "Where are you?"

"Still twenty minutes out and Joel is probably another five minutes behind me. I wanted to be sure you were still at the Sunny Side Up Café."

"We are." He scanned the street outside. It was still too early to be bustling with people, and he couldn't deny feeling nervous about how exposed they were. Should they stay there? Or go somewhere else? Eyeing Bailey, he decided not to head anywhere else unless they had no choice. "If we have to go on the move, I'll let you know."

"Sounds good. I have not heard back from the rental company yet on the cabin. Hopefully, the place is still available."

"If that doesn't work, we'll figure something out." He'd wanted to stay near Cody, if only to access the records related to the Sweet Water Pub and Grill, but he'd take Bailey to Greybull and beyond if necessary.

All that mattered was keeping her safe.

"I can find other rentals too. Let's give them some time. See you soon." Kendra ended the call.

"Your sister is on her way?" Bailey asked.

"Yes. I probably should have mentioned that you and my sister Kendra are the same age."

"Oh, so she knows me, but I won't remember her." Bailey's face fell.

He wished there was a way to make this easier for her. But short of miraculously filling her mind with the missing memories, he was stuck. An older couple entered the café. He didn't know them, but he didn't perceive them to be a threat.

Doris returned to refill his cup. She smiled at

seeing their empty plates. "I hope everything tasted okay."

"It was great. Bring the bill when you have time." He glanced at Bailey, then added, "We're waiting for my sister."

"That's fine, we're not too busy." Doris stacked their plates and took them away.

When his phone rang again, he quickly answered. It wasn't one of his sibs, it was Sergeant Howell. "Hey, Tom."

"Where are you?" Tom sounded annoyed. "You shouldn't have left the gas station."

Trevor decided there was no point in arguing. "I know you need our statements. We'll swing by the Cody police station as soon as I have a replacement set of wheels."

"Where are you?" Howell repeated. "I'll come to you if I have to."

"I'd rather you didn't." Trevor kept his tone even. "I said we'll come to you when we have a car."

"Listen, Trevor, this is serious stuff. That gas station is a mess, and the poor kid running the place had to be taken to the hospital to be treated for shock. I need to know what is going on."

"How about you start with digging into Clark's death?" When he mentioned Bailey's dead husband, her gaze snapped to his. "You and I both know the two incidents are related."

"Two incidents? More like five!" Howell's voice rose in agitation. "Have you talked to Griff yet?"

"No, but I plan to do that soon." He was getting the sense the local police were feeling overwhelmed. "You want FBI assistance on this?"

"I want this gunman caught and arrested." Howell sighed. "Okay, I get it. You don't want anyone to know where you are. Just get your butts into the station as soon as possible. And yeah, maybe you should call Griff. We need all the help we can get."

"I will. See you soon." He ended the call.

"They want the FBI to take over the investigation?" Bailey's eyes widened. "Why does that worry me?"

"Because it's a small-town police department, and you know as well as I do their resources are limited." He reached across the table to take her hand. "My brother-in-law Griff will help. My other brother-in-law Doug Bridges will pitch in, too, if needed. We'll get to the bottom of this."

"I'm scared." Bailey's voice had dropped to a whisper. "I'm afraid this guy will kill me and my baby."

"I won't let that happen." He caught sight of a pair of headlights coming down the street. When they slowed and turned into the parking lot, he sprang to his feet, which made Archie scramble out from beneath the table. Then he relaxed when he recognized an SUV, not a large pickup truck. He bent to give Archie a reassuring pat. "We're fine, boy. I think that's Kendra. She made good time."

His sister emerged from the SUV. The back hatch opened, and her K9, Smoky, jumped out. The dog looked like a giant ball of white and brown fluff, but she was an excellent tracker like the rest of their K9s. His sister strode inside and crossed to their table.

"Bailey, it's nice to see you again." Kendra slid into the seat beside her.

"Kendra, Bailey is having some trouble remembering her past after her car crash," he quickly said.

"Oh, you poor thing!" Kendra slipped her arm around Bailey's shoulders in a quick hug. "That's okay. It's not a problem. This is my K9, Smoky." Her K9 stood at Kendra's side. "Friend, Smoky. Bailey is a friend."

Smoky sniffed Bailey, her curly tail wagging. Bailey stroked the dog's soft fur. "Seems like I should remember such a pretty dog."

"Ah, well, you'll remember soon enough." Kendra shot him a concerned glance. "Joel will be here soon. Do you want to stay here, or should we move on?"

"It might be better to move on." He wasn't sure why he was feeling on edge. "I promised Sergent Howell that we'd go in to provide our statements after the gas station shooting. Maybe Joel can meet us there."

"Okay, let's go." Kendra jumped out of the seat. "Come, Smoky."

Bailey slid out of the bench seat, following Kendra. He stood and gave Archie the heel command. Normally, the K9s played together like maniacs, but they could be well behaved when necessary.

Giving the heel command told Archie it was not playtime.

Kendra and Smoky led the way outside. Bailey followed his sister. Trevor scanned the area, half expecting the black truck to materialize. Early light dawned on the eastern horizon, but the overcast sky indicated snow might be on the way. Kendra and Bailey took the front seats, so he was standing beside the passenger door, waiting for Archie to jump in, when he glimpsed the truck.

"Go, Kendra! Go!" He jumped into the back seat, slamming the door behind him. The moment the back hatch was closed, Kendra shifted into reverse and drove backward, away from the road.

He was impressed by his sister's ingenuity, until the driver of the truck slowed to follow.

"Hurry." Trevor pulled his weapon, rolled down his window, and prepared to fire. Kendra wrenched the wheel to the side, just as gunfire erupted from the truck.

Sick of this guy shooting at them, he extended his arm out as far as possible to return fire. He fired three times, yelling, "Go, go!"

Kendra did as instructed, hitting the gas and bouncing up and over the curb that was behind the café.

He peered behind them, praying the black truck wouldn't follow. But being found again so soon after the gas station was sobering.

This guy must know the Sullivans were helping Bailey. Maybe even noticing Kendra's SUV and following her to the café.

None of them were safe. Whoever this guy was, he didn't seem to care how many Sullivans he took out of the picture in his quest to kill Bailey.

6

———————

Bailey gripped the armrest so tightly her fingers went numb. Kendra had gotten them away from the café and was driving through the back streets of Cody, intent to keep the gunman from following them.

She admired Kendra's quick response to the gunfire. As if she'd been through something like this before. Glancing at the pretty redhead behind the wheel, Bailey wished she could remember her.

"Keep driving around for a few minutes, Kendra," Trevor said. "I'll call Joel. We'll have to get to the police station soon to give them an update on recent events. After that, we'll need another plan."

"Sounds good." Kendra's tone was remarkably calm. "I wish I understood how he knew we were at the café."

"I assume he must have spotted your SUV and followed you." Trevor paused, then said, "Hey, Joel. Change of plan. We were found at the café."

While Bailey couldn't hear the other side of Trevor's conversation, she could tell Joel was asking questions about what happened. She drew in a deep breath, hoping to calm her racing heart. The doctor had suggested rest and being in familiar surroundings.

Impossible for her to do either of those things.

"It's okay." Kendra must have read her mind, because she reached over to touch her hand. "We're going to keep you safe."

"I know." She knew they'd try to do that. But the way this guy kept popping up when they least expected him was concerning.

One of these times, a bullet would hit its mark.

The thought of something terrible happening to her baby made tears sting her eyes. Then she remembered Trevor's prayer. He'd prayed twice now before meals. Was that something she normally did? She wasn't sure but decided to try.

Closing her eyes, she opened her heart to the Lord. *Please, Lord Jesus, protect me and my baby. Amen.*

A sense of calm washed over her. She opened her eyes, feeling stronger with the knowledge that she wasn't alone. Not only did she have the Sullivans around her, but God was covering her too.

Bailey wished she could remember some Bible passages. Maybe they'd come back to her when the rest of her memory returned.

"I think we'll need a rental car," Trevor was saying. "Something that wouldn't be associated with our ranch."

Kendra made another right-hand turn, then turned left a few streets later. The youngest Sullivan sibling kept her eye on the rearview mirror. Kendra's ability to remain calm under fire was impressive. Bailey had given up trying to figure out where they were. Having amnesia was not only terrifying, but it also made her feel incredibly helpless.

"Yep, see you at the police station," Trevor said. Bailey turned in her seat to see he'd ended the call. "Okay, Kendra, let's make our way back to the police station. Joel is going to work on getting a rental car for me."

"Sounds good." Kendra made another turn. "I didn't notice anyone following me through town. I hate knowing I may have led the gunman to you."

"Not your fault," Trevor said. "I think this guy knows Bailey. And if he knows her and her brother, it's not a stretch to assume I'm involved with keeping her safe."

"You think he knows me that well?" Bailey was shocked. She turned to look at Trevor. "You mean, like a friend of the family?"

Trevor hesitated, then shrugged. "Something like that. Cody isn't that big. Locals who've lived here their entire lives would know you, your husband, me, and your brother. It's the only way I can figure out that they keep finding us."

She sat back in her seat, her mind whirling. For some reason, she'd assumed this was some stranger who'd come after her. Not someone she knew on a first-name basis.

Yet Trevor was right. Cody might be the fifth largest city in the state, but it held a small-town vibe. If she had her memory, she was sure she'd recognize the people they ran across.

"I assume I've lived here my entire life?" she asked.

"Yes. Same as us," Kendra confirmed.

She nodded, thinking again how awful it was that she probably knew the man who had tried numerous times to kill her. Rubbing her fingers into her temples, she struggled to remember—anything.

To no avail.

Kendra pulled up to the Cody police department. The building didn't look familiar. With a sigh, she pushed her door open.

"Wait for me." Trevor jumped out of the back seat with Archie on his heels. Kendra opened the back hatch for Smoky. Trevor came around to Bailey's side. "Stay close, okay?"

She managed a nod, feeling a bit shaky as she slid out of the car. Trevor put his arm around her, urging her toward the front of the building. Archie, Kendra, and Smoky trailed behind.

They walked through a vestibule to a main desk where a woman sat behind what Bailey assumed was bulletproof glass.

"Good morning, we'd like to speak with Sergeant Howell if he's available," Trevor said. "Tell him the Sullivans are here with Bailey Adams."

"Of course. Come on back." The woman reached down and pressed a button. A locked door clicked open.

Trevor grabbed it. "Thanks. After you, Bailey."

She walked into the back, glancing around curiously. Again, nothing looked familiar, but she wasn't sure she'd ever been there before either. Surprisingly, nobody seemed to care that there were two dogs accompanying them.

"This way." Trevor rested his hand on the small of her back, steering her toward a small office. A tall man with dark hair and a mustache stood and gestured for them to come in.

"Please have a seat, Bailey." Tom Howell looked to be in his mid-forties. His expression was grim, but his eyes were kind. "I'm sorry to hear you've been in danger."

"Thank you." She sat in one of the two chairs.

Kendra sat in the chair next to her, while Trevor hovered behind them. "Trevor has been doing a remarkable job in keeping me safe, but we need help. This guy is escalating, and I'm afraid he'll find me again."

"I understand." Howell's gaze flicked to Trevor, then back to her. "If you don't mind, I'd like you to start at the beginning."

"The beginning?" She frowned. "I'm sorry to say I don't remember anything prior to my car accident. Trevor will have to fill you in on that part. I only know that once I was discharged from the hospital, we headed to my house. Trevor opened the door first and found the place trashed. From there, we headed over to the Elk Lodge. We were able to get some sleep, but then a stranger cut through the glass in my room and tried to crawl through the window. Trevor and Archie chased him off." She paused, then added, "I think he fired at Trevor too. We left the hotel and drove around for a while until we needed gas. I was in the hallway when the gunfire rang out, and we had to leave the gas station on foot." Reiterating the events made her exhausted. "We ordered breakfast at the Sunny Side Up Café and waited for Kendra to arrive. Just as we were leaving, the black truck arrived and started shooting again. Thankfully, Kendra was able to get away."

Howell's gaze held sympathy. "I'm sorry you had

to go through all of that. I take it your memory hasn't returned?"

"No." She tucked a strand of her hair behind her ear. "I wish it would. You have no idea what it's like to not recognize people who know you."

"I'm sure it's difficult." Howell's gaze flicked to Trevor. "Do you have anything to add?"

"Just that the guy in the black truck seems to recognize the Sullivan K9 SUVs. I know they're not marked anymore," Trevor added, "but I think he must know us well enough to recognize our crate area. I think he drove past the gas station, recognized my car, and then turned around and came back to open fire. I also think he must have noticed Kendra driving through town and followed her to the café. It was shortly after she arrived that we headed out. I think we surprised him by leaving so soon and that's why he fired at us again."

"So he knows you and Bailey." Howell sat back in his chair, his expression thoughtful. "I wish I could say that narrows things down for us. But it doesn't."

"Have you found anything useful from reviewing Clark's accident?" Trevor asked.

"No." Howell grimaced. "But I haven't had much time to look at my notes either."

Bailey tamped down a flash of impatience.

"Don't you think you should make time? This guy keeps trying to kill me!"

"Yes, I know. But to be honest, our investigation didn't find evidence of foul play, so I'm basically starting from scratch." Howell sounded a bit defensive.

Her baby kicked, a reminder that stressing out wasn't helpful. Bailey drew in a deep breath and let it out slowly. "I understand."

"You need to talk to the current owners of the Sweet Water Pub," Trevor said. "They're the ones who benefited the most from Clark's death."

"I spoke with Aaron Norman months ago, but he's just the assistant manager. Norman told me that Clark was a co-owner with an investment group by the name of Plymouth Properties. I've reached out to Plymouth several times, without a response. They're based out of New Jersey, and I suspect this is just one small property for them in the big scheme of things."

Bailey frowned. "You're saying Plymouth Properties was given full ownership of the pub after Clark's death?"

Howell shifted in his seat, looking uncomfortable. "Yes, but keep in mind, the original paperwork I saw indicated they'd already owned eighty percent of the pub. Clark was a minority partner and manager."

"Still, twenty percent should have gone to Bailey," Trevor said. "Unless I'm missing something."

"The terms of the agreement indicated the property would default to Plymouth upon Clark's death." Howell grabbed a file folder from a pile on the corner of his desk. "Here, you can see for yourself."

Bailey scanned the paperwork. It was dated three years ago, and she wondered if that was before she and Clark were married. If so, it would make sense that she wasn't a beneficiary. Although shouldn't Clark have updated the agreement after they'd tied the knot? Maybe he'd intended to but never got around to it. With a sigh, she handed the document to Trevor.

"I'd like a copy of this," Trevor said after a moment. "I think Bailey should have her lawyer review it."

"Yeah, sure." Howell stood, took the paperwork from Trevor, and left the office.

"Trevor, when did Clark and I get married?" She turned to look up at him. "I noticed the agreement was signed a little over three years ago."

"You and Clark were only married for eighteen months before he died." Trevor rested a hand on her shoulder. "That may explain why the document wasn't updated to include you, but it should have been amended after your marriage. And I think as his wife you still have rights."

"Maybe." She tried to imagine how she'd felt at becoming a widow after only eighteen months of marriage. Especially being pregnant.

She must have grieved over the loss, and it seemed wrong that she couldn't remember Clark. Her husband. The father of her baby.

Was that part of the reason her mind had shut down? Had her grief been too much to bear?

Maybe, but she couldn't afford to be left in the dark. Grief or not, she desperately needed to remember Clark and the rest of her past soon.

Before the gunman found them again.

TREVOR WAS glad to have at least one piece of the puzzle surrounding Clark's passing. Yet he wasn't sure why the investment group wasn't investigated more closely. Sounded to him that a 20 percent ownership in the pub was enough of a motive to kill Clark. Especially since the money had not gone to Bailey.

None of that explained coming after Bailey now, though. Why try to kill her seven months after Clark's death? Unless they were concerned about her coming after them for her share of the money.

And how much cash were they talking about?

Trevor found it hard to believe it was more than a couple hundred thousand dollars at the most.

They'd need to get a financial evaluation done on the Sweet Water Pub to know for sure. Maybe it wasn't even that much.

Archie was stretched out behind Bailey's chair. Smoky was near Kendra. They both lifted their heads when Tom returned, handing Trevor a copy of the agreement. He folded it and tucked it into the inside pocket of his jacket. "Do you know anything about the Plymouth Properties group?"

"Not much. That was my next step." Tom returned to his seat. "I'll see what I can dig up today."

Trevor nodded, intending to ask his brother-in-law Griff to do the same. The FBI might have more resources to get the answers they needed. "Okay, is there anything else you can tell us? What about the gas station video?"

"We're still combing through the video of the gas station closest to Bailey's home." Tom grimaced. "I wish I had more. All we know is that a guy wearing a black hat and black clothes driving a black truck has tried to kill you. A name, a make and model of the truck, or a license plate would be helpful."

Trevor narrowed his gaze. "And if I had that, I'd tell you. The guy's reckless shooting at us makes it difficult to get details. Oh, wait. Here's the shell casing Archie found." He tugged the brass from his pocket.

"Thank, I'll get this to the lab. And I'm not judging you," Howell said. "It's just that telling my officers to look for a black truck won't help if we can't narrow the search down to a particular make and model."

"I'm aware." Trevor took a step back. "We've provided our statements and gave you the shell casing. Now we need to find a safe place to stay. We'll be in touch."

"When you talk to Griff, have him call me." Tom gave him a knowing look. "I promise there won't be a turf war. We both want the same thing, to find and get this guy behind bars."

"I will." He gave the cop an appreciative nod. "Thanks."

Bailey stood as Archie scrambled to his feet. He let her out of the office first, then followed with Archie. Kendra and Smoky followed.

"Joel's here," Kendra said, showing Trevor her phone. "He's at the car rental place. He'll meet us here with a new ride soon."

"Great. I need to feed Archie while we wait."

"I'll grab food from the SUV." Kendra left the police station, returning a few minutes later with a couple of collapsible bowls and a container of food.

He set them out for Archie and gave him the

hand gesture to eat. Archie pounced on his food with enthusiasm. He stroked the dog's back, then turned to Kendra. "Thanks. Now that Archie has been cared for, what about a rental property?" Having the Sweet Water Pub agreement had him changing his mind about the need to stay in Cody. Maybe they were better off heading somewhere else. Yet the threat of snow was a factor they couldn't ignore. He couldn't risk harming Bailey or her unborn child.

"Hang on." Kendra worked her phone, then nodded. "Yep, that cabin Joel used a few months ago has been approved. You and Bailey can stay there for the next few days."

He glanced at Bailey. "What do you think? Should we stay in town? Or head to Greybull?"

"Have I been in Greybull?" Bailey glanced between him and Kendra. "The doctor suggested I stay in familiar surroundings. I'm sure a cabin doesn't count, but being in the city where I lived might help."

"I'm sure you've been in Greybull, but I know you've never lived there." He sighed. "Okay, we'll stick with the cabin for now. We can always head to Greybull later."

"Okay, I'm texting you the information," Kendra said.

His phone dinged, and he quickly memorized

the info. Then he powered down his phone and handed it to his sister. "We'll need to grab groceries and disposable phones before heading out to the cabin."

"Yeah, I figured." Kendra took his phone. "What about Bailey's device?"

"I left it at the café." He wished he'd have tossed it in the garbage, but it was too late now. "We'll buy her a replacement once this is over."

"I'm sure I can buy my own phone," Bailey said.

He wasn't about to argue, instead leading the way outside with Archie. Joel pulled up in a black SUV that looked similar to the make and model they normally used, without the crate area in the back.

"Thanks, Joel." He opened the driver's side door. "I can take it from here."

"I think I should come with you," Kendra said with a frown.

"No, sis. There's no need for you to do that." He exchanged a look with Joel and knew his older brother agreed with him. "We'll be safe at the cabin. I'll text you our new phone numbers when I have them."

"I have a pair here for you to use." Joel gestured to the bag on the passenger seat. "I brought them along. Also, there's extra K9 gear in the back, including food and the vest and booties you requested for Archie. Last but not least, I threw in a laptop computer. Figured you may need to do some research while at the cabin. Don't worry, it can't be traced to us. It's a brand-new device."

He was humbled by his brother's thoroughness. Joel, well, all his siblings really, had learned a lot from being in similar situations throughout the past months. "Thanks. All we need now is groceries."

"I wish you'd let one of us go with you." Kendra frowned. "I'm not helpless. I can shoot a gun as well as any of you."

"I never said you were helpless." He knew Kendra was sensitive to the fact that they'd tended to protect her. "I just think we'll blend in on our own. Besides, you and Joel need to drive the two SUVs back to the ranch." When she still scowled, he added, "I promise to call you first if I need backup."

"Okay." She finally relented. "Although I really wish you'd all stop treating me with kid gloves. I admit it was my fault I fell down that ravine last year, but that could have happened to anyone."

He knew she was right about that. "Nobody holds that fall against you, Kendra."

"Could have fooled me," she groused. Then she shook off her sour mood and gave Bailey a quick hug. "Take care of yourself. Come on, Joel. I'll drive you back to the rental car company."

"Keep in touch, bro." Joel gave him and Bailey a nod. "We're here if you need us."

"We should be fine now that we're completely off-grid." At least, he hoped so. Trevor went around to open the passenger door for Bailey. Then he told Archie to jump into the back seat. It wasn't as safe as having the K9 in the crate area, but being fired upon wasn't exactly a better option.

"Your family seems nice." Bailey glanced at him as they pulled out of the parking lot of the police station. "It must be wonderful to have so many brothers and sisters."

He chuckled. "Sure, if you like living in chaos. I will say the twins, Joel and Justin, were always close to me and Kendra. The four of us played together and hung out together even as adults."

"Nine kids." Bailey smoothed her hand over her pregnant belly. "Looks like I'll only have one. But she'll be the most loved little girl in the world."

He tipped his head to the side. "You remember you're having a girl?"

Her eyes widened. "I—don't know. I mean, that just came out of my mouth without me thinking about it." She gripped his arm. "Am I having a girl?"

"You are," he confirmed.

"That's wonderful." She shot him a hopeful look. "Do you think I'm starting to remember?"

"Maybe." He patted her hand. "Keep trying to relax, okay? That may be the best thing you can do."

"I've been trying to relax." There was an edge to her voice. "It's not my fault some crazy man keeps shooting at me."

"True enough." Trevor hoped that having a rental car would help them avoid the driver of the black truck. That is, if his theory of the guy knowing the Sullivan SUVs was correct. And they no longer had their usual phones either.

Still, he kept a wary eye on the rearview mirror as he drove through town. As before, he took the back roads whenever possible. He found the grocery store closest to the northwest side of town without difficulty. He couldn't leave Archie in the car, though, as the vehicle wasn't equipped with their standard safety precautions.

He shoved the gearshift into park, then glanced at Bailey. "I need you to stay out here with Archie. I won't be long. I'll just grab the basics and be out as quickly as possible."

Apprehension darkened her eyes, but she nodded. "Okay. Will you get me prenatal vitamins? I'm supposed to take one each day."

"No problem." He pushed out of the car and strode quickly inside. Trevor went up and down the aisles as quickly as possible, then had to run back to get the vitamins. He sighed in relief when he returned fifteen minutes later to find Bailey and Archie waiting patiently.

So far, so good, he thought as he stored the groceries in the back. Now to get her to the cabin where they could hide out for—he wasn't sure how long it would take the Cody police to find this guy. Even with Griff's help.

Tom had been right to point out they had little to go on. The more he thought about Plymouth Properties, the more he was starting to think this could be a murder-for-hire scheme.

Black Hat was a local, though, that much he was certain of. Okay, maybe the Sullivan name was well known throughout the state, but his friendship with Miles wasn't known beyond the local community.

"I wish I could remember your sister." Bailey's tone was wistful. "It seems like I could use a friend."

He nodded. "I know Stacy is a friend of yours too." At her blank look, he added, "Stacy White. She works with you at City Hall."

"Oh." She shrugged. "Maybe if I saw her, I'd recognize her."

"I can show you a few pictures," he offered. "We'll use the laptop Joel left in the back. Social media is generally useless, but in this case, it may help."

"That would be great." Bailey straightened in

her seat, then her expression fell. "I left the photo of me and Miles in your SUV."

"Well, that didn't work to help you remember, right? So don't worry about it. I'm sure we'll get it back."

They drove for a while in silence. A few trucks passed them on the road, but they didn't slow down or seem to pay them any attention. When they reached the road that would take them to the cabin, he put the SUV in four-wheel drive, as a plow hadn't been by recently.

The cabin itself wasn't far. He pulled in, eyeing the untouched snow surrounding the property. At least they'd know if anyone tried to approach the place.

"Let's get you inside." He got out and trudged through the fresh powdery snow to open her door. Then he let Archie out too. "I'll turn up the thermostat, start a fire, and then grab the groceries."

"Okay." Bailey followed him and Archie inside. "It's nicer than I thought."

"Yeah." He was about to head over to the thermostat when she caught his hand. He glanced at her in concern. "Is something wrong?"

She bit her lip. "I can't stop thinking about the fact that someone I know is trying to kill me."

"You're safe here." He drew her close. "We're off-grid."

She leaned against him. "I wish . . ." Her voice trailed off.

He bent his head to brush a chaste kiss on her temple. "Don't worry about anything. Just get some rest, okay? The more you rest, the more likely your memory will return."

She didn't move for a long moment. Then she drew back and surprised him by leaning up to press a light kiss along his cheek. "You're an amazing man, Trevor Sullivan."

He hoped she wouldn't notice his ears turning red. Bailey didn't remember him, so her sweet admission shouldn't matter. Maybe once her memory returned, she'd regret her impulse to kiss him.

But he wouldn't regret it. It was all he could do to take a step back, rather than gathering her close for a real kiss.

7

Bailey watched as Trevor crossed the room to turn the heat up, then head over to the fireplace. There was something so warm and inviting about a fire. Archie followed Trevor like his shadow, standing as Trevor stacked logs as if supervising.

Why had she kissed Trevor? She was supposed to be a grieving widow. Not to mention carrying her dead husband's child. She should be ashamed of her attraction to him. Yet it was hard to ignore the man who'd put his life on the line for her several times over the past twenty-four hours.

Was her husband, Clark, like Trevor? Handsome, kind, and caring? She thought he must have been, or why would she have married him?

Why couldn't she remember?

She moved into the kitchen, still wearing her winter coat. The cabin was slowly warming up now that the furnace had kicked in. The interior of the cabin was nicer than the brief glimpse she'd gotten of her own house, and she wondered how much it cost to rent the place. Kendra and Trevor hadn't seemed concerned about the expense. The Sullivan K9 Search and Rescue Ranch must have been doing well.

"There." Trevor rose and headed for the door. "Sit down, Bailey. I'll get the groceries."

"Okay." She wasn't helpless, but there was no denying her lack of sleep was catching up to her. She yawned and wished she could have a cup of coffee. Her headache had dulled a bit, but it hadn't gone away completely.

Now that they were safe, she should be able to follow the *get some rest* part of the doctor's orders. Trevor's idea of using social media to find people she might have known was a good one too. The key to catching this guy depended on her memory returning. She would do whatever was necessary to make that happen.

Trevor made several trips from the rental SUV to the house. He brought in groceries along with supplies for Archie. She had never realized how much stuff he must have kept in the SUVs that were specifically designed for their K9s.

She rose and crossed the room to begin putting food away. She was touched that Trevor had purchased herbal tea and hot chocolate for her. She pulled out the large bottle of prenatal vitamins and set it aside for later.

"I'll get that," Trevor protested, shrugging out of his coat and hanging it on a peg on the wall. "Sit down for a bit."

"It's not like I've been running around." She stepped back to give him room to work. Sharing the kitchen with him brought a strange intimacy to the situation. She hadn't noticed it as much in the hotel suite. Then again, she'd been so tired she'd fallen asleep the moment her head hit the pillow.

"How did you and Kendra know about this place?" She settled back into the kitchen chair, looking around curiously. "Because Joel stayed here?"

"Yep." He glanced at her over his shoulder. "Joel and his now wife, Trina, and their son, Ben, stayed here back in August. Ben still talks about the time he accidentally got too close to a grizzly bear cub. The mama bear was not happy, roaring loudly at him. Thankfully, Joel wasn't forced to shoot her."

Her eyes widened. "I didn't know we had grizzlies out here."

"Some have migrated from Yellowstone." He

shrugged and went back to putting food away. "Not to worry, they're getting ready to hibernate by now."

"That's good." She suppressed a shiver. As if she didn't have enough to worry about with the black-hat guy and the black truck. "Sounds like you and your siblings get into a lot of interesting situations."

"That's one way to put it." He flashed a wry smile. "Our goal is to serve the community. Sometimes that's more dangerous than we anticipate."

Like his agreeing to help her, she thought with a sigh.

"Okay, I figure we'll wait a few hours to have lunch. I hope you don't mind if I make more coffee, though." He filled the carafe and turned the machine on. Then he turned from the counter and crossed to the bag he'd tossed onto the living room sofa. "Now that we're settled, I need to get in touch with my brother-in-law."

"Griff is the FBI agent, right?" She could clearly remember the things he'd told her recently. Too bad it wasn't as easy for her to recall events from the past.

Like her husband, Clark.

"Yep." He pulled out the disposable phone and punched in a number. After a brief pause, he said, "Griff? It's Trevor. I need your help."

She waved at him. "Put it on speaker."

Trevor nodded and came to join her. "Hang on,

Griff. Bailey Adams is with me, and I'd like her to hear this too." He lowered the phone and put the call on speaker. "Okay, here's the situation. We have reason to believe someone wants Bailey dead. First, her car was struck with enough force to send her into the culvert. After being checked out at the hospital, we went to her place and found it completely ransacked. From there, we went to the Elk Lodge where some guy tried to climb into her window. He fired at me when Archie and I followed him. Then the same guy shot up the gas station where we were getting food and fuel. Lastly, he found us at the Sunny Side Up Café and took more shots at us there."

Griff audibly sighed. "And you asked Kendra and Joel for help?"

"Yes, but they should be back at the ranch soon." Trevor looked annoyed. "We've talked to the police several times, but they don't have much to go on. Archie did find a shell casing outside the Elk Lodge that I left with Howell. I was hoping you could dig into Clark Miller's background for us. He was killed about seven months ago, also in a car crash. His death was ruled an accident, but now that Bailey is in danger, the two incidents must be connected."

"Clark Miller. Do you have a date of birth?" Griff asked.

"I'm sorry, I don't remember." Bailey tried not to

sound defensive. "After the car crash, I've been suffering from amnesia."

"Amnesia?" Griff sounded surprised. "That's unusual."

"We're hoping her memory returns soon," Trevor said. "In the meantime, we need to understand what's going on. Clark was the co-owner of the Sweet Water Pub and Grill along with an investment firm by the name of Plymouth Properties. I'm hoping you can find him that way."

"That helps." Bailey heard clicking noises and knew Griff was typing on a computer. "Do you know anything about the shooter?"

"No, other than he drives a large black truck." Trevor grimaced, holding her gaze. "We've only seen him in the darkness. I never got a close enough to identify the make and model, much less a license plate."

"What about other casings?" Griff asked.

"No, I didn't get any from the gas station attack. I had to get Bailey out of there, so there wasn't time to search. But there should be video, right? Howell was going to check video from the gas station closest to Bailey's house too."

"I can work on the video angle. I'm sure the police have picked up shell casings from the scene of the recent shooting," Griff said. "Yet bullets and shell casings won't help much until we have a gun to match them with."

"I know. In the meantime, we're off-grid, which is why we're using one of the disposable phones," Trevor said.

"Yeah, I figured," Griff said with another loud sigh. "I've learned over this past year to answer any number that pops up on my phone. Tell me more about this pub. What was it called? Sweet Water?"

"Yeah. I have a copy of the ownership agreement. I'll take pictures and send them to you in a few minutes via text. Bailey isn't on the agreement, so Clark's twenty percent ownership has reverted back to Plymouth Properties upon his death. Not sure the value of that ownership is worth killing for. And doesn't really explain why Bailey has been targeted now."

"Hmm. That's interesting." Griff was silent for a moment. "People have been killed for less, so it's worth investigating that angle."

"I agree." Trevor looked relieved to have his brother-in-law on board. "Anything you can dig up for us would be great. Don't worry, I warned Sergeant Howell that you'd be in touch."

"Good. It's nice to have the locals on board with the plan."

Bailey glanced at coffeepot. She would love to have some, but she knew caffeine wasn't good for the baby. She rose to fill a cup for Trevor. He smiled at her gratefully and mouthed thanks.

"Is there anything else you can tell me about the pub?" Griff asked.

"No. Unfortunately, I haven't been there." Trevor frowned. "Wait, it's relatively new. The ownership agreement was signed three years ago. So it hasn't been around for long."

"Okay, I'll see what I can come up with," Griff said. "You just concentrate on being safe. Speaking of that, have you spoken to Chase?"

"No. He'll be my next call," Trevor said. "I've been a little busy."

"Yeah, but you know how Chase can be. He hates being the last to know stuff like this. Later, Trevor. Take care, Bailey." With that, Griff ended the call.

Trevor sipped his coffee, his expression thoughtful. She nudged the phone toward him. "Call your brother."

He rolled his eyes. "Fine. But he'll be cranky."

"Only because he cares." She rose and moved down the hall to find the bathroom.

After using the facilities, she stared at her image in the mirror. The bruise on her temple had gotten darker and spread a bit beneath her pale skin. She searched her blue eyes, praying for a spark of recognition. But it could have been a stranger staring back at her.

Bailey feared using social media to spark her memory wouldn't work. Seeing her own face should have been familiar enough.

As she returned to the kitchen, she secretly admitted how much she liked Trevor. If not for Black Hat chasing after her with a gun, she'd enjoy spending more time with him.

Yet that was a terrible way for a relatively new widow to think. Wasn't it?

Nothing made sense to the point Bailey knew she couldn't trust her emotions. Not until her memory returned.

TREVOR STARED up at the ceiling as Chase reamed him out. "You know I hate being the last to know this stuff, Trev. And what were you thinking dragging Kendra into danger?"

"I didn't think she'd be in danger." Trevor tried to remain calm in the face of his oldest brother's anger. "I figured she'd drop off her SUV with me and ride home with Joel."

"And how did that work out?" Chase's tone rose. "Some guy showed up at the café and took shots at you! It's a miracle nobody was hurt!"

"I know, I was there. Trust me, I wasn't expecting the shooter to show up at the café." He swallowed a sigh. "Besides, it's not like Kendra is helpless in difficult situations. She's done her share of SAR missions. You and Maya tended to keep me and Kendra out of the loop, but we're more than capable of handling stress and danger."

"We only did that because you're the youngest." Chase sounded slightly calmer now. "I know you're both capable of defending yourselves. I made sure you can hit what you're aiming at. I just don't like knowing you're in danger."

"I love you too, bro," Trevor teased. "Don't worry about us. We're fine. We've reported these incidents to the police and have gotten Griff involved too. We're currently off the grid and plan to stay that way until this guy is found. It's bad enough that he's targeted Bailey, but she's seven months pregnant. I can't risk anything happening to her baby either."

"Yeah, that makes things more complicated," Chase agreed. "What else do you need from us?"

"Nothing at the moment." He scanned the cabin, then glanced over as Bailey entered the room. "We're safe. But you could ask Kendra to find another rental property in case we need to go on the move. Maybe something outside of Cody."

"I can do that," Chase agreed. "Do you want one of us to head out to provide backup?"

"Not now. I'll let you know if things change." The last thing he wanted was to have a couple of Sullivan SUVs heading for the cabin. He smiled at Bailey reassuringly. "Like I said, we're safe here."

"I hope so." Chase sounded annoyed. "Next time, fill me in right from the beginning. I could have driven out to support you."

"Kendra is fine. So am I. I'll be in touch if needed. Goodbye, Chase." He lowered the phone and ended the call. He tried to cut his older brother some slack, knowing Chase felt responsible for keeping the family together after losing their parents. But he'd also taught them to be independent and to perform SAR missions.

Not letting Kendra help only undermined her ability. Granted, Trevor had done his fair share of trying to protect the youngest sibling too.

"Sounds like you and Chase are close." Bailey returned to her seat at the table. "Am I close with my brother, Miles?"

"Yes, you are." He reached over to touch her hand. "Miles would be here if he wasn't in Alaska working under a contract. I promised him I'd look after you. If things change, he'll drop everything to get here."

A smile tugged at her lips. "That's nice."

Feeling restless, he stood and crossed to the supplies he'd dumped in the corner of the room.

Pulling out the brand-new laptop case, he carried it back to the table. "Let's get this up and running so we can search for pictures that might spark your memory."

"I'm willing to try." Her smile faded. "It's hard to imagine this will work when I don't even recognize my own face."

"Hey, you're doing fine." He set the laptop down and plugged it in. He knew from Kendra that the cabin had internet access, something he'd normally avoid. Since they were using a brand-new laptop, he doubted it could be used to track their location.

Crossing over to the router, he made a note of the password. Less than a minute later, they were online.

Bailey pulled her chair closer to his, leaning forward to see the screen. He tried not to notice that her dark-brown hair smelled like flowers.

He cleared his throat. "Okay, let's start with social media." He tapped the mousepad to search the internet.

"Do you have a profile page?" Bailey asked.

"No, but the ranch has a website." At her questioning glance, he shrugged. "We're pretty well known. I don't see that it's necessary to have a big social media presence."

She frowned. "Don't you need donations to keep the ranch going?"

"We get plenty of dog food donations." He didn't want to get into the financial aspect of the ranch. "Let's try your name first."

Trevor typed Bailey Adams into the search engine. Several people showed up, but none with Bailey's face in the profile. He narrowed the search to Cody and got no results. He hesitated, then tried Bailey Miller. He knew she'd changed her name back to Adams after her husband's death, but she may not have bothered to update her social media pages.

Still no match. He frowned. "Apparently, you're not on social media either."

"I don't know what to say, other than it's possible I like my privacy." She gestured to the screen. "I don't see the point of putting personal information out in the world for everyone to see. I mean, I must talk to my friends in person, right?"

"Right." He leaned forward and tapped in her brother's name. A moment later, he found Miles Adam's page. He turned the screen toward her. "Here's your brother."

"He has a full beard in this photo," Bailey said. "In the picture you took from my house, he only had a mustache."

"That photo was a few years ago," Trevor admitted. "This one here is more recent." He leaned forward to see better. "Looks like he updated this a few weeks ago while he's been in Alaska." He clicked through the other images. As he didn't have an account, and Bailey didn't either, their access was limited.

"Wait, is that my brother standing with a woman?" Bailey stared at the picture. "Do you think they're dating?"

"I'm not sure." Based on the way Miles had his arm around the pretty woman, he'd say yes, but he didn't want to speculate. "When I spoke to Miles yesterday, he didn't mention meeting anyone. She could just be a friend."

"Like we are?" Bailey asked.

He hoped his ears weren't turning red again. The memory of her chaste kiss was still too fresh in his mind. His feelings for her were not as friendly as they should be. But that was his problem, not hers. Striving for a casual tone, he nodded. "Yep, just like that."

"Okay." Her gaze lingered on his for a moment, then turned back to the screen. "How long as Miles been in Alaska?"

"Six months." He frowned. "I remember asking him if you were okay with his leaving, and he assured me you were doing fine. He was hoping to be home at Christmas when his contract is up."

"He'll be here when the baby is born, then, which is all that matters." Bailey scrolled through another handful of pictures. She landed on another one featuring her and Miles together. There was no sign of her baby bump, so he assumed it was taken earlier in the year. She lightly touched her brother's image. "We both look happy here. Do you think this was before or after Clark's death?"

"I'm not sure." He moved the cursor to see better. "This was taken in April. You must not have been showing very much because you don't look pregnant here." He glanced at her. "You do look happy. I guess that's a good thing."

"Yeah." Her furrowed brow belied her words.

He suddenly realized her concern was that she wasn't mired in grief over losing Clark. And now that he saw the picture, that made him rethink things too. Was it possible things weren't as great between them as he'd assumed?

Or was that just wishful thinking on his part?

That he could even hope for something like that made him feel ashamed. He was raised better than that and wouldn't wish an unhappy marriage on anyone. Trevor shook off the disturbing thought and jumped up from the table, eager to put distance between them. "I'm hungry. How about we have sandwiches for lunch?"

"That sounds good." Bailey didn't glance over at him, her gaze still focused on the computer. After a long moment, she pushed the computer aside. "I still can't believe I don't recognize my own brother."

"Hey, your memory will return in time." He forced himself to sound positive. "You like chicken, right? I bought sliced chicken breast from the deli."

"I do." She grimaced. "Interesting how I know things I like but can't remember making meals." She leaned forward and snagged a box from the table. "I'll take my prenatal vitamin now since I missed taking it at breakfast."

He kept himself busy pulling food from the fridge. He set their sandwich fixings on a plate—sliced chicken, cheddar cheese, lettuce, and tomato. Healthy enough, he hoped, for a pregnant woman.

Setting the platter on the table, he grabbed two glasses and the quart of milk he'd purchased. He remembered Bailey had always liked drinking milk with meals.

"Thanks." She took the glass and used the milk to wash down the vitamin. "Everything looks delicious."

It wasn't the fried chicken their housekeeper Anna made every weekend, but it would suffice. He cleared his throat and bowed his head. "Dear Lord Jesus, we thank You for this food we are about to eat. We ask You to continue keeping us safe in Your care. Grant us the strength and wisdom we need to find this man who seeks us harm. And most of all, Lord, we ask You to restore Bailey's memory. Amen."

"Amen," she echoed. "That was nice, Trevor. Thanks."

"Anytime." He couldn't understand why he was so aware of her. He quickly made a sandwich and took a big bite. It was barely noon, and the rest of the day seemed to yawn wide and empty before them.

He had no idea how they'd get through the day. He was already feeling antsy.

"We need to see if Clark has a social media page." She pulled the computer closer.

"I hadn't bothered since he's gone." He eyed her warily. "I'm sure you or someone would have deleted it by now."

"Maybe. But I feel like we should still check." She ate with one hand, poking at the keyboard with the other. "Since I'm not on the site, I may not have thought about deleting his profile."

He leaned forward as she did the search. Then she stopped and turned toward him, her gaze stricken. "I forgot that I don't remember what Clark looks like."

"I'll find him for you." He took over control of the laptop. He doubted they'd find anything, but she was right in that it couldn't hurt to look. None of the

Clark Millers on the screen looked like the guy he remembered.

"Maybe one of Clark's friends?" Bailey sighed. "Not that I know who they were."

"There was one guy I met at his funeral." Trevor tried to summon his name. "Max Nelson." He typed that name into the search engine.

The top match was the guy he remembered. Encouraged, he clicked on the image, surprised that Max didn't have any privacy settings in place. From there, he found a picture of Max and Clark fly-fishing. Clark held up a trout, grinning widely.

"Here. See what you think." He didn't offer anything more specific.

Bailey stared at the screen. Then the color drained from her cheeks, and she jumped up from her seat and bolted down the hall toward the bathroom.

"Bailey?" He jumped up to follow, stopping short when he heard her retching.

What in the world was going on? Had she recognized her husband? If so, why on earth would that make her sick to her stomach?

8

Shaky, Bailey rinsed her mouth out and sank down on the commode, resting her forehead on the edge of the sink. The wave of nausea had hit hard; she'd barely made it to the bathroom in time. She still didn't feel very good, but the urge to be sick had passed. Placing a hand on her belly, she straightened and took several deep breaths. Was this a response to the stress she'd been under? Or was there something going on with her pregnancy?

Lifting her gaze to the ceiling, she begged God to protect her daughter.

"Bailey? Are you okay?" Trevor's concerned tone reminded her she wasn't alone.

"Yes." She slowly rose to her feet. A quick glance at her reflection made her realize she still looked incredibly pale. "I'm coming."

The image of the two men on the computer screen flashed in her mind. They'd seemed familiar, but she hadn't had time to study their faces. Trevor likely wanted her to do that now, so she opened the door to step into the hallway.

"You're not feeling well." His gaze searched hers. Then he took her hand, leading her toward one of the bedrooms. Archie followed, as if he was concerned about her too. "I think you need to lie down and rest."

"No, really, I should keep searching the computer." Her protest was weak, as the idea of resting held a definite appeal.

"Not now. You can do that later when you feel better. Here, you should take the master suite." He pushed the door wide. "Having quick access to a bathroom is important."

The way he stated the obvious almost made her smile. "Thanks." She moved toward the bed, sinking down onto the edge. "I don't understand why I was sick."

He hovered in the doorway. "Was it the photograph on the screen?"

She slowly shook her head. "I don't think so, but I'm honestly not sure. Maybe I should take another look at it."

He hesitated. "Let's hold off on that. Try to get some sleep. I'll make some soup for you when you wake up."

She gave up trying to argue. Soup sounded good, but sleep sounded even better. "Okay, thanks again."

"Sleep well." Trevor stepped back. "Come, Archie." The K9 followed him into the hall so Trevor could close the door behind him.

Remembering the man who'd crawled into her hotel room, Bailey decided to sleep in her clothes. She kicked off her shoes, pulled back the covers, and climbed in. Resting her head against the pillow felt wonderful. Yet as exhausted as she was, she didn't immediately fall asleep.

The abrupt nausea concerned her. She must have had morning sickness early on in her pregnancy, but she couldn't remember. Was this morning sickness now? It seemed too late for that. Then again, she had been in a bad car crash. Maybe the nausea was related to that.

It has to be stress, she thought wearily. Too much fear and anxiety over her lost memories while dodging the man who'd kept trying to kill her. Even now, she found it hard to believe they were truly safe. She trusted Trevor. He'd done a good job of getting her out of harm's way over the past twenty-four hours.

He would keep her safe.

She smoothed her hands over her belly, doing her best to relax. Sleep would help her feel better.

Yet deep down, she was worried there was something wrong with her pregnancy. And silently vowed that if she didn't feel better after a nap, she'd ask Trevor to take her to the hospital.

Hoping and praying that leaving their cabin refuge wouldn't put them at risk of being found by the killer.

Trevor finished eating and cleaned up the kitchen. He found some canned soup in the cupboard, and while it wasn't as healthy as Anna's homemade chicken noodle, it would suffice for Bailey once she woke from her nap.

He sat at the table, staring moodily at the image of Clark and Max. Bailey hadn't mentioned her memory returning, but he was convinced this picture may have caused her abrupt onset of illness. Maybe, deep down, she had recognized either Clark or Max and had been afraid of them on some subconscious level.

The other possibility was that the stress of the past few hours had caught up to her. He kicked himself for not getting her to a safe house like this cabin sooner. He knew the doctor had suggested she rest.

Instead, he'd dragged her from one place to the next, including the police station to provide their statements. He needed to do better moving forward.

He rose and paced the length of the room. Archie looked up at him, his ears perked forward. A glance at his watch indicated it had been a while since the dog had been outside, so he shrugged into his coat and stepped into his boots.

"Come, Archie." He opened the front door. A blast of chilly air hit him in the face. It wasn't as cold as it normally was in January, but it was bad enough that he hunched his shoulders against the wind.

Archie leaped through the snow with enthusiasm, his tail wagging. His K9 might be a lab, but the goofy dog loved snow as much as Maya's husky, Zion, and Chase's Norwegian elkhound, Rocky, did. Along with Kendra's Alaskan malamute, Smoky, the three dogs were equipped with thick fur to protect them in the winter.

"Get busy." He scanned their surroundings, glad to see the snow around the property was still undisturbed. Well, except for his footprints and Archie's.

Archie got down to business. Trevor eyed the dark clouds, practically tasting the threat of snow in the air. November was often a gloomy month in Wyoming, and he hoped that they didn't get dumped on by a foot of snow.

After cleaning up after his K9, he headed

back inside. He refilled Archie's water bowl, then glanced down the hallway. Bailey's bedroom door was still closed, and as he shed his winter gear, he considered calling Maya or Jess. Both of his sisters were pregnant and could maybe shed some light on Bailey's sudden nausea.

Maya answered on the first ring. "Hello?" Her voice was cautious, and he belatedly remembered he was using a disposable phone.

"It's Trevor."

"It's good to hear from you." There was a pause, then she asked, "What's going on? Do you need more backup?"

"No, we're safe," he hastened to assure her. Chase had obviously filled her in on what was happening. "I'm calling with a pregnancy-related question."

"I'm not an obstetrician," she protested. "I only know as much as I've experienced firsthand. Well, and in talking to Jess and Wynona about their experiences too. By the way, we suspect Libby is pregnant. Pretty soon the ranch will be full to bursting with the next generation of Sullivans."

"That's great news about Libby. I understand you're not an expert but give me your opinion anyway." He stared out the window at the wooded landscape beyond the cabin's clearing. "Bailey is seven months pregnant and just experienced a sudden onset of nausea and vomiting."

"Did she eat something that didn't agree with her?" Maya asked. "I used to love some foods, like bacon, but once I became pregnant, the mere scent of Doug cooking it sent me to the closest bathroom."

"She was having a chicken breast sandwich with lettuce, cheese, and tomato. She didn't even add mayo."

"Hmm. That doesn't seem like the type of food to cause that reaction," Maya admitted. "Maybe she has the type of morning sickness that lasts all day."

"It's possible. But this is the first bout I've witnessed since yesterday. And she hadn't mentioned suffering from all-day sickness before." He turned away from the view. "Granted, she may not remember her pregnancy symptoms. She's been under a lot of stress. We've basically been on the run since yesterday."

"Absolutely, stress could be the cause of her nausea and vomiting." Maya paused, then said, "Chase mentioned she was in a car crash, right? And has lost her memory? Maybe there's something else going on with her pregnancy."

"I thought of that, and the doctor told us to be on the lookout for bleeding. He didn't mention nausea and vomiting."

"I get that, but everyone is different. Since you asked for my opinion, I'll say that if it happens again, you should take her to the hospital to be evaluated. Best to let the experts tell you if there's something to be concerned about."

"Yeah, that sounds like a good idea." He was glad to have his sister's perspective. "I appreciate your insight. She's resting now, and I'll see how she feels when she wakes up."

"Has she gotten much rest?" Maya asked.

"No. And that's my fault."

"I doubt that, Trevor. From what Chase said, you're doing an admirable job of keeping her safe. This is the bad guy's fault, not yours."

He didn't necessarily agree, but he let it go. "The good news is that I think we're safe here."

"Good. That may be all she needs," Maya said. "That level of stress isn't good for her or the baby."

"I know. Okay, thanks, Maya. I'll be in touch if anything changes."

"Be safe, Trevor." There was a hint of concern in Maya's tone. He knew she was worried about him, the same way Chase was. Maya just handled it differently.

He ended the call and tucked the disposable phone back into his pocket.

It was too early to follow up with Griff on what he may have found, so he returned to the computer to see what he could learn about Plymouth Properties. Unfortunately, he didn't uncover anything more than what he'd already been told. They were incorporated in New Jersey, which he found odd. Companies on the East Coast didn't usually venture this far west to invest in property. A good day at the Sweet Water Pub and Grill likely didn't bring in much cash compared to restaurants in the bigger cities.

So why had they come all this way? He tried to find a list of other businesses in Wyoming to see if they were also owned by Plymouth Properties, but a simple search didn't reveal anything helpful.

He bit the bullet and called Griff. His brother-in-law answered quickly. "Hey, Trevor. I'm still working on your problem."

"Sorry to be a pest." He didn't bother going into detail about Bailey's sudden illness. "I'm going crazy here doing nothing."

"I hear you. I will say I have not been able to find the individual names of the owners of Plymouth Properties."

He frowned. "Is that unusual?"

"Not really. The government tried to put in a rule that all owners had to be listed by name, but it never went through. In my experience, most people don't bother to list them as it's not required."

Another dead end. "What about finding out

what additional properties the company owns? That must be listed in some database."

"I'm running a list, hold on for a moment." Griff paused, then said, "Looks like most of their property is in New Jersey and New York. There are seven other businesses outside of those two states. Two happen to be in Wyoming. The Sweet Water Pub and another place called the Wagoneer, which is located in Cheyenne."

Cheyenne was a good six-hour drive from Cody. Not exactly convenient if the owners wanted to visit their respective restaurants. Then again, Wyoming was so far from New Jersey and New York that he was having trouble figuring out why they'd branched out west in the first place.

"So nothing suspicious about them," he said after a moment. "Nothing to indicate they'd have killed Clark on purpose."

"Not yet, but I plan to keep digging. I find it interesting the company has so many restaurants," Griff admitted. "Those types of places don't always stay solvent. I mean, chain restaurants can succeed, but the average restaurant doesn't rake in tons of cash. And many don't survive their first few years in business."

"That was my thought too. I can't imagine the Sweet Water Pub brings in anything close to what they make in New Jersey. The average wage is less here, and people don't necessarily go out to dinner that often."

"Yep. I'll reach out to my colleagues on the East Coast, see if they have any insight," Griff agreed.

"Did the Cody police say anything about the shell casing?" Trevor figured that was a long shot.

"No, but I asked Logan to fly it down to the lab in Cheyenne along with some from the gas station shooting. They appear to be a match, but that's all I know." Griff sighed. "Things don't move as quickly out here as I'd like at times like this. The long distances between cities are a hindrance, especially in bad weather."

He thought about the impending storm. "I hope Logan doesn't get caught in a blizzard."

"He's a good pilot. He took Jess with him, and they were planning to stay in Cheyenne if it starts to snow." Griff didn't sound concerned. "They know their limits. Logan isn't going to take any chances with Jessica's pregnancy."

Trevor could relate to that sentiment. "Okay, Griff. Thanks. I have one more question if you don't mind."

"What's that?"

"I'm wondering if the local police interviewed Clark's friend, Max Nelson. I don't know the guy, but I remember meeting him at Clark's funeral."

"You think he's involved?" Griff asked.

"I have no idea, but we suspect the shooter knows Bailey and some of our family too. I just think it's worth an interview."

"I'll ask Sergeant Howell to reach out to him. I would like to continue working the Plymouth Properties angle."

"That's fine." He figured it was better to have the local police ask questions rather than bringing in the FBI. That may scare Nelson off. "Please keep me in the loop if you find anything more."

"Will do. And Trevor? Don't get yourself killed." Griff ended the call.

He couldn't help but smile as he pocketed his phone. Griff might not be a blood relative, having married his sister Alexis, but the federal agent adapted to being part of their large family. His older siblings had used Griff's FBI expertise over the last few months, most recently when Justin had needed help in catching an escaped convict.

They were fortunate to have Griff on hand as needed.

Feeling restless again, he stood and resumed his pacing. Archie rose from his position in front of the fire, stretched, and joined him. He knew his K9 would be able to track Bailey's bad guy if they could only find him.

He headed into the kitchen to figure out what they should have for dinner. If Bailey was feeling better, soup may not be enough. There was chicken, small red potatoes, and green beans. Healthy enough for a pregnant woman.

As the minutes stretched into one hour and then two, he grew worried. Archie sensed his unease, tracking him with his large brown eyes as he went down the hallway to listen outside Bailey's door.

Hearing nothing alarming, he told himself she was fine. Then he cracked the door just enough to see her sleeping.

Slightly reassured, he quietly closed the door and returned to the kitchen. He opened the computer and went back to Max Nelson's social media. He scanned the comments, searching for anything unusual.

One comment caught his attention since it was written by Clark on the same day as his death.

Still up for a brew later?

Nelson had liked the comment and replied with a thumbs-up emoji.

He sat back in his chair, wondering if Sergeant Howell had known Clark had made plans to meet up with his buddy Max the day he'd crashed. Did it matter? From what he'd learned about investigating crimes over the past year, the last person to see someone alive was always interviewed first.

He vaguely remembered Clark's crash being late at night. Another reason the police had deemed it an accident. But he also knew that Clark hadn't been intoxicated when he'd crashed. Or at least, not over the legal limit. He pulled out his phone and called Howell. The cop didn't answer, so he left a message.

"This is Trevor Sullivan. Did you interview Clark's buddy, Max Nelson? He met with Clark the evening he died for a drink at the Sweet Water Pub." He hoped Tom didn't take offense to his question. "Just curious if he was the last one to see Clark alive. Please call me back when you have time, thanks."

"Trevor?" Hearing Bailey's voice, he spun in his seat. Then he jumped up to cross over to her. Every time he moved, Archie scrambled to his feet.

"How are you feeling?" To his eye, she looked better. "Are you hungry? Should I heat up some soup?"

"I feel better." She smiled, and he had to shove his hands into his pockets to keep from pulling her into his arms. "And yes, I would love some soup, maybe some toast as well."

"Coming right up." He turned to head into the kitchen while Archie greeted Bailey as if she had been gone for days instead of napping for a few hours. "I can also make a cup of herbal tea."

"That would be great." She lowered herself into the chair, stroking Archie's fur. "I'm not sure what happened earlier. The sandwich tasted fine going down."

He debated telling her about his conversation with Maya but decided to wait. If she felt worse again, he'd let her know about Maya's suggestion of going to the hospital.

Busying himself in the kitchen, he filled an electric kettle with water and turned it on. Then he set about heating the soup on the stove.

"Did you find anything interesting?" Bailey asked as he filled a mug with hot water and brought it to her with the variety pack of herbal tea.

"Just that Clark had a meeting with his friend Max Nelson the evening he died." He turned to put the bread in the toaster.

"A business meeting?"

"No, it sounded social." He glanced at her. "They were having a beer at the pub."

She shrugged. "I guess that doesn't surprise me. I imagine Clark spent a lot of time at the pub."

The derogatory note in her voice was interesting. "You didn't approve?"

"I—don't remember." She stared at her tea. "But if you asked me now if I'd like to be married to a man who owns a pub, I'd say not in a million years."

The firm and somewhat annoyed tone surprised him. "I wonder why you married him, then."

"I don't know how to answer that since I don't

remember him or our life together." She took a cautious sip of her tea. "Maybe I didn't feel that way at first but grew to dislike the pub over time."

"That makes sense." The toast popped. He buttered it, filled a bowl with soup, and carried the plate and bowl to the table. "Here you go."

"Thanks." She folded her hands together, blushed, and asked, "Um, will you say grace? I don't know why, but I have trouble finding the right words with my memory loss."

"Of course." He was touched by her request and almost mentioned the fact that she didn't normally pray before meals. But he was hoping this was the beginning of her faith journey and simply complied. "Dear Lord Jesus, we thank You for this food Bailey is about to eat. We ask You to continue to keep Bailey and her baby safe in Your care. Amen."

"Amen." She took a bite of the toast. "This hits the spot."

He watched her with the intensity of a hawk tracking a mouse. "Let me know if you start to feel sick again."

"I'm fine." She ate one piece of toast, then started on the soup. "Actually, I wouldn't mind more toast."

"Coming right up." He was relieved she wasn't running to the bathroom to puke. Maybe that had been more about stress and lack of sleep. The two-hour nap seemed to have done wonders for her.

She ate in silence for a few moments. Archie snored softly from beneath the table. "Have you learned anything new about the investigation?"

"I spoke to Griff. He's still digging into Plymouth Properties. Turns out they own a place in Cheyenne too. It's called the Wagoneer." He eyed her closely. "Does that sound familiar?"

"No." She frowned. "Cheyenne, huh? I think I've visited the state capital once."

"You remember that?" His pulse kicked up. Was this the start of her memory returning? Maybe rather than coming in one fell swoop, it would be more of this gradual familiarity with things.

The latter option made more sense, now that he thought about it.

"Sort of. I mean, I can see the capital building in my mind." She sipped more soup. "To be fair, I could have seen it in a picture."

The toast had popped, so he buttered it and carried it to her plate. Then he sat beside her. "Do you remember if you were with anyone at the capital?"

"No." She frowned. "Don't get all excited over a vague image in my mind. I'll let you know if my memory returns."

"I understand." He squashed his enthusiasm.

"When you feel up to it, we can look at more social media posts."

She nodded. "I'm good. Let's do it."

He waited until she'd finished her toast and soup. After clearing the dishes away, he returned to the table. "If you get upset, let me know and I'll shut it down."

"Okay, but I'm pretty sure I'm fine now." She rested her hand on his arm. "Thanks for your concern."

"You scared me," he admitted. Tapping the track pad, he woke up the computer. He went back up to the photo of the two men he'd shown her earlier. "Do you know these men?"

She stared at the screen for a long moment. "There's a familiarity about them, but I don't have a clear memory of either of them." She glanced at him. "Which one is Clark?" Before he could answer, she tapped the guy on the right. "This one?"

"Yes, that's correct." He tipped his head to the side. "Was that a guess?"

She nodded and sighed. "He looks more familiar than the other one, but I can't bring a full memory of him into my mind. To be honest, I can't really imagine being married to either of them."

Maybe being faced with familiar people in her life was working. Trevor took control of the keyboard again, bringing up the website for the Sweet

Water Pub. He turned the screen toward here. "How about this?"

She gasped, her eyes going wide. "Yes! I was there!" Then she frowned. "How is it that I can remember a place but not the man I married?"

"Don't be too hard on yourself. The good news is that you're starting to remember." He reached for her hand. "Getting some sleep probably helped. Maybe by tomorrow morning, you'll remember more."

"I hope you're right." She clung to his hand. "Because this being lost in the dark is for the birds."

He leaned in to kiss her, brushing his lips lightly across hers. Then he quickly straightened, mentally kicking himself. What was he thinking?

They needed her memory to return. And kissing her wasn't likely to help one bit.

Except to remind him of what he'd never have.

9

———————

Bailey tried to ignore the shimmering awareness stretching like a live wire between her and Trevor. His brief kiss had left her longing for more. Looking away, she took a deep breath, then swallowed hard. Talk about an inappropriate response. She'd just been shown a photograph of her dead husband, and here she was keenly aware of another man.

What kind of grieving widow was she to be so attracted to Trevor?

Pregnancy hormones running amok. That had to be the reason she was so drawn to him. Her emotions were all over the place. Not her fault, considering the circumstances. She didn't remember her husband, so she couldn't miss him.

She'd been targeted by a gunman, that was enough to terrorize anyone, especially knowing her baby's life was at risk too. Yes, that had to be it. Likely, this was nothing more than the primal reaction to being with a man who'd protect her with his own life if necessary.

Would Clark have done the same? She wanted to believe he would have. Men protected their families, didn't they? Yet seeing his image on the screen hadn't filled her with a sense of longing, or even of sorrow.

For some unknown reason, she'd only felt relief. And that didn't make any sense.

"Would you like more tea?" Trevor released her hand and jumped up from his seat. His movements were so abrupt Archie jumped up from beneath the table, looking around curiously. "I'll make it for you."

"Thanks." Even that bit of kindness made tears prick her eyes. She quickly wiped them away, knowing she needed to get a grip. Trevor was her brother's friend. He was being nice out of a sense of duty, nothing more. As if sensing her distress, Archie crossed to her side and licked her hand. She smiled and stroked his incredibly soft red fur. Archie might be known to track people, but she thought he'd be a great emotional support dog too.

"I think we should continue with searching the internet for familiar places."

"I agree." Trevor flashed a warm smile as he filled the kettle with water. "I'm encouraged by you remembering the Sweet Water Pub."

"It would be better if I could remember Clark or his friend Max." She gave Archie a pat, then reached over to manipulate the cursor to bring the photograph back up on the screen. The two men were smiling at whoever was taking the picture. Yet as she examined their faces more closely, she sensed a wariness in Max's eyes.

Pregnancy hormones? Her imagination? She had no idea.

"We'll try to find your friend Stacy White next." When the water began to boil, he filled a mug and brought it to the table. He leaned down to give Archie a reassuring rub. The dog settled on the floor between them.

"You said I work with her at City Hall." She chose an orange-flavored herbal tea bag and added it to the steaming water. Then her eyes widened. "I forgot to call to let them know I wouldn't be in."

"I took care of that." He turned the laptop toward him. "They'll understand."

Would they? Her head ached as she struggled to remember walking into work, setting her purse down, and turning on her computer.

It seemed like something she would do, but she couldn't actually remember doing it. It was getting harder to separate things she knew, such as how to operate a computer, from memories of working at one. With a sigh, she took a tentative sip of her tea. The warmth seeped through her bloodstream.

"Take a look at this." Trevor gestured to the image on the screen. The single-story building was built with tan brick and brown trim, and it had a flagpole out front.

"I'm assuming this is City Hall." She grimaced. "I can't say I remember being there before my accident, but I know we passed it during our drive around the city."

"We did." He typed on the keyboard. "What about this?"

An image of a pretty woman's face filled the screen. Bailey caught her breath, a brief flash of memory popping into her mind. She and Stacy were having lunch at the Hitching Post. She raised an excited gaze to his. "That's my friend Stacy. I remember having lunch with her."

"Do you remember when? I mean, like recently?" Trevor pressed.

She frowned, then shook her head. "No. I just remember sitting across from her in a booth at the Post. I can't recall if there was snow on the ground or not."

"That's okay. Any memory is a step in the right direction." Trevor's tone was encouraging. "We're making headway, Bailey. God has answered our prayers. Your mind is beginning to heal and with that healing will come your memories."

She regarded him thoughtfully. "You really believe that, about God answering our prayers. You're not just saying the words."

"I truly believe in God, that he sent his only son to walk among us, preaching God's word. And that Jesus died to save us from our sins." He didn't blink or look uncomfortable at discussing such things. "I know He's watching over us."

She stared at him, drawing comfort from that thought. "I wish I could remember Bible verses I've learned. Or even a church service I attended."

"In time." He glanced back at the computer. "I'm trying to think of other places you may have been that will spark your memory."

"Maybe the doctor's office?" She smoothed her hands over her abdomen. Archie lifted his head to look at her, then lowered it again. "I must have been there often in the past few months."

"True." The corner of his mouth quirked up in a smile. His fingers worked the keyboard, and she was mesmerized by the strength of his hands. "Here, this is the only clinic in town. Looks like they offer OB services."

Leaning in, she gazed at the building on the screen. Despite knowing she'd been there regularly, the place didn't spark any memories. Because they were routine visits? Nothing memorable? She sighed. "Sorry, but I don't recall being there."

"Hey, that's okay. You're doing great." He patted her shoulder. "Don't stress. We know that's not good for you or the baby."

The memory of her sudden nausea made her swallow hard. He was right. She'd started to remember, but pushing it wasn't smart. Concentrating only made her headache worse.

"You're right. I need a break." She turned away from the computer, cradling her mug in her hands. The fire Trevor had started earlier in the stone fireplace was still going strong. He must have fed more wood into the blaze.

Watching the flames was mesmerizing. Soothing. Calming.

"I was planning to have baked chicken for dinner." Trevor's statement had her turning toward him. "I know you just ate, so I'll wait a while before making it."

"Sounds good." She sipped her tea, which was getting cold. "I'm surprised you know how to cook."

He barked out a laugh. "Trust me, our parents expected us to pitch in and help with all aspects of the ranch. Including cooking, cleaning, laundry as well as general ranch chores. Now we have a house-keeper who holds down the fort while we're off doing SAR missions. Anna is an amazing cook, but we all fend for ourselves most of the time. Except on weekends, when Anna likes to cook large meals for the family."

"The entire family? All nine of you and the respective spouses?" That sounded akin to feeding a small army.

"Yep." He smiled. "You'll have to join us once this is over."

"Oh, I don't know about that." She felt her cheeks flush at the thought of joining family dinner. That seemed a bit too personal.

"You're more than welcome." He stood and paced the kitchen. Archie crawled out from beneath the table to stare up at him. He gave the dog a pat, then turned toward her. "I wish I knew why your house was trashed. It feels as if the gunman was looking for something."

"Like what?" She didn't understand where he was going with this. "If this guy wanted something from me, why not stick around after the crash?" She sighed. "At least, I don't think he stayed around."

"I got there pretty quick and may have scared him off." Trevor shrugged. "We may have to head back to your place at some point to take a closer look."

She didn't like that idea for several reasons. Not least of all, the bad guy knew where she lived and might have been waiting for her to do just that. "I'm sure he found whatever he was looking for."

"I'm not convinced of that." He turned to face her. "Otherwise, why is he still coming after you?"

"How should I know? Maybe he just doesn't like loose ends." She set the empty tea aside and pressed her fingertips into her temples, massaging the tense muscles.

"Or maybe he thinks you still have whatever he wants."

"That's ridiculous." She glanced down at her badly wrinkled clothes. "I don't even have fresh maternity clothes to wear, much less something a gunman would kill for."

"If you don't mind, I'd like to go through your purse." Trevor gestured to the quilted bag she'd draped over the back of a chair. "I should have thought of it sooner."

Bailey almost refused. A woman's purse was personal. Then again, it wasn't as if she had anything to hide. Did she? No, that didn't seem right. She couldn't imagine a scenario where she'd keep a secret that might harm her unborn child. "Go ahead."

"Thanks." He eyed the purse as if it were a snake that might bite him. But that didn't stop him from grabbing the bag and pulling items out one by one.

A wallet. Car keys. Tissues, lip balm, a scrunchie to use in her hair. All routine, everyday things.

When the bag was empty, he riffled through her wallet. Then he smoothed his hands over the fabric of the bag, as if looking for a secret pocket.

"Nothing unusual." He returned the items he'd removed.

"Wait, can I see those keys?" She held out her hand. He dropped them into her palm. There were a few keys on the chain, the key fob for her car, what looked to be a house key, and a smaller key, maybe to a locker? But there was another key on the ring. She stared at it. Did this open the garage? Or the back door?

"What is it?" He leaned close.

"Probably nothing." She stared at it a moment longer, then tossed it into her bag. "I don't know why it caught my eye."

He fished the key ring back out and took another long look. "It's completely different from your house key. I wonder if it opens the pub?"

"Why would I have a key to the pub?" She spread her hands wide. "I don't have any sort of ownership in the place. And I can't imagine Clark gave me a key."

"Maybe not." He eyed the key, then tossed the ring back into her purse.

"Hopefully, I'll remember the key when my

memory returns. Excuse me." She stood to make her way to the bathroom. The tea had worked through her system.

Yet even as she did so, the key niggled at the back of her mind. What was it for? And would unlocking that door, wherever it was, help her to remember why someone might want her dead?

TREVOR SET THE BAG ASIDE, feeling guilty for rummaging through Bailey's purse. His sisters would never have allowed him to do such a thing. Well, maybe they would if their life was on the line.

Archie stood silently at the front door. He grabbed his coat, shoved his feet into his boots, and opened the door. "Let's go, boy."

His K9 eagerly headed out. Trevor noticed snow flurries were starting to fall. They were light now, but he knew they could easily get worse. He hunched his shoulders to keep the snowflakes from sliding down to melt on the back of his neck.

Archie sniffed around the rental vehicle, then galloped over to lift his leg on the closest bushes. Trevor scanned the area, seeing nothing amiss.

There was no way Black Hat could know their location. Yet he was concerned that they may get stuck if the thick clouds overhead dumped several inches of snow on them. The large black truck would easily be able to plow through the drifts.

The rental SUV had four-wheel drive, but the undercarriage was lower, so it could get stuck. Seeing no fresh footprints in the snow made him feel better.

"Let's go, boy." He gave Archie the hand signal to come. His K9 abandoned his exploration of the bushes to bound toward him. Then Archie stood and gave himself a shake to get rid of the snow.

He went back into the cabin, kicking the snow from his boots before stepping across the threshold. Archie trotted to the fireplace. Seeing that Bailey was still in the bathroom, he crossed over to add another log to the blaze, then detoured into the kitchen.

Opening the fridge, he removed the package of chicken. He would have loved some of Anna's fried chicken, but an oven-backed version would have to suffice. They had green beans and little red potatoes to accompany the meal. Healthy food for Bailey and her baby.

As he prepared the meal, he thought about the key Bailey had noticed. The fact that she'd given it an odd look didn't mean much. She couldn't remember her own husband, much less a particular key. Yet he wouldn't be able to rest until he knew exactly what door the key would open.

"I'm going to sit by the fire." Bailey's voice had him turning around. Her skin was pale again.

"Are you okay?"

"Fine. Just tired. I'd like to rest for a bit." She walked into the living room, bypassing Archie who was back to his usual position near the fire.

"You'll tell me if you start to feel sick again, right?" He glanced at the window where the snow was coming down faster now. "It's snowing, so if we need to make the trip into town, the sooner you let me know, the better."

"I'm fine." She sighed as she settled into the corner of the sofa. She smoothed her hands over her abdomen. "I'm going to do some deep breathing exercises."

"Okay." He forced himself to turn away. His hovering over her wouldn't help. He had to trust her maternal instincts. Bailey wouldn't risk harming her child.

His phone rang, startling him. He grabbed it from his pocket. The number was familiar, but not one of his siblings. Belatedly remembering the message he'd left for Sergeant Tom Howell, he quickly answered. "This is Trevor."

"I got your message." Tom sounded exhausted, and considering the guy had been woken up well before sunrise, it was hard to hold it against him. "Per your suggestion, I drove out to see Max Nelson.

He wasn't home, so I left my card with a note to call me when he gets in."

He bit back a flash of impatience. It wasn't as if they had oodles of time on their side. Bailey was in danger, and the sooner Clark's buddy Max was interviewed, the better. "What about going to wherever he works?"

"I checked the Sweet Water Pub, he wasn't there." Tom's tone had gotten testy. "He's a truck driver. I assume he's on the road making deliveries. I can't drive around the entire state looking for him. I don't have a phone number for him either."

He swallowed a sigh. "Okay, I guess I didn't realize he was a truck driver. Sorry."

There was a brief pause. "Anything else you'd like me to do for you? More leads you want me to follow up on?"

Trevor wasn't going to apologize for trying to find Black Hat. "What about the gas station video? Were you able to get a closer look at the black pickup truck?"

"Unfortunately, there is no video from the gas station your perp shot up." Now Howell sounded disgusted. "I guess it broke down a week or so ago and hasn't been repaired yet. In looking at the gas station video located close to Bailey's house, I haven't found anything unusual."

That made him frown. He knew Black Hat

couldn't have damaged the video on purpose, there's no way the guy would know that Trevor and Bailey would stop there for fuel. The guy would have had to take out all the gas stations in the entire city and that was highly unlikely. Just bad luck that they'd stopped at the one station that didn't have a working video camera. "What about shell casings?"

"Yeah, we found several casings that match the one you found outside the Elk Lodge. Griff has sent them to the lab in Cheyenne. Good thing, as driving would be out of the question."

"Yeah, I hear you."

"I'm sure they'll match," Tom went on. "But without a weapon to compare to, we won't learn much."

"I know." He tried to think of another avenue to pursue, but he was fresh out of ideas. "Thanks for trying to find Max Nelson."

"Yeah." Howell grunted. "I'm calling it a night. My officers are going to be busy enough with this stupid snow."

"Okay, take care." He lowered the phone, battling a keen sense of disappointment. He'd really hoped interviewing Max Nelson would reveal a clue as to what was going on. He hadn't anticipated the guy wouldn't be home. As a truck driver, Max could be anywhere.

Another dead end, he thought as he placed the baking dish into the oven.

Eyeing the clock, he decided to feed Archie. He had brought in a pile of the K9s supplies, so he crossed over to find the dog food and collapsible food dish.

Archie ran into the kitchen the moment he opened the containers, his dark-brown eyes focused on his food. "You're something, Arch." He filled the bowl and stepped back. Archie sat, staring at him expectantly. He didn't make the dog wait to punish him, but to remind the K9 who was in charge.

A few months ago, a serial killer set out poisoned dog food to try to hurt Alexis's dog, Denali. The well-trained K9 had not eaten the food, so Denali hadn't been hurt. But that was exactly the reason they worked with their K9s to make sure they only ate the food their handler provided.

"Okay, boy. Go get it." He nodded at the bowl.

Archie pounced, his tail wagging as he gobbled his food. To slow him down, Trevor stopped him halfway and made him sit again. Archie didn't like it but sat patiently waiting for the signal.

"Take it easy, would you?" Shaking his head, he waited a full minute, then gestured to the bowl. "Go get it."

Archie finished the rest of his meal in record

time. Then he licked his chops as if satisfied with his performance.

"Goofy dog." He cut and seasoned the red potatoes, then set them aside as they wouldn't take long to bake. Glancing over at Bailey, she appeared to be asleep. But then her eyes opened, and he knew she'd just been resting.

"What was that about Max Nelson?" She stretched and pushed herself up off the sofa. "I heard you talking about him."

"Sergeant Howell stopped by his home to talk, but he wasn't there." He crossed to the computer, struck by an idea. He pulled up the guy's social media page and scrolled through the pictures. "Apparently, he drives a truck for work and is probably out on the road somewhere."

"What kind of truck?" Bailey stood behind him, peering over his shoulder. Her flowery scent teased his senses. He kept his gaze on the screen with an effort.

"No clue. I'm hoping to find a picture of him that will provide that information." He scrolled through the familiar pictures, then stopped at one. Max wore a gray shirt with his name over the breast pocket. On the pocket itself was a well-known beer logo embroidered into the fabric. "He delivers beer?"

"Maybe that's how he and Clark met." Bailey

moved closer, resting her hand on his shoulder. "I never liked beer."

He risked a quick glance at her profile. "Is that a memory?"

"No. But imagining the taste makes me feel sick to my stomach." She straightened and dropped into the chair beside him. "You would know more than I do if I've ever had beer."

"You don't drink at all from what I remember." He shrugged. "Your father drank too much, so you and Miles avoided drinking. My family doesn't drink either."

"So we have that in common." She waved a hand at the computer. "I don't know why you think it's important to talk to Max. I doubt he knows anything."

"Maybe not. But he met with Clark shortly before his death. I believe they were at the Sweet Water Pub." He shrugged and stood. "I'm not a cop, but even I know it's important to talk to the last person to see him alive."

She tipped her head to the side. "How do you know I wasn't the last person to see him alive?"

He hesitated. "I think Miles told me the two of you were together that night. He was with you when you received the call from the police about his death."

"Oh." She stared down at her belly. "Well, I still

don't think that means Max is involved. Or knows anything."

He crossed over to slide the potatoes into the oven and to cook the green beans. "You're probably right. It's just something that should be done at some point. Maybe Clark confided in his buddy."

"Confided what exactly?" She stared at him intently. "Are you suggesting we were having marriage troubles?"

"No, I was thinking more along the lines of work troubles. Maybe a disagreement between Clark and the majority owners of the pub."

"That makes sense."

He still thought it was strange that Plymouth Properties hid their members' names and that they'd spread out from New Jersey to open two restaurants in Wyoming. He was tempted to call Griff again but held off. His brother-in-law would call if he found something.

It didn't take long for dinner to be ready.

"I can't believe I'm hungry again," Bailey groused as he brought the steaming dishes to the table. "Everything looks amazing. You're quite the cook."

"I don't starve, that's for sure." He grinned and reached for her hand. "Let's say grace."

"Of course." She gripped his fingers and bowed her head.

"Lord Jesus, we ask You to bless this food we are about to eat. We ask for Your grace, wisdom, and strength as we seek those who would do us harm. In Jesus's name. Amen."

"Amen." She clung to his hand for another second before releasing it. "That was nice."

Trevor cleared his throat and held the chicken platter for her. He was dangerously close to falling for Bailey in a big way. He waited until she'd served herself, then piled food on his plate.

Archie crawled under the table. Their K9s were so well trained they wouldn't even eat a dropped morsel of food without permission.

They ate in silence for a few minutes. Trevor took note of the swirling snow outside. It was coming down harder now, and he imagined the rental SUV was completely covered.

He made a mental note to head out to brush it off, just in case they had to leave in a hurry.

"This was delicious, thanks." Bailey smiled and pushed back her chair. "I'll wash dishes."

"No, really, let me." He jumped to his feet, startling Archie. "You should rest."

"I hardly think washing dishes is taxing." She rolled her eyes. "It's the least I can do."

"I'll help." He was about to carry his dirty dishes to the sink when his phone rang again. This time, he recognized Tom Howell's number from earlier. "Hey, Tom, what's up?"

"I just learned that Max Nelson was in an accident out on Highway 14. Halfway between Cody and Greybull." Trevor froze, his grip tightening on the phone. "He didn't make it," Howell continued. "He was killed in the crash."

He drew in a harsh breath. Was Max's death an accident?

Or murder?

10

———

The grim expression on Trevor's face indicated he'd received bad news. She turned from the sink and leaned back against it, holding his gaze. She didn't like being in the dark about what was happening.

Archie lifted his head from his spot on the floor between them, then lowered it again. The K9 seemed to sense when there was trouble. When the K9 huffed out a sigh and closed his eyes, she found herself wishing she could fall asleep so easily.

"Any indication it was intentional?" Trevor asked.

She couldn't hear the reply. Trevor's expression didn't change, so she suspected it wasn't anything good.

"Okay, thanks. Keep me updated on your investigation." He lowered the phone, slipping the item back into his pocket. He stood without moving for a long moment. Then he cleared his throat. "That was Tom Howell. Max Nelson is dead."

"What?" If she hadn't been leaning against the sink, she may have fallen to the floor. "When? How?"

"Trucking accident on Highway 14." He gestured to the snow falling outside. "Could be that he lost control of his rig in the storm."

He could have, but she wasn't buying it. She slowly shook her head. "Three accidents? Clark, then me, and now Max Nelson? I find that hard to believe."

"I know." Trevor scrubbed his hands over his face. "I share your concern. Tom doesn't have any reason to believe Max's crash is anything but an accident, especially considering the weather, but he's coordinating with the state patrol officer who found Max's truck and trailer to investigate."

Dazed, she scrambled to make sense of the news. "I can't believe he's dead." She hadn't remembered him, but she wouldn't wish something like this on anyone. "I can't help but wonder if Max was silenced because he and Clark were friends. Because Black Hat thought he knew something he shouldn't." Another thought struck. "Or maybe they were involved in something illegal? They could have stolen stuff from the Sweet Water Pub. Money, beer, or something else entirely."

Trevor's gaze narrowed. "Do you think Clark is the type to break the law?"

"I don't know!" She lifted her hands in frustration. "I don't remember him or my life with him before his death."

"It's okay. I'm just asking." His tone was soothing.

She forced herself to take a deep breath. Stress wasn't good for the baby. Calmer, she continued. "I guess I feel like they must have been involved in something sinister to have been killed." She smoothed her hands over her abdomen. "I don't want to believe I was a part of it, though. I don't think I'd put my baby in harm's way by doing something like that."

"Trust me, Bailey, there's no way you're involved in anything illegal. That's not your nature." Trevor's smile was strained. "I think the shooter has gone after you because they're afraid of what you know."

What she knew was a big fat pile of nothing! She closed her eyes for a moment. "Maybe I should put up a billboard sign that says I have amnesia, so there's no reason to kill me."

"It's going to be okay." Trevor crossed over join her at the sink. "I promise I won't let anyone hurt you."

"I know." She turned and filled the sink with warm water. Trevor would do his best to protect her, but he was only one man. Sure, they'd gone off-grid, but how long would that last? The man after her didn't have superhuman powers, but she couldn't help feeling vulnerable.

Reminding herself stress wasn't good for the baby, she focused on washing dishes. When Trevor stepped close and pulled out a dishtowel to help, she swallowed the urge to lean on him for support.

She'd been leaning on his sweetness and strength more than she should.

"You know, you could be right about something illegal going on at the pub," he said after a long moment of silence. "Could be that Clark uncovered whatever was going on and was silenced before he could report his suspicions to the police."

It was a credible theory. Even the most likely one. What did it say about her that she had so readily jumped to the conclusion that her husband was a bad guy? She should be thinking the best of him. That the man she'd married was an innocent victim in this.

"You're right." She strove to sound confident. "Maybe Clark confided in Max, sharing his suspicions about the illegal activity. That's why they've both been killed." After a beat, she added, "Maybe they think Clark confided in me too."

"I've considered that, but why now?" Trevor frowned as he dried a plate and put it away. "Why come after you and kill Max Nelson all these months later?"

"Something must have happened recently. If I could remember, that would help." Her head throbbed painfully, and she was starting to feel queasy again.

"Don't worry about it." Trevor patted her shoulder. "There's nothing more we can do tonight."

She nodded, knowing he was right. But that didn't make her feel any better. Her headache seemed to be growing more intense, so she finished the last of the dishes and turned away. "I'm going to get some rest."

"Okay." His brow furrowed as he regarded her. "You'll tell me if you think we should go to the hospital."

"Of course." Her tone came out harsher than she intended. She sighed, then added, "I'm fine. Just tired."

Skirting Archie's sleeping form, she headed to the master bedroom. Her two-hour nap seemed like days ago. She felt just as exhausted as before.

The doctor had recommended rest. A luxury considering her current situation. She hadn't gotten a full night's sleep since waking in the wrecked car. Sleep would heal her broken mind. After all, she had started to remember a few things after her nap. Not exactly helpful things, but every little bit counted.

After using the bathroom, she crawled into bed, wearing her badly wrinkled clothes. She closed her eyes and took several deep, calming breaths. The pain in her head eased a bit, and the nausea receded too.

She must have slept but woke when she heard a thudding sound. Fear spiked through her, and she sat up, blinking the sleep from her eyes. Sliding off the bed, she moved to the door, opening it a crack.

"Lie down, Archie." Reassured by Trevor's low husky voice, she relaxed. "It's time to get some sleep."

The sound she'd heard was nothing more than Trevor taking his K9 outside to get busy. She silently closed her door and leaned against it. Even though she'd been sleeping, her instincts had gone on high alert at the slightest sound.

So much for no stress, she thought with a sigh.

Pushing away from the door, she crossed to the window and peered out. The snow had stopped falling, leaving a fresh blanket of whiteness covering the terrain. It was pretty, sparkling a bit in the moonlight. And also, she realized, irrefutable proof there was nobody out there aside of her and Trevor and Archie. Not a single footprint in the snow.

Safe. They were safe here at the cabin. After using the bathroom, she crawled back into bed.

Closing her eyes, she silently prayed for peace and that her memory would return in the morning.

TREVOR DIDN'T SLEEP WELL. He awoke often, inwardly groaning when he realized only an hour had passed since the last time he'd awoken. Archie snored softly beside him, which should have been reassuring. His K9 had better instincts than he did. Yet, he was worried his sixth sense was telling him something, so each time he woke, he got up off the sofa and moved from window to window to make sure nobody was outside.

The pristine snow was untouched, at least in the back of the cabin. In the front, he and Archie had made all sorts of tracks.

The last time he'd taken Archie out to get busy, he'd taken the time to brush the snow off the rental SUV. He'd also turned the vehicle around so that it was facing down the driveway. He'd wanted to make sure they'd have a clean getaway if needed.

Paranoid? Yep. The news of Max Nelson's death nagged at him. Probably the main reason he couldn't sleep.

He knew from hanging around with cops over

the past six years doing SAR work that they didn't believe in coincidences. Even Howell had sounded grim about Max Nelson's untimely death. And it irked Trevor that the cop hadn't gotten a chance to interview Clark's good buddy about the night they'd shared a beer, shortly before Clark's death.

Archie lifted his head to watch him move through the living room and kitchen. "Go back to sleep," he whispered. Archie continued to watch him. With a sigh, he went down the hall to the bedrooms. Bailey's room and the one directly across the hall from it both overlooked the backyard.

The snow remained untouched. But as he turned away, a dark shape caught the corner of his eye. With a frown, he moved to the side of the window and focused on it. The dark shadow was in the woods, likely an animal. Not a bear, but maybe a moose?

He watched the area for several long moments. The shadow disappeared. He blinked and looked again.

His imagination? Maybe. Either way, the shadow was gone, so he turned and padded back to the living room.

Archie had shifted on the sofa, taking over his pillow. Rather than pulling it away, Trevor went back to the bedrooms to grab a second one. By habit, his gaze went to the woods.

The dark shape was back.

The hairs on the back of his neck rose with alarm. An animal wouldn't stand there watching, then turn to leave only to return a few minutes later.

He watched the shadow for several long seconds. Then he backed out of the room to shove his feet into his boots and to grab his weapon. Archie opened one eye, but then sat up, his tail thumping on the sofa.

Trevor debated his next move and decided there was only one thing he could do. Get Bailey out of there as soon as possible.

"Come, Archie." He kept his voice low, glad he'd had the foresight to pack the K9's things in the SUV. He shrugged into his coat, grabbed Bailey's coat and purse, then hurried down the hall, Archie trailing in his wake. He quickly opened her door and poked his head inside. "Bailey. We need to go."

She woke abruptly, turning toward him while shoving her hair from her eyes. Seeing him with his coat and holding her things, her eyes widened with alarm. She scrambled from the bed. "What's going on?"

"I think someone is out back." He gestured to her shoes. "Please hurry. We need to get away from here."

With a nod, she shoved her feet into her shoes and walked toward him. He helped her with the coat, handed over her purse, then grabbed her hand. "Stay behind me. We need to be as quiet as possible."

"Okay." Her voice was barely a whisper. He led the way down the hall, glad he hadn't used any lights. To be honest, the snow outside provided enough illumination for him to see well enough.

And that worried him because he knew the same could be said for whoever was lurking outside.

At the front door, he paused. Leaning in close, he whispered into her ear. "I need you to get into the passenger seat. Don't slam the door, close it quietly. I'll take care of Archie, then drive us out of here."

She nodded, her face pale. He squashed a flash of guilt—nobody should have been able to find them there—but didn't waste another second. He opened the front door and swept his gaze over the area. He didn't see anything alarming, but he knew the moment the car made any sounds, the guy lurking out back would charge around to the front.

The snow muffled their footsteps. Bailey hurried to the passenger-side door. He opened the driver's side, then the back for Archie. The rear hatch made a clicking sound, but it didn't seem too loud.

The moment Archie was in the back, he closed the hatch and rushed to get in behind the wheel. He pressed the start button, knowing the noise of the engine would draw attention. He quickly shifted into drive and hit the gas. The SUV lurched forward, the tires grinding into the fresh snow thanks to the four-wheel drive.

The crack of gunfire wasn't entirely unexpected. He kept driving without glancing at the rearview mirror. He hadn't heard the thud of a bullet striking the vehicle. The SUV fishtailed a bit, but he pushed the speed as much as possible, desperate to get away.

When he hit the road, he swept his gaze both ways. There wasn't another vehicle nearby that he could see. Had the intruder gone in on foot from another location? And how on earth had they been found?

There were no ready answers to the questions rolling around in his mind. Fighting them back, he concentrated on putting distance between them and the gunman.

"Are we safe now?" Bailey's voice cracked. "I don't understand. I thought we'd be safe at the cabin!"

"We should have been." He couldn't imagine how they'd been found. And if not for his inability to sleep, the gunman may have gotten inside. He swallowed against the bitter taste of failure. "I don't know how he found us. I'm sorry."

Bailey buried her face in her hands, clearly struggling to maintain control. He kicked himself up and down for not doing a better job of protecting her.

Was it time to take her to the Sullivan ranch? He didn't want to put his pregnant sisters and sisters-in-law in harm's way, but it seemed like the safer option. At least with his other siblings there, they'd have strength in numbers. Not to mention ten dogs to alert them to trouble. Eleven dogs, if he counted Joel's newest puppy, King.

He focused on driving, then abruptly tapped the brake when he saw deep tire tracks veering off the road. Peering into the trees, he tried to spot a vehicle, but it was too dark to see anything beyond the trees.

The black truck was likely back there, somewhere. If he was alone, he'd have driven in to get a better look. But he couldn't take that risk with Bailey in the car.

No, his job was to keep her safe. He pulled out his disposable phone and held it toward Bailey. She was still sitting with her head down, so she didn't see him.

"Bailey, please call 911." At his voice, she lifted her head and swiped away her tears. "Let the dispatcher know a car went off the road, about a mile down Hawthorn Drive."

"Okay." She sniffed, took the phone, and made

the call. In the back, Archie rested his chin on the back of the seat, watching them.

Trevor would have felt better with a crate compartment for his K9. Especially if the black truck appeared behind them. He pushed their speed as high as he dared over the slick snow-covered roads. The plows hadn't made it this far.

"Put the call on speaker," he whispered when she began to speak.

Bailey nodded and did so. "Yes, we're on Hawthorn Drive. We heard gunfire and noticed tire tracks going into the woods. Please have someone come and check the area."

"I will send officers to the area. Please give me your name and is this phone the number I can reach you at?"

"I—um, I'm just a concerned citizen." She ended the call and dropped the phone into the center console cupholder. "I don't know why I said that."

"It's okay, I should have anticipated the dispatcher would ask. She may call back too." When the phone rang, he sighed. "Just ignore it. I have a bad feeling the gunman will be gone long before the police arrive."

That made her turn in her seat to look behind them. "He might follow us!"

"There's nobody back there. We're in the clear." *For now*, he silently added. Considering it was three in the morning, their options were limited. He considered heading to Greybull but wasn't sure that would work. Not when he didn't know how they were found in the first place.

"I don't feel very good." Bailey's low voice concerned him. "My head hurts, and I feel sick to my stomach again."

"Like before? When you got sick in the bathroom?" He tried not to show the extent of his panic. "Do you think we should go to the hospital?"

"I don't know." She rested her head against the window and closed her eyes. "Give me a few minutes. I'm sure this is just stress related."

He swallowed hard and took the long way into town. More to avoid the black truck than anything else. Heading to Greybull wasn't smart. Not when they may need to go to the hospital at any moment.

He focused on driving, silently praying for God to protect Bailey and her unborn child.

"I'm not sure what to do," Bailey whispered a few minutes later. "It could be my imagination, but I feel as if something is wrong."

"We'll go to the hospital." He decided this wasn't the time for a debate. "It can't hurt for you to be checked out. Besides, the doctor told you to return to be seen if your condition changes."

"I think he meant bleeding, but yeah, maybe that's for the best." She shifted in her seat. "For one thing, I need to use the restroom. For another, I just don't feel good. It's weird, because sometimes I feel normal, and other times, like now, I feel terrible."

Since he knew next to nothing about pregnancy, he couldn't argue. "The worst that can happen is that the doctors say you're fine and discharge you out of there." He forced a smile. "At least that will buy us some time until I can figure out where to go next."

"Yeah." She rubbed her temples. "I guess feeling like a fool is no big deal. It's better to be safe than sorry."

"They won't think you're being foolish." He eyed the rearview mirror. Still no sign of the black truck. Or any other vehicle for that matter. Taking the next right-hand turn, he headed toward Main Street. The hospital wasn't far from the Hitching Post and the Elk Lodge. Maybe this change in their destination would shake the gunman off their tail. The guy wouldn't anticipate they'd head back to the hospital.

Or so he hoped.

The parking lot to the north side of the emergency department entrance was almost completely empty. Only one car sat out there, and it was covered in snow, as if it had been there for hours. Pulling into the closest spot to the door, he shifted into park and glanced at Bailey. "Can you walk? Or should I get a wheelchair?"

"I'll walk." She pushed open her driver's side door and looped her purse over her shoulder. He opened the rear hatch for Archie and slid out from behind the wheel. Archie bounded toward him, tail wagging as if anticipating the search game.

"Sorry, buddy." He bent to stroke the dog, then hurried around to take Bailey's arm. "Go easy, it's slippery."

She didn't answer but stepped carefully through the partially plowed driveway. He escorted her through the glass doors, glad there was no sign of the black truck. He hoped the police had gotten to Hawthorn Drive in time to find the driver. Yet he also knew the town of Cody only had two squads on duty during the midnight tour. It was well past bar time, though, so maybe one of the officers had gotten there quickly.

"My name is Bailey Adams, and I'm not feeling well." Bailey rested her hand on her abdomen. "I was here yesterday after a car crash. The doctor told me to return if there was a change in my condition."

"Of course, we'll get you back right away." The woman behind the desk jumped up. "Follow me."

Trevor was surprised there wasn't anyone else in the waiting room. He trailed after Bailey, with Archie at his side. Thankfully, the hospital staff didn't ask him to leave with the dog, because that wasn't happening.

"Sit down here and a nurse will be with you soon." The woman flashed a smile, then left. True to her word, a nurse came in to see Bailey. It wasn't Emily Ross this time; he didn't recognize this caregiver.

"My name is Harper. I understand you're not feeling well?" Harper raked a gaze over Bailey. "Have you noticed any bleeding or abdominal discomfort?"

"I've been having weird flashes of nausea along with episodes where my headache gets worse." Bailey rubbed her temple. "Like right now, it's bad."

"I'm going to get a set of vital signs." Harper glanced at him, then turned her attention back to Bailey. "We'll start with a blood pressure."

"Okay." Bailey held out her arm. Harper put a stethoscope in her ears and pumped up the blood pressure cuff. After a long two minutes, Harper frowned and pulled the scope away. "Let's get you lying down with your feet up."

He sensed the tension in Harper's voice. "What's wrong?"

"Her blood pressure is pretty high." Harper moved to the cardiac monitor. "I'm going to get you hooked up to our equipment."

Trevor turned away to give Bailey privacy. He hoped the blood pressure issue was temporary, a result of his waking Bailey in the middle of the night to get her out of the cabin.

"Okay, your pulse is a little fast, so take some deep breaths for me," Harper instructed. Trevor risked a glance over his shoulder to see the rapid clip of Bailey's pulse dancing across the heart monitor.

"What about my baby?" Bailey asked. "Will you check her heart rate too?"

"Yes. In a moment." Harper took another blood pressure reading. This time, there was no mistaking the concern in her expression. "Still pretty high. Just relax for a bit, I'm going to get the doctor."

Harper hurried away. Trevor stepped up to take Bailey's hand. She gripped it tightly. "I think something's wrong."

He was getting the same impression. "You're in the right place, Bailey. Help is on the way. Deep breaths now. Close your eyes and relax."

Bailey's eyes flashed with anger, but then she did as he'd suggested. Ten seconds later, Harper and a female doctor wearing a long lab coat came into the room.

Releasing Bailey's hand wasn't easy, but Trevor pulled away and stepped back to give them room. "I'm Dr. Schaffer. When did you start feeling poorly?"

"I haven't felt great since the car accident,"

Bailey confessed. "But the nausea and vomiting started earlier this afternoon."

"Vomiting?" Dr. Schaffer gently palpated Bailey's abdomen as Harper got a fetal monitor device ready. A few minutes later, the rapid beat of the baby's heart filled the room.

"Yes." Bailey seemed calmer upon hearing the baby's heart rate. "I threw up once. But I feel sick to my stomach again now."

"Hmm." Dr. Schaffer turned to Harper. "Let's get a urine protein test. I'd like to rule out preeclampsia."

"What's that?" Bailey asked.

"It's a condition some pregnant women suffer, characterized by high blood pressure, sometimes nausea, along with spilling protein in the urine." Dr. Schaffer put a hand on Bailey's arm. "I don't want to alarm you, but it's something to be concerned about. We can try to keep you on bed rest for a while, see if that helps."

"What if it doesn't?" Trevor asked. "What other treatment options does Bailey have?"

"The most effective treatment is to induce labor," Dr. Schaffer admitted.

"No! It's too early!" Bailey's horrified gaze clung to his. "Please, don't do that."

"We'll see what your urine test shows," Dr.

Schaffer said. "If you have a mild case, bed rest and medication may do the trick."

Bed rest and meds or inducing labor. Trevor battled back a wave of panic. He wasn't sure how he would keep Bailey and her baby safe under either of those conditions.

Feeling helpless, he bowed his head and silently prayed. *Dear Lord Jesus, keep Bailey and her baby safe in Your care!*

11

―――――――

Struggling to remain calm, Bailey stared up at the doctor in horror. "Please, there must be something you can do. I don't want to have my baby this early!"

"I understand your concern." Dr. Schaffer's voice was soothing. "But keep in mind your baby is far enough along that she'll be okay. She'll likely need to be in the neonatal intensive care unit for a while, but she'll be fine."

Neonatal intensive care? Bailey glanced at Trevor, his grim expression sharing her fear. "Is this my fault?" She pushed the question past her tight throat. "Did I cause this by being upset or stressed? I was in a car crash two days ago, is that why I'm having difficulty now?" She thought about how the gunman had been following them for the past two days. "If I promise to stay calm, will my blood pressure return to normal?"

"This is *not* your fault." Dr. Shaffer's tone was firm. "Preeclampsia is just one of those conditions that sometimes occur in a pregnancy. It's rare in the big scheme of things. Only seven percent of pregnant women experience this complication, and it's almost always with first-time pregnancies. You didn't cause this, Bailey. Please trust me on that." The doctor's kind smile was only slightly reassuring. "And we don't know for sure how bad your condition is until we get that urine sample."

"Speaking of that, do you think you can use the bathroom?" Harper asked.

"Yes." She'd almost forgotten her need to empty her bladder. Trevor slid his arm behind her shoulders to help her sit up. She flashed him a grateful look. His unwavering support made tears prick her eyes. She realized God had been watching out for her when He sent Trevor to her side. Without him, she'd be lost in a world of hurt.

And now this. Possibly delivering a premature baby! She couldn't bear to think about it. Despite Dr. Schaffer's comments, she knew that premature babies could develop complications with their heart or lungs.

"Easy," Harper cautioned, taking a few minutes

to disconnect her from the heart and baby monitor. "Slow and easy."

Bailey focused on taking slow, deep breaths as she allowed the nurse to help her into the bathroom. A few minutes later, the urine sample was on its way to the lab. Harper helped her back to bed, and Bailey was glad to see Trevor was still there too.

"How long will it take to get the results?" he asked.

"Not long." Harper covered her with a blanket. "I'll let you know when we have them. For now, just rest."

As she settled back against the pillow, she realized the diagnosis of preeclampsia made sense. The increase in her headache and the sudden onset of nausea must have been when her blood pressure was high.

Deep down, she was convinced the stress she'd been under over the past two days hadn't helped matters. Maybe stress alone doesn't cause preeclampsia, but it hadn't helped either.

"I'm sorry." Trevor's low, anguished voice broke into her thoughts. "If I had done a better job of keeping you safe . . ."

"You have kept me safe." She reached for his hand. "I'm here now. And maybe my condition isn't as serious as it sounds." She wanted to reassure him that it wasn't his fault.

All blame rested with the gunman. What sick person targets a pregnant woman? A flash of anger hit hard, and she had to remind herself to let it go.

Getting upset wasn't helpful. She was in good hands at the hospital.

Trevor pulled up a chair and sat beside her. Archie shifted positions on the floor at his feet. Remembering how she'd considered Archie to be a therapy dog, she kept her gaze on him, relishing his sweet face.

"Trevor? Will you put Archie up here by me for a while?" She scootched over to make room. "Just for a few minutes."

"Sure." He lowered the side rail and patted the gurney. "Up, Arch. Get up."

The red lab gathered himself and leaped gracefully up onto her gurney. The K9 leaned in to lick her, then stretched out beside her. She rested her hand on his silky fur, then closed her eyes.

She must have dozed, because she awoke when her door opened. Dr. Schaffer was back. Trevor shot to his feet and took her hand.

"I have your urine protein results," Dr. Schaffer announced. "You definitely have preeclampsia, but in my opinion, your condition isn't severe. You do have some protein in your urine, but not as much as I feared."

Bailey glanced at Trevor, then back to the doc. "What does that mean?"

"I've put a call in to the OB doc on call to come in and see you," Dr. Schaffer said. "I think you can be managed conservatively with bed rest along with some medication to keep your blood pressure down, but we'll see what the OB says. He or she may have another thought."

Bed rest? She winced, wondering how on earth they'd manage that. "I don't want to take medication."

"I understand, but there's a medication that's safe to use in pregnancy." Dr. Schaffer said. "We wouldn't recommend anything that would hurt your baby. You need to understand that preeclampsia could lead to you having seizures. That would be very bad for your unborn child."

She swallowed hard, doing her best not to panic. Seizures? She wasn't prepared for this! She strove to sound calm. "Will bed rest and medication cure this condition?"

"No, unfortunately the only real cure for preeclampsia is to deliver the baby." Dr. Schaffer gave her an encouraging smile. "Obviously, the longer we can keep that bun of yours in the oven, the better. Our goal would be to wait as long as possible, providing time for your baby's lungs to continue to develop. We'd like to avoid your daughter needing to be placed on a ventilator after birth. But we need to balance that with the risk of you suffering a seizure."

A ventilator! She swallowed hard at the image of her premature daughter connected to a breathing machine that flashed in her mind. She couldn't imagine anything worse. Well, except for open heart surgery or something like that.

Obviously, this was all a bigger deal than she'd realized. Of course, she'd take the medication if that would help prevent her daughter from being born earlier than normal. "But you think my case is mild."

"Well, mild for now," Dr. Schaffer corrected. "I'm cautiously optimistic. But you'll need to be monitored closely from now on, at least once a week maybe twice. Depends on how well your blood pressure remains in good control." Dr. Schaffer turned to leave. "The OB doctor on call will likely have additional ideas for what we can do for you. He'll be here soon."

The door shut behind the doc. Bailey stared up at Trevor. "Bed rest."

"I know. We'll find a way to make that happen." He gently squeezed her hand. "Try not to worry."

"Yeah." She grimaced. "Easier said than done. I never expected this, Trevor. High blood pressure, protein in the urine, and possible seizures? That all sounds so scary to me."

"It is scary, but you're in good hands, Bailey." He reached for her hand. "Let's pray."

She was touched by his offer. With a nod, she bowed her head and opened her heart. "Dear Lord Jesus, please keep my baby safe in Your care. Amen."

"Amen," Trevor murmured.

She continued to cling to his hand, the other buried in Archie's fur. "I never prayed out loud before."

A smile lit up his green eyes. "You'll get used to it."

Would she? She closed her eyes and focused on the beat of her baby's heart. She would put her fears and worries into God's hands.

A moment later, there was a knock at the door. She opened her eyes. "Come in."

A different OB doctor from the day before came into the room. He was older, balding, but he had kind eyes. "I'm Dr. Clayton. I understand you're experiencing some complications with your pregnancy."

"Yes." She was glad he didn't ask for Archie to be put back on the floor. "I guess I have some protein in my urine."

"I saw the lab results." Dr. Clayton gently palpated her abdomen. "You're two days over thirty weeks pregnant, which is good, but I'd like to see if we can get you to thirty-four or thirty-five weeks gestation before we deliver."

"How about waiting until I'm full term?" She gave him a hopeful look. "If my condition is mild . . ."

He shook his head. "I'm sorry, Bailey, but that's not likely. We may be able to buy some time, but in my experience, preeclampsia gets worse as the pregnancy progresses. Take heart, though. Even a few more weeks will help tremendously. I'm sure you've been told about the risk of seizures. That's something we cannot allow." He patted her arm. "Having preeclampsia is an added stress on your body. The good news is that babies who are under some stress like preeclampsia tend to have better lung development as they grow. That's important. We'd like to avoid putting your baby on a ventilator if possible."

She tried to nod, her head swimming at his explanation.

"We'll start you on a low-dose blood pressure medication that is safe for pregnant mothers. I'm also going to perform an ultrasound to estimate the size of your baby. That will help us know what we're dealing with." He turned to leave. "Be back in a minute."

"Okay." She blinked back tears. If Dr. Clayton

was right about being able to hold off four to five weeks, she'd have her baby between Thanksgiving and Christmas. That hadn't been a part of her plan. She wasn't due until January! The holiday didn't matter as much as making sure her baby was healthy enough to survive being born premature.

"I'm going to call my siblings to make arrangements for you to stay at the ranch." Trevor's voice pulled her from her thoughts. "That's the safest place for you to be on bed rest."

"But you mentioned your sisters are pregnant." She wanted nothing more than to be safe, but the thought of putting others at risk didn't sit well with her. Their babies were just as important as hers. "I don't think exposing them to danger is smart."

"I don't like it either, but I don't see an alternative." His expression turned grim. "You need to stay on bed rest long enough for your baby to grow and develop. If the doctors don't keep you here, the ranch is the only viable option."

She stared at him. "I think you better run that past your brother, Chase. If this guy follows us to the ranch . . ."

"He won't." Trevor sounded positive, but she wasn't convinced. After all, this guy had found them at the cabin where they were supposed to be off the grid. How had he managed that anyway?

Her head started to throb, so she closed her eyes

again and focused on breathing. If this was her blood pressure spiking up, she was determined to bring it down naturally. She'd also take the medication he ordered for her too. Anything to keep her baby safe and growing stronger.

Dr. Clayton returned a few minutes later pushing an ultrasound machine.

"Down, Archie," Trevor said.

Archie stood and leaped off her gurney to the floor. He stretched, then trotted toward the door. Bailey knew the dog probably needed to go out and gave Trevor a nod. "Go ahead. I'll be fine."

He hesitated. Dr. Clayton glanced at him, then said, "You can stay. This will only take a few minutes."

She shrugged, indicating that was fine with her. He took a step back to make room for the additional equipment. Archie came over to stretch out beside him.

"Cold gel," Dr. Clayton said as he bared her belly. She felt self-conscious about her belly showing until Dr. Clayton put the probe in the gel and moved it around. Then her gaze was fixated on the ultrasound screen.

"See, here's the head." He moved the probe in a slow circle. "Here's the body." He manipulated the probe easily, using markers to indicate spots on the screen. Dr. Clayton continued with the exam, then finally lifted the probe. "Good news, your baby is already three pounds."

Three pounds sounded so small! She tried not to show her dismay. "But most babies are born at seven pounds or more, right?"

"Some full-term babies are born at six pounds." He removed the goop with a paper towel and then covered her abdomen. "This is a period of growth for your baby, all her organs are functioning well. If we can hold off four to five weeks, your baby will be five to six pounds. That's a reasonable size for a preemie."

She tried to share his optimism. But she kept thinking about how her baby was still only three pounds. That her young daughter would need to double in size over the next few weeks seemed almost impossible.

And she prayed again for Lord Jesus to protect her baby girl.

"I'm going to order blood pressure medication for you," Dr. Clayton said. Trevor knew the guy assumed he was the father of Bailey's child, and he didn't bother to correct the man. For the moment, he was the only support system Bailey had. And it surprised him how much he wanted to be with Bailey. Not just now, but after this nightmare was over. "I'd like you to be monitored here for a while before discharging you."

"You're not keeping her?" Trevor tried not to sound disappointed. "Shouldn't she have close observation?"

"If the medication works, she'll be fine resting at home," Dr. Clayton said. "But you need to follow up with your doctor in a few days. It will be important to continue checking your urine for protein."

"Okay, thank you," Bailey said.

Trevor wasn't sure how they'd manage a doctor visit so soon, but he was determined to find a way. He really needed the Cody police to step up their game. Black Hat guy needed to be found and arrested ASAP.

He crossed to Bailey's bedside. Seeing the baby on the ultrasound screen had filled him with awe. He reached for her hand. "Will you be okay alone for a few minutes? I need to take Archie outside."

"Of course." Her smile didn't reach her eyes. "I'm fine."

He knew she wasn't, but he didn't argue. He had been encouraged by the doctor's words, but apprehension still lingered in Bailey's eyes. "Hey, you're going to be okay. So will your baby. Just hang in there. I'll make some phone calls." He glanced at the time and grimaced. "Although I'd rather wait until a more reasonable hour to contact my family. They tend to be up early, but it's only four twenty."

"Sounds like they'll watch me for an hour or so after I take the first dose of medication." Bailey shifted on the gurney. "That gives us some time."

"Yeah, that's a good thing." He released her, noting that Archie was standing by the door again, his K9's signal that he needed to go out. "Rest now. I'll be back soon."

She nodded and closed her eyes.

Resisting the urge to kiss her, Trevor went to open the door. Archie padded out, instinctively heading through the department to the main entrance. He glanced at the nurses and doctors chatting in the center of the room, but they didn't pay him or Archie any attention.

Even the OB doctor hadn't seemed to mind Archie's presence. He bent to pat his dog on the head. "You're a good boy, Arch."

His K9 wagged his tail in agreement.

As he passed the front desk, he saw a Cody police officer standing there with a man sporting a bruise on his temple. Trevor recognized him as Heath Anderson. He frowned, remembering his recent call to Tom Howell. "Hey, did you guys find anything off Hawthorn Drive? Maybe a black truck?"

"Not me, I was breaking up a fight in town." Anderson jerked his thumb toward the guy standing beside him. "Two brothers slugging it out, can you believe it?"

He could, although his fights with his siblings had rarely escalated to physical blows. Yet they had wrestled a lot when they were younger. The guy standing beside Heath was old enough to know better. "Did someone else respond?" he asked.

"Yeah. Jeff Riley went out to investigate. I haven't heard him respond with an arrest, though."

Trevor's hopes plummeted to the soles of his feet. "Do you think you can check with him? I'd really like to know if this guy is in custody."

"Yeah, sure." Anderson lifted a hand to his radio. "Unit 8, I'm at the hospital with Sullivan. Do you have anything on the reported vehicle off Hawthorn Drive?"

There was a long silence, before Trevor heard a male voice respond. "Negative. Tracks indicate the vehicle left the area."

Left the area. Trevor swallowed a groan. The chances of the cops finding this guy were shrinking.

How long before this guy discovered where they were and tried again? Trevor still hadn't figured out how they'd been found at the cabin in the first place. They'd only gone online with a clean laptop and used disposable phones. What else could he do to protect Bailey?

"Ten-four, Unit 8." Anderson glanced at him and shrugged. "Sorry, Trevor. No sign of your guy."

"Yeah, I heard. Thanks for asking." He moved toward the doors. "Come, Archie."

The cold air was a brutal slap to the face. Not that Archie seemed to notice. The dog bounded across the parking lot to the closest snow pile to get busy.

Anderson's police car was parked near his rental SUV. But there were still no other cars in the lot. He supposed it was a good thing the hospital wasn't too busy.

Hunching his shoulders, he waited for Archie to finish, then called the dog over. He debated feeding him, but it was still early. "Let's go, boy." He turned to head inside. Anderson and his bruised perp were gone, already taken back to a room.

Staying in the empty waiting room, he pulled out his phone and sent a text to Chase. *Need a safe place for Bailey to be on bed rest. Call me.*

He wasn't sure how his oldest brother would feel about Bailey staying in Trevor's cabin on the ranch. There were now four pregnant women on the ranch, including Chase's wife, Wynona, and Shane's wife, Libby.

The cabin should have been safe, but it wasn't. The Elk Lodge certainly hadn't worked. He couldn't imagine another hotel would be any better.

He lifted his gaze to the ceiling, praying for answers.

When his phone rang, Chase sounded grumpy and sleepy. "What happened to staying at the cabin?"

"We were found." Trevor paced the length of the room. Archie was stretched out on the floor, watching him. "I don't understand how, Chase. We used disposable phones, a clean computer. Kendra made the reservation, but I can't imagine this guy has the ability to hack into the rental property website to find us."

"We may need someone other than family to find a place," Chase said.

A flash of anger hit hard. That was not what he wanted to hear. "We're at the hospital. Bailey has been diagnosed with preeclampsia. It's a condition that requires medication and bed rest to protect the baby from being born too early. If her condition worsens, they'd deliver her despite the fact that her baby is only three pounds!" Realizing his voice was rising, he did his best to dial it back. "This is serious, Chase. I wouldn't ask if it wasn't. I need to bring Bailey to the ranch."

"Preeclampsia?" Chase sounded wide awake now. "I've never heard of it."

"It's not something we were taught in EMT training either. Our focus was always on emergency situations like when the placenta breaks away from the uterus." He stopped pacing and sighed. "Listen, Chase, I wouldn't ask if it wasn't important. If you'd have heard this doctor talking about the risk of a premature baby, along with the possibility of Bailey having seizures if her blood pressure doesn't get under control, you'd understand. I can't keep waking her up in the middle of the night to go from one hotel or rental property to the next. She needs to be on bed rest while we keep her safe."

"Okay, fine. I hear you. Bring her to the ranch." Chase sounded resigned. "At least we have plenty of people here to help her. And the dogs will let us know if anyone gets too close."

The wave of relief was overwhelming. "Thanks, Chase. I appreciate your willingness to do this for her."

"Hcy, I'd want someone to do the same for anyone in our family." His gruff older brother's voice softened. "Adding one more pregnant female to the bunch shouldn't be a problem."

But it was a risk, and Trevor knew it. He stared out at the hospital parking lot. Anderson's squad was still parked out there, and knowing the police officer was inside the emergency department gave him an added sense of security. "I'll call you when we're able to leave," he said. "Sounds like they're going to start her on a blood pressure medication and want to watch her for a bit afterward to make sure her level comes down."

"That's fine. I'll make sure Anna knows you and Bailey are coming. She'll want to make breakfast for you."

"That would be great. See you soon." Trevor disconnected from the call. It felt good to have a plan. He didn't love placing his family in danger, but Bailey deserved to be safe.

It dawned on him that he should let Miles know about Bailey's diagnosis. His buddy wasn't scheduled to return to Wyoming until Christmas, but if she had the baby early, Trevor was sure Miles would cut his contract short. Even if that meant sacrificing his bonus.

Later, he decided. It was too early to call Miles now. Besides, he really wanted to talk to Tom Howell again. He didn't like treating the sergeant as his personal source in the department, but there had to be something more they could be doing to find the black truck or the shooter.

Frowning when Tom didn't answer, he left a message. "Hey, call me when you get this. I spoke with Heath Anderson. Jeff Riley didn't find the truck or the shooter. I need to know if you got any tire impressions. Maybe that will help us narrow down the make and model of the vehicle. Call me."

With a sigh, he pocketed the phone. He didn't

like feeling as if he were running the investigation. Jeff Riley had probably already asked for the crime scene techs to come out to look at the tire tracks.

He turned to head back into the emergency department when a pair of high, square, bright headlights caught his eye. Moving closer to the glass doors of the emergency department, he narrowed his gaze, watching them approach.

They belonged to a truck—of that much he was certain. His heart thudded painfully against his sternum. A black truck?

Without thinking it through, Trevor ran outside. His feet slipped on the slick surface, but he didn't go down. He stared hard at the truck as it rolled past. It was dark in color. Hard to say if it was black or a dark gray.

As it went by, he stared hard at the license plate, hoping to get a number. Only there wasn't one. He caught a glimpse of a paper taped to the back window above the truck bed.

A temporary plate. But the writing was too faint for him to see it clearly in the dark. Trying not to overreact, he turned to rush back inside. He needed to find Anderson to let him know.

Maybe it was nothing. But at that point, he couldn't afford to leave any stone unturned. He wanted that truck found, identified, and the driver brought in for questioning as soon as possible.

12

———————

After taking the new blood pressure medicine Dr. Clayton had ordered, Bailey closed her eyes and tried to relax. The only good thing about all of this was that she felt safe here in the hospital.

When Harper had brought her medication in, Bailey had asked about staying overnight. It felt awkward, as she doubted most people would not want to spend more time in the hospital than necessary. Harper had grimaced and said she didn't think Dr. Schaffer would agree, but she promised to ask.

Bailey sighed, knowing it was a futile request. Hard to justify the expense of a hospital stay when the doctor's orders were to take medication and to stay on bed rest. Her case was mild enough that the doctor had mentioned that she could get up to eat and use the restroom, so it wasn't like she couldn't move around a bit.

Yet she was scared to leave. Frightened to know the black-hat guy was out there, waiting for her. Her memory hadn't returned either, despite getting some sleep. She tried not to overreact to her impending discharge. Trevor had promised to call his brother about the idea of her staying at the ranch.

That thought brought more guilt. What if Black Hat found her there? Would he hurt the other pregnant women? Feeling her muscles tense, she drew in a slow breath and rubbed her hands over her belly.

No stress. No stress. The words became a mantra in her brain.

"Hey, how are you feeling?" Trevor's voice had her opening her eyes. Had she fallen asleep? She glanced down, smiling when she saw Archie standing beside him.

"Fine." She belatedly realized her headache was better, and she wasn't feeling as sick to her stomach. In fact, she was aware of the gnawing hunger rumbling in her abdomen. "I wouldn't mind breakfast."

"Me too. Hopefully, we'll be able to eat soon." His tone was light, but his expression remained serious. "Chase is on board with us heading to the ranch."

"Great." She shoved the guilt aside. "I'm glad."

"Yeah." He glanced down at Archie, then patted the gurney. "Up, boy."

Archie gathered himself and leaped gracefully up onto the gurney. She reached out to stroke the K9's soft fur. Like before, he settled down beside her, resting his head between his paws.

There was a knock at the door, then it opened. Bailey was surprised to see one of the local cops standing there. "Trevor? You wanted to talk to me?"

"Yeah." Trevor shot her a quick glance. "It's probably nothing, but when I was out in the waiting room making calls, I noticed a large dark truck passing by. I ran outside to try to get the license plate, but there wasn't one."

The officer whose name tag read Anderson frowned. "That's odd."

"Well, there was a temporary plate number taped to the back window, but I couldn't read it." Trevor shoved his hands into the front pockets of his jeans. "I was hoping you would put out a BOLO for the vehicle so we can find out who owns it."

Bailey noticed the hesitation that crossed Anderson's features. "I don't know, Trevor. Having a temporary plate isn't a crime."

"I get that, but what if it's a ruse? A way to keep us from identifying the vehicle and owner?" Trevor didn't back down. "Anyone can tape a piece of cardboard with a fake temporary license number. And this guy has been escalating. I don't think it's too much to ask to find the truck and ask the driver a few questions. If it's legit, fine. But if it's not, then we need to know that too."

The officer blew out a sigh. "I guess it can't hurt." He lifted a hand to the radio attached to his uniform. "Unit 8, please be on the lookout for a dark truck without a license plate but has a temporary number tacked to the back window."

"Roger that, Unit 7" was the response.

"Thanks." Trevor grimaced. "I know I might be paranoid, but how many dark trucks are driving around the city at this hour? Especially when we already know this guy was out near the rental cabin?"

"Lots of dark trucks out here in Wyoming," Anderson countered. "But I get your point."

Bailey tried not to panic, despite her concern about how Trevor had noticed a black truck going past the hospital. As much as she hated to admit it, Officer Anderson had a point about the prevalence of trucks in the state. Yet the timing bothered her. What if that guy knew they were at the hospital?

What if he followed them to the ranch?

"Anything else?" Anderson asked.

"Not that I can think of." Trevor gestured toward her. "I have a feeling we'll be here for a while yet."

She almost corrected him but decided against it.

Maybe Dr. Schaffer would take pity on her and allow her to stay. Then again, would her medical insurance cover that? She had no idea. She assumed being the receptionist for City Hall meant she had insurance, and she made a mental note to ask Harper about it.

"Okay. Let me know if there's anything else you need." Anderson glanced over his shoulder. "I have to get this guy booked before I can head back out on patrol."

His comment reminded her that there were only two officers on duty for the entire city. How would two cops manage to find this guy? She tried not to let the despair overwhelm her.

"Thanks again, Heath," Trevor said.

The cop turned away. Bailey continued to stroke Archie's fur, taking solace in the dog's presence. "You know him on a personal level?"

"Yeah, Heath was in Kendra's grade at school. I don't know the other cop, Jeff Riley, as well. He's new to the force. Just started six months ago." Trevor stepped closer, quickly eyeing the monitor overhead. "Have they rechecked your blood pressure yet?"

"No." The word barely cleared her throat when the door opened revealing Harper.

"How are you feeling?" Harper's tone was cheerful.

"Better," she answered honestly. "My headache is gone, and I don't feel as sick to my stomach as before."

"I'm glad to hear it." Harper moved to the other side of the bed to do a blood pressure reading. She smiled when she finished. "Your blood pressure is much lower. Your heart rate has come down nicely too. I'll let Dr. Schaffer know. I anticipate you'll be discharged shortly."

"Great." Bailey forced a smile. "I'm relieved to know the medication is working. Oh, by the way, can you tell if I have medical insurance?"

Harper looked surprised. "You don't know what insurance you have?"

"I don't remember." Wasn't that the truth? "If you could let me know, that's one less issue for me to worry about."

"Of course." Harper crossed over to the computer mounted in the corner of the room. She logged on, tapped several keys, then glanced at her. "You do have insurance, through the City of Cody."

She nodded. "Thanks for verifying that for me."

Harper typed more keys, no doubt entering her blood pressure reading. "Okay, I'll be back in a few minutes."

A long silence fell between her and Trevor after Harper left. She sighed. "Guess we'll have time to get breakfast."

"Yeah." Trevor stared at the baby monitor for a moment, before catching her gaze. "I know Anna will make breakfast for us if you can wait long enough for us to get to the ranch. I'd rather hit the highway now when there's less traffic."

Her gaze clung to his. "Is that because you want to make sure we're not followed?"

"Yep." She was impressed he didn't try to lie or sugarcoat the truth. "I wasn't happy to see that black truck going past a few minutes ago. I still think it could belong to your Black Hat."

"If he is, then I pray the officers will find him very soon." She shivered despite the warmth of the room. "Too bad we can't eat here at the hospital."

"That's an option." Trevor's expression turned thoughtful. "In fact, I like that idea. We'll still be early enough to make sure we're not followed, yet that will also give the cops time to track down the truck."

"Great." She felt better at the thought of staying within the sanctuary of the hospital for a little longer.

It took Harper about ten minutes to return. "Okay, Dr. Schaffer has signed your discharge paperwork. Let's get you disconnected from these monitors."

"Down, Archie," Trevor said. The red lab rose, licked her hand, then jumped down to the floor.

Trevor turned away, and she was touched by his attempt to give her privacy. She didn't remember her husband, but she couldn't help but wonder if Clark had a personality that was similar to Trevor's. Sweet, kind, protective, and caring.

She could easily imagine herself married to a man like Trevor. Which begged the question, had she ever gone out with Trevor? He was her brother's best friend, and he'd told her they'd known each other for years.

And if they hadn't dated, then why not? Had she rejected him at some point? Or worse, had Trevor never expressed any interest in her? Based on her keen awareness of him, the latter option felt more likely.

Either way, it was too late for them now.

TREVOR WARMED to the idea of having breakfast here at the hospital. Not only would that buy them some time, but he could feed Archie as well. Despite his eagerness to get Bailey to the safety of the family ranch, he was concerned about the black truck he'd seen earlier.

No matter how many times he told himself not to be paranoid, he was convinced the shooter was nearby. He trusted the Cody police, but their re-sources were limited.

He'd follow up with Griff once they reached the ranch. His brother-in-law must know something useful about the Plymouth Properties by now.

"All set." Harper's voice had him turning around. Bailey looked better. Her cheeks weren't as pale as they had been, her mouth less pinched with pain. She was beautiful, and it was all he could do not to cross over to pull her into his arms and kiss her. A totally inappropriate thought for a woman who had no memory of the love she'd had for her dead husband.

"What about the prescription for my blood pressure medicine?" Bailey asked.

"You can pick that up in our pharmacy here, but not until seven," Harper said. "But that's only forty-five minutes from now."

Trevor hadn't realized how long they'd been there. "Perfect. We'll eat breakfast, then grab your meds before we head home."

"Another good reason to eat here." Bailey reached for her coat. He hurried forward to hold it for her. "Thanks." Her voice sounded breathless as she looped her purse over her shoulder.

"Anytime." He glanced at the nurse. "Does she need a wheelchair?"

"I'll grab it for you."

"Oh, really?" Bailey looked disappointed.

"You're not on strict bed rest," Harper said. "You can be up for meals and to use the bathroom. But it can't hurt to use the wheelchair since you're on a new medication. I wouldn't want you to get dizzy and fall."

"We'll wait for the chair," he said firmly.

Bailey sighed and sat back on the edge of the gurney.

Harper brought the wheelchair. He helped Bailey sit down. "Thanks," he told Harper. Then he added, "Come, Archie."

He pushed Bailey's wheelchair through the doorway. Archie trotted ahead as if he owned the place. Rather than returning to the waiting area, Trevor steered Bailey down a hallway. He knew where the cafeteria was located since he'd worked as an EMT for a few years. Also, he and his siblings had spent some time there a year ago after Kendra had suffered her bad fall.

"I can smell bacon and eggs," Bailey murmured as they went through the hospital corridor.

"Me too." They reached the cafeteria a few minutes later. "Let's find a table. I need to grab food and dishes for Archie out of the SUV."

"Sure."

He scanned the room. It was early enough that most tables were empty. Yet there were several hospital staff members heading toward the food line. She gestured to a table in the back. "That should work. I can wait there for you."

He pushed her to the table. Then he locked the wheels into place. "Stay, Archie." He gave his K9 the command to sit. Archie lowered his haunches beside Bailey. "Guard."

The K9's tail thumped against the floor.

Trevor retraced his steps through the long corridor back to the emergency department entrance. The snow had stopped, which was nice. But his rental was covered in snow. He quickly brushed it off, then opened the rear hatch. He pulled out his backpack, then stepped back to close the door.

There were more cars in the parking lot, none of them a black pickup truck with a temporary license plate. He figured the hospital would get busier now that dawn was breaking over the horizon.

He paused, second-guessing his decision to stay. Then he pushed the doubt aside. Bailey needed her blood pressure medication for her newly diagnosed preeclampsia. That meant they didn't have an option but to wait here for at least forty-five minutes. Might as well eat during that time.

He strode quickly back into the cafeteria. Bailey was still seated in her wheelchair, stroking Archie's fur. "I don't know what it is about Archie," she said as he approached. "His calm demeanor makes me feel better."

He dropped into the chair across from her. "When we were training our K9s, Maya and Chase expressed some concern over Archie's easygoing nature. They thought maybe he was too nice of a dog to be successful in search and rescue missions. Maya suggested I use him as a therapy dog instead." He opened the backpack to remove the collapsible bowls. "Archie proved them wrong about his tracking ability. He has an excellent nose and has successfully found many lost people. But I have noticed he's good with victims too."

"He's amazing," she agreed.

"Give me a minute to fill this with water from the sink." He rose and crossed to the handwashing sink. He offered Archie the water, then filled the second bowl with food. Archie's dark eyes watched with interest as he set the bowl on the floor. Archie sat perfectly still, waiting for the command. "Go get it, boy."

Archie quickly bent to eat, his tail wagging with excitement.

When Archie was finished, he tucked the bowls away, then stood. "I'll get our food, just tell me what you'd like."

"Bacon and eggs, over easy, with toast and orange juice." She opened her purse and pulled out the bottle of vitamins he'd gotten for her.

"Got it. Stay, Archie." His K9 stretched out under the table, satiated after having his own breakfast.

It didn't take long for him to get their respective meals, including a large coffee for himself. He was running low on cash but figured the blood pressure medication wouldn't cost too much.

Thankfully, he had more than enough fuel in the rental SUV to get them to the ranch.

It felt good to have a safe destination for Bailey. He smiled at her, setting the tray on the table. Then he took his seat and reached for her hand. "I'd like to say grace."

"Okay." She glanced around the cafeteria as if self-conscious about praying in public. Hard to blame her since he knew she didn't normally say grace before meals.

"Dear Lord Jesus, we thank You for this food we are about to eat. We ask You to continue keeping Bailey and her daughter safe in Your care. Amen."

"And Trevor too. Amen," she murmured.

He smiled at the way she included him in their prayer. He hoped that once her memory returned, she'd continue on her faith journey. He really wanted her to continue to know God and to accept Jesus as her savior.

For now, he'd settle for keeping her safe. He dug

into his meal with enthusiasm. The coffee was great and helped battle against his fatigue. Two nights in a row without getting much sleep was catching up to him.

But that would change once they reached the ranch. Not only would Bailey be able to enjoy her bed rest, but he could catch a quick nap too.

"This is good," she said between bites.

He nodded. "When Kendra was here as a patient last year, we ate here a lot. The food isn't half bad. Although it's difficult to mess up breakfast."

"I didn't realize Kendra was a patient here." She eyed him over her glass of orange juice. "She's okay now?"

"Oh yeah. She's fine. Broke her pelvis, though, in a bad fall." He shook his head. "It was rough for a while, and my older siblings tend to treat her with kid gloves."

"I can imagine you're all protective of her." Bailey downed her prenatal vitamin, then drained her juice. "Thanks for the OJ. Those vitamins have a bad aftertaste," she said wryly.

"I can only imagine." He glanced under the table at Archie, then continued eating. By his watch, the pharmacy would open in ten minutes. Perfect timing. They could be on the road heading south well before most of the city awoke.

"Tell me about the ranch," Bailey said. "I assume you have a large ranch house?"

"The property used to be a dude ranch. There's one main ranch house, with a huge dining area where we gather for family meals. Then there are ten individual cabins that each of us uses as our own place. Chase recently moved into the main ranch house, so his cabin is currently the guest house. Maya and her husband, Doug, have added on to their cabin, expanding their master bedroom and creating a home office space."

"It sounds like you basically live alone."

"Not really, there's always activity going on." He finished his coffee. "We've added an air strip and a hangar for Logan; he's a charter pilot married to my sister Jessica. He owns three planes, if you can believe it. Oh, and then there's the barn and corral. We have four horses that we sometimes use for our search missions." He glanced under the table at Archie. "Not to mention ten dogs roaming around. When they're off duty, they know it's playtime and run around the ranch like crazy."

"Ten dogs?" She frowned. "You have an extra K9? That seems strange."

"No, I forgot to mention Doug's sister, Emily, and her husband, Owen, live on the ranch now too. Emily is the nurse you had your first night here, remember? They have a chocolate lab named Bear who is training to be a SAR dog. He's coming along nicely and will be ready to head out on his own by next spring. And I should add there's a new black lab puppy named King. Eleven dogs now." He shook his head ruefully. "No wonder it's chaotic."

"Wow. That sounds like your ranch is a busy place." She finished her toast and pushed her plate aside. "Thanks, that was great."

"Do you want anything else?" He was pleased she'd eaten everything. Important fuel for her growing baby. "We have a few minutes before the pharmacy opens."

"No, thanks. I'm stuffed." She eyed his empty coffee cup. "I miss coffee."

He felt guilty for enjoying his coffee when she couldn't. "Sorry, next time I won't get any."

"Don't be silly. I don't begrudge you coffee." She sighed. "I just miss it. But it's worth avoiding caffeine for baby Naomi."

"Naomi?" He hadn't known she'd chosen a name. Then it hit him. "You remember her name?"

Her eyes widened. "Yes. Naomi is my mother's name. I—I remember writing that down in a baby book." Then her shoulders drooped. "I'm sure the baby book was destroyed during the break-in."

"We'll find it." He hoped the baby book was salvageable. If nothing else, it may spur more memories. "I'm thrilled your memory is starting to return."

"Me too." She sighed. "Although remembering key information about Clark and his work at the pub would be far more helpful." She frowned, and added, "If that's what's going on here."

He figured that had to be the reason she was in danger. "Your memory will return soon." He rose and lifted their tray of dirty dishes. "I'll carry this to the tray line. Then we'll head to the pharmacy."

Archie slept beneath the table until he returned. Releasing the brakes on Bailey's wheelchair, he rolled her away from the table. Archie crawled out, stretched, then followed.

"We should have asked where it's located." Bailey glanced back at him as they crossed the room.

"Pretty sure it's in the corner of the lobby." He pushed her wheelchair out of the cafeteria and turned to the left. The lobby wasn't far, and again, he was surprised to see several employees in scrubs milling about. He remembered Emily saying she worked twelve-hour shifts from seven in the morning until seven thirty at night. This must be the early crew reporting to work.

The pharmacy wasn't open yet. He pushed Bailey off to the side so they wouldn't be in anyone's way and considered heading out to bring the SUV around to the front. Not that it was a problem to push her through the hospital back to the emergency department. He glanced at his watch again. Hearing a click, he glanced over to see a woman with long blond hair unlocking the glass door to the pharmacy.

"It's open. Sit tight, I'll be back soon." Without giving Bailey a chance to say anything, he crossed the lobby to enter the pharmacy. Archie trailed along beside him, sniffing the floor with interest.

"May I help you?" The blond-haired woman glanced up from her computer.

"I'm here to pick up a prescription for Bailey Adams." He gestured to where she sat in the wheelchair. "She's been discharged from the emergency department."

"One moment please." She worked the keyboard for a moment. "Okay, I see it. Give me a minute or two to get this filled for you."

"Of course." He bent to scratch Archie behind the ears. "We're heading home, boy."

Archie thumped his tail on the floor.

He straightened, watching the pharmacist as she plucked a bottle off the shelf and carried it to a counter. Preparing the prescription didn't take too long. She returned to the cash register and pushed the bag toward him. "That will nineteen dollars and fifty-two cents."

Archie growled as he pulled cash from his

pocket. With a frown, he glanced at his K9, then looked back through the glass door.

A man wearing scrubs was wheeling Bailey through the lobby toward the front door.

"No, stop!" He tossed the twenty-dollar bill down and grabbed the blood pressure medication. "Get him, Archie!"

His K9 wheeled away and ran through the lobby. Trevor was hot on the dog's heels. He dodged a staff member who was walking while looking at her phone, barely missing her.

"Stop him! Stop!" he shouted as he burst through the open door. Archie had already snaked through when the woman on the phone had walked in. Archie was barking loudly, doing a good imitation of an attack dog.

"Trevor!" Bailey's voice was terrified. "Help!"

The man in scrubs wore a coat along with a paper hospital mask concealing his face. He glanced over his shoulder, then gave Bailey's wheelchair a hard shove, sending her skating across the driveway straight toward a snowbank.

Trevor put on a burst of speed, but it was too late. The guy in scrubs darted to the left, jumped into the front seat of a black pickup truck, and roared away.

13

Bailey hit the snowbank hard, falling face first when the wheels of the chair came to an abrupt halt. She tried to break her fall with her arms, protecting her abdomen, but her forehead still hit the snow hard enough to make tears spring to her eyes. She closed her eyes for a moment, then pushed herself up and over onto her back. Archie bounded next to her, licking her cheek.

"Bailey! Are you all right?" Trevor's familiar face popped into her line of vision.

She looked up at him, a flash of memory hitting hard. "You helped me when I fell off your horse. Archie licked me, just like he did now."

Shock registered in his eyes, and he nodded. "Yeah, I did. Archie reached you before I did, then, too. I'm glad you remember that. Are you hurt?"

"My hand." She lifted her right hand. Her fingers were red and swollen from where she'd tried to stop the stranger from wheeling her outside. They'd gotten caught in the spokes of the wheel. "I don't think they're broken, just bruised."

"I'm so sorry." His gaze filled with self-recrimination. "I never expected anyone to pretend to be a hospital staff member to get close to you."

"It's not your fault." She sat up on the snow, eyeing the wheelchair. She would have preferred to walk, but she was concerned that this little escapade had already caused her blood pressure to rise. Something she couldn't afford if she wanted her baby to grow bigger before being born. With a sigh, she stood. Trevor tucked her prescription pill bottle into her purse, then wrapped his arm around her waist, guiding her back into the chair.

"What happened?" Trevor asked.

"At first, I thought the guy was legit. He muttered something about a test that the staff had forgotten to do. I didn't try to stop him until I realized we were headed outside. I grabbed the wheels, but he had gained momentum." She looked down at her red and swollen fingers. "I should have realized he wasn't a real staff member."

"I'm so sorry." He looked miserable as he turned her chair around to push her back inside. "We need to get out of here."

"Trevor, how did he find me here at the hospital?" She frowned as the event replayed in her mind. "Not only did he find me, but he also had time to dress in scrubs to fool me. He knew I'd been seen in the emergency department. He claimed I needed another test, so that's why I went along for a few minutes."

"That's my fault. I ran outside the emergency department entrance to get the license plate of the black truck. He must have seen me in his rearview mirror and knew then we were there." He sounded grim. "If I'd just stayed inside, this wouldn't have happened."

"I doubt that mattered. Besides, it was important to try to get his license plate, right?" She turned to look up at him. "We should probably call the police to report this."

"Yeah." Trevor's features appeared carved in stone. "I'll call Sergeant Howell. I know from back when Doug Bridge's sister, Emily, was taken from here, there are two hospital security cameras, one overlooking the emergency department parking lot and the other overlooking this front entrance."

"Will they share the video with us?" The thought of getting a glimpse of this guy's face or his black truck filled her with hope. They needed something, anything, to go on. Clearly, she wasn't safe there at the hospital.

Would that hold true for the ranch as well? Would this guy track them down no matter where they went?

"They'd better share the video." Trevor's tone was clipped. "This guy pretended to be a staff member, that should make them eager to find him."

She nodded. "I hope so."

Trevor pushed her through the lobby until he reached the main desk. "I want to talk to someone in hospital administration or in security."

The woman behind the desk frowned. "I don't think Stan is here yet."

"Then give me whoever is in charge." Trevor's tone was lined with steel. "Someone dressed as a staff member just tried to kidnap Bailey."

The woman's gaze bounced from Trevor to her and back to Trevor. Then she noticed Archie and recognition dawned. "Oh, you're one of the Sullivans?"

"Yes. Trevor Sullivan."

"Your brother helped my nephew Colton when he got lost. I'll find Stan or someone else right away." She lifted the phone, more than anxious to help.

"Guess it pays to be a Sullivan," she murmured.

"It shouldn't be that way," Trevor agreed. "But right now, I'll take what we can get."

A moment later, a short round man walked toward them. "You're Trevor Sullivan? Related to Maya and Doug Bridges? I'm Stan Beck. I'm in charge of security."

"Yes. This is Bailey Adams. Some guy dressed in scrubs and wearing a paper face mask tried to kidnap her. I need to see your video for the camera outside the front lobby. We know he's driving a black truck, but we don't have a license plate."

"Of course. This way." Surprisingly, Stan gestured for them to follow him. "I normally would ask for a warrant, but hearing this guy was pretending to work here and was dressed in scrubs is concerning. We'd want to tell the police about this ourselves."

Bailey felt a little foolish being pushed in the wheelchair down a narrow hallway toward a small office. There was barely enough room for Trevor and Stan to fit in the cramped space, much less her wheelchair. Trevor slipped into the room, leaving her wheelchair blocking the doorway. Archie squeezed into the room, then stood in front of her, his dark eyes seeming to watch Trevor.

"Hang on a minute while I pull up the video." Stan manipulated the computer screen on his laptop. "After Doug Bridge's sister was kidnapped, we got approval for two more cameras to be added to the perimeter of the building. One in the ambulance bay, since that's where Emily was taken, and a second one outside the emergency department."

"That's good to know. We'll need to look at the video from the emergency department too." Trevor's eyes gleamed with anticipation. "I saw the black truck outside the ED entrance earlier, maybe around six in the morning? I couldn't get the license plate because he had a temporary license taped to the back window."

"That should be easy to spot. Let's start with the lobby camera first." Stan tapped the keys, then turned his screen so that she could see. "This is our guy, right?"

"Yes." Her voice was strained as she watched the image of her being pushed outside in the wheelchair by a tall man in scrubs.

"He looks to be about six feet tall with dark hair." Trevor tapped the screen. "Can you back up so we can get an image of him walking into the hospital?"

"Yep." Stan did so, then made a face. "It's not helpful. He's wearing that face mask when he comes inside too. He doesn't have a hospital ID badge on either."

"That's a bummer." Trevor sounded annoyed. "Okay, then I need you to zoom in to get a better image of that black truck parked off to the side."

"Okay." Stan turned the computer screen back

and worked the keyboard. After another long moment, he shook his head. "Unfortunately, there's no front license plate. I can say it's a black GMC. Does that mesh with what you saw earlier?"

"A GMC? Yeah, I'm sure that's the same truck I saw earlier." Trevor waved at the computer. "Pull up the emergency department video. Specifically around the six o'clock time frame."

Stan didn't argue. He went back to work, taking what felt to Bailey as an inordinately long time, before he said, "Okay, I think I found that truck."

"Let me see." Trevor leaned forward, bracing his hand on the desktop. Stan obliged by turning the screen again so they could both watch the video. It was hard for her to see beyond the two men.

"There, freeze the video. That's the truck." Trevor stepped back so she could see it too. "Do you recognize it?"

She stared at the image. Those square headlights looked familiar. Because she'd seen them prior to her crash? She sighed. "Maybe. It's hard to say for sure."

"That's okay. I know what I saw." Trevor turned his attention back to Stan. "I need you to zoom in on that temporary license number."

"Sure thing." Stan did so, bringing the image into focus. "Interesting that the temporary license number doesn't start with the same two digits all other Wyoming plates to," Stan said with a frown. "Shouldn't it reflect the county it was purchased in?"

"Yeah, it should." Trevor's expression hardened. "I'm pretty sure it's fake, and not even a good fake. Anyone who lives in Wyoming would know enough to use the two-digit county code."

Bailey shivered. She wasn't cold; it was the knowledge that this stranger wasn't from the area. She thought about how Trevor had mentioned the owners of Sweet Water were incorporated in New Jersey. "He's from out of town?"

"I'm leaning that way, but we'll see what Tom Howell thinks." Trevor looked at Stan. "I need copies of these videos. I'll share them with the Cody police and my brother-in-law Griff with the FBI."

Stan nodded solemnly. "You got it."

She gently flexed the red, swollen fingers on her right hand, her thoughts whirling. Why had the guy wheeled her toward the truck rather than simply killing her? It was a change in tactic that didn't make sense.

Then she opened her purse and rummaged inside for the keys. Pulling the ring out, she stared at the key that didn't look like either her house or garage key. A flash of Clark asking for her keys flashed in her mind. She'd been annoyed with him for some reason and vaguely remembered throwing the keys at him with more force than she should have. Instead of getting mad at her, he'd taken them and left.

He must have added the key to the ring containing her other keys at that time. But if that was the case, why hadn't she noticed? Why had she been upset with him?

Why was someone trying to kill her?

Or maybe, she realized, the goal wasn't to kill her but to get the key back. Yet that didn't make sense either. The guy wearing scrubs hadn't tried to grab her purse. It would seem logical for him to do that if he'd suspected she had something of Clark's. The purse was the only thing she'd had with her this entire time. Aside from the clothes on her back and her winter coat. Nothing else, just the purse.

Her house had been searched sometime after her crash. Was it possible Black Hat didn't know what he was looking for? That he was searching for something other than a key?

"Bailey? Are you feeling sick again?" Trevor asked, his gaze full of concern.

"No, but I think this key is important." She held it up for him. "I just remembered Clark asking for my keys."

His gaze sharpened. "What brought that on?"

She was hurt by the doubt in his tone. "I have no idea why that memory came into my mind. I only recall being annoyed with Clark, but I don't remember him clearly or why I was upset." The memory fragments were almost worse than having no memory. It was like fitting pieces of a puzzle together without an image to work with.

"I'm glad you're starting to remember." Trevor patted her arm as Stan worked on their copy of the video. "I think we'll stop at the Cody police station before we head to the ranch. Maybe they can figure out what that key opens."

"Okay." She didn't want to argue, although she was feeling tired again. Sitting in a chair was similar to being on bed rest, wasn't it?

She stifled a yawn and moved her chair back from the doorway to give Trevor and Archie room to leave. Deep down, she wondered why she'd remembered Trevor first over the man she'd married.

Likely because Trevor was her lifeline. He was here in the present, helping her. Supporting her. Caring for her.

Yet somehow, she had the distinct impression she wasn't happily married.

TREVOR TOOK the USB drive Stan held out to him. "Both videos are on there," Stan said.

"Thanks." He dropped the thumb drive into his pocket. "I appreciate your cooperation."

"I'll need to report this up the chain myself." Stan grimaced. "Never a good thing when someone pretends to work here while committing a crime. The only good news is that he didn't have a hospital ID badge. I was worried he may have stolen one."

Trevor hadn't considered that possibility. He was torn between getting to the ranch as quickly as possible and speaking with the local law enforcement about the few clues they'd managed to unearth.

It made the most sense to visit the police station while they were here. It wasn't far, and it was better for the local cops to have all the information they needed. But he'd also call Griff too. He needed all hands on deck.

Bailey's preeclampsia diagnosis changed things. The near miss outside the lobby had shaken him. Not just because they guy had almost succeeded in kidnapping her, but the rough treatment could have hurt her baby.

It had been a risky plan attempting to snatch her in the daytime, yet also simple enough that it may have worked. If not for Archie's growling, Trevor may not have noticed in time.

They needed answers and fast.

He wheeled Bailey through the hallway toward the emergency department. He was anxious to get out of there.

"I don't think I was happily married." Bailey's statement seemed to come out of the blue.

He frowned, still pushing her forward. "What makes you say that?"

"I don't know. My first memory of Clark was being annoyed." She rubbed the injured fingers on her hand. "I just think if I had been happy, the memories would come easier."

He wasn't sure about that. The traumatic crash on the heels of telling him she thought she was being followed seemed like more than enough of a reason for her brain to have shut down. But now that she'd said the words, he wondered if she was on to something. Maybe her being angry with Clark had contributed to the amnesia.

"All we can do is hope your memory continues to return." He reached the emergency department lobby, noticing more people had gathered there now. He scanned the faces but didn't see anyone that fit the description of the man who'd tried to grab Bailey.

"I'll walk from here," Bailey said as he crossed the waiting room. "That way we can leave the wheelchair inside."

"Okay." The doctor had said she could be up to eat and use the bathroom. The distance from here to his rental SUV parked near the doorway wasn't far. He pulled the key fob and hit the automatic start. The engine roared to life.

He kept a sharp eye out for trouble as he escorted her to the SUV. He opened the rear hatch for Archie, who bounded inside. He would need to give the dog time to get busy outside but thought that could wait until they reached the Cody police station.

Less than a minute later, they were back on the road. There were more vehicles and people out and about as the overcast sky gave room to a glimpse of the sun. He'd missed his chance to get Bailey to the ranch early enough to avoid traffic. Now it would be harder to spot a tail.

The police station wasn't far. The car had barely warmed up when he pulled into the small parking lot. He put the car in gear and turned to Bailey. "You feel up to walking inside?"

"I'm not an invalid." Her tone was more exhausted than annoyed. "I can walk a few steps."

He nodded. "Wait for me." He let Archie out, then ran around to her side of the car. "I'm sure this won't take long."

"I'm hoping they'll have more officers on the road looking for the black GMC truck." She looped her purse over her shoulder. "Maybe they'll even have an idea about the key."

"Yeah." Trevor was feeling better about his decision to come there. Between the video, the key, and the more detailed description of the truck, he felt they were finally closing in on this guy.

And he sensed the bad guy was beginning to feel the pressure too.

He opened the door to the police station for Bailey. There were a couple of hard plastic chairs off to the side of the small lobby area. He gestured toward them. "Sit for a minute. I'm not even sure Howell is in yet."

She didn't argue. Archie stayed by his side. Since he knew they weren't in danger there, he didn't ask his K9 to guard.

"Trevor Sullivan here to see Sergeant Tom Howell," he said to the receptionist. Digging in his pocket, he held up the USB drive. "There's been another attempt against Bailey Adams, and I have video evidence I'd like to share with him."

"One moment please." She made the call, speaking low so that he couldn't hear. She looked surprised as she lowered the phone. "Sergeant Howell is available. Do you know where his office is?"

"Yep. Thanks." He turned to see Bailey making her way toward him. He slid his arm around her waist. "You'll let me know if you start feeling bad."

"Yes." She leaned against him. "I won't risk my baby."

He knew she wouldn't and was glad her tumble onto the snowbank hadn't hurt. The way she'd looked up and remembered him had warmed his heart. But he also knew he couldn't express his growing feelings for her until all her repressed memories had returned.

And if they didn't? He shied away from that thought.

"You're becoming a real pain in the behind," Howell groused when they entered. "I haven't gotten a good night's sleep since this started."

"Join the club. The attempts are escalating, so there's no time to waste sleeping." He stepped aside so Bailey could sit in the chair. Then he placed the USB drive on Howell's desk. "This is video of the attempted abduction of Bailey from the hospital lobby. There's also video of a black GMC truck going past the emergency department with what I believe is a fake temporary license plate."

"Oh yeah?" Despite his earlier words, Tom looked interested. "Let's take a look."

"Make yourself a copy," Trevor said. "I need that USB for Griff."

"Yeah, okay." Howell uploaded the video. After a few seconds, he whistled between his teeth. "Can't believe he was brazen enough to take her out through the front door."

"To a black GMC truck." Trevor waved a hand. "Keep watching."

Howell's expression darkened as the second video rolled across the screen. "I heard the BOLO go out about the truck with temporary plates." He held Trevor's gaze. "Why do you think it's fake?"

"No two-digit county designation." He shrugged. "Would think even a legit temporary plate would have one."

"So you think someone from New Jersey obtained this truck and is using the temporary tag to avoid being traced." Tom sighed. "That's a reasonable assumption."

"I thought so. Oh, and we have a key that we'd like your thoughts on." Trevor turned to Bailey. She pulled the key chain out and handed it to him. "We noticed this key doesn't match the one that's obviously for the house and car. Any idea what it might open?"

"Too small for a padlock." Tom turned the key over in his hand, examining it from all angles. "I haven't seen a key like this before, but I can ask around. See if it looks familiar to any of the officers."

He hesitated. "I'd rather not leave it here. Maybe you can take a picture of it?"

"That works." Tom set the key on his desk and used his cell phone to take a picture. Then he handed the key back. "You've made some ground on this case."

"I wish it was more." He handed the keys back to Bailey. "We really need your officers to find that truck."

"We're not sitting around eating donuts." Tom's tone was sharp. "Both officers on duty last night did their best to search for it between calls."

"I know. I ran into Heath Anderson at the hospital, and he followed up with Jeff Riley who was out searching for the truck." He swallowed his frustration. "I understand your resources are limited."

"I've requested overtime for my officers." Tom tapped the computer screen. "I think when the chief sees this, he'll gladly approve my request."

"Good." He glanced at Bailey, who looked relieved to know more officers would soon be out on the street. "If you need us, we can be reached at the ranch."

Tom arched a brow. "Surprised you're leaving town."

"Bailey needs to rest." He didn't see a reason to go into detail about her diagnosis. "We have ten dogs and a puppy that will alert us to trouble."

"Yeah, okay. I get that." Tom hit a few keys on his computer, clearly making a copy of the video from the USB drive. Then the printer whirled as he printed a copy of the picture of the key. When those things were finished, Tom rose to his feet and handed the USB drive back. "I'm going to get this picture out to the team ASAP. Between this key and the additional information on the black truck, I'm sure we'll have this guy in custody by the end of the day."

"Thank you, Sergeant Howell." It was the first time Bailey had spoken since entering the office. "We appreciate your quick response."

Tom's gaze softened. "That's our job. Yours is to stay safe." He clapped Trevor on the shoulder, easing past him with the photo in hand. "The Sullivans are more than capable of keeping an eye on you."

"I know." She pushed up from the seat, but Trevor put a hand on her shoulder.

"Why don't you stay here for a few minutes? I need to take Archie outside to get busy. He hasn't been out since eating breakfast."

She nodded and settled back down. "Okay. I'll wait here."

Trevor turned away. "Come, Archie." He led the dog out through the cubicles, noticing Tom veered off to join a group of uniformed officers gathering in what he assumed was the staff breakroom. Satisfied he'd done what he could to get things rolling, Trevor led Archie outside.

"Get busy, Arch." The red lab sniffed the parking

lot with interest but didn't take long to get down to business.

He crossed to the SUV to dig a plastic baggie from the backpack. He quickly cleaned up after his K9, thinking about the ride home.

There was a detour he could take to avoid the main highway, but that would add thirty minutes to the already forty-plus minute drive. Not to mention, he wasn't sure that the lesser traveled Route 3 had been plowed since the recent snowfall.

No, it was probably better to head straight south.

"Come on, Archie," he called to his K9. The dog bounded toward him, tail wagging. Normally, he'd have taken the time to play with Archie a bit, but that would have to wait until they got to the ranch.

He headed back inside. The receptionist was on the phone, so he waited a minute for her to wave him through.

When he reached Tom Howell's office, though, there was no sign of Bailey. He frowned, wondering if she needed to use the bathroom. He turned to ask Tom when he saw the guy speaking to his team. The video was up on a screen, and he had already distributed copies of the key picture to the five officers standing there.

"Hey, have you seen Bailey?" he asked.

Tom frowned. "She's not in my office?"

"No." A niggle of unease snaked down his back. "Where are your restrooms?"

"Right here." Tom indicated the two restrooms located right next to the break room. Both doors were open. There was no sign of Bailey.

His pulse spiked into triple digits. "She can't have gotten far. Is there a back exit?"

"Yeah, this way." Tom rushed through the cubicles to a rear door. The sergeant quickly pushed through it in time for Trevor to see the red glow of taillights in the distance.

Trevor stared in horror, two things hitting him with the force of a cannon ball to the chest. First, someone within the police department was involved. And second, the black-hat guy had Bailey.

14

Bailey stared in horror at Cody police officer Jeff Riley. When he'd asked her to go with him, she hadn't argued. Until he'd forced her out the back door of the police station at gun point.

Now stuck in the back of his police cruiser, her thoughts whirled. Never had she considered the possibility that a Cody police officer was involved. Swallowing hard, she silently prayed this man wouldn't kill her and her baby.

"Where are you taking me?" Her shaky voice betrayed her terror. "I don't understand what's going on. Did you know I lost my memory in the crash? I'm no threat to you or whatever you're involved in."

Riley glanced at her using the rearview mirror.

Then he quickly looked away, almost as if he regretted his actions. "Boss wants the money your husband stole from him."

"Money? What money?" She should have known this was about money, yet his comment made her feel more desperate than ever. "I don't have any money!"

He didn't say anything, but she noticed his fingers tightened on the steering wheel. His unease was the only thing she had going for her. In her condition, fighting him off would be next to impossible. Even if she could break free, how far would she get? She splayed her hands over her abdomen and took several deep breaths.

"Officer Riley, I'm supposed to be on bed rest. I've been diagnosed with an illness that could cause my baby to be delivered prematurely." Again, his gaze flicked to hers in the rearview. At least he was listening. "Please don't do this. I'll give you all the money I have, but I'm begging you not to harm me or my baby."

"He just wants the cash. That's all."

"Don't be stupid!" Her sharp comment caught him off guard. He looked at her again, and the hint of regret in his gaze fueled her forward. "Your boss, whoever he is, won't let me walk away. Not after all of this." She waved a hand at the police cruiser.

"The list of crimes is growing by the minute. Kidnapping! Attempted murder!"

"Shut up!" His voice was sharp, but she sensed he was rattled.

"Are you willing to throw your entire life away for this boss of yours?" She continued to push. "Trevor probably already realizes I'm gone. He'll know someone from inside the police station is involved. It won't take him long to put two and two together to realize you're the one who kidnapped me."

"I said shut up." His tone lacked heat. He continued gripping the wheel as if he wanted to turn around. But then she saw the sign for the Sweet Water Pub and realized it was too late.

"Please turn around. Turn the squad around and take me back to Trevor." She didn't try to hide her desperation. "Don't kill me and my unborn child. Don't do this!"

He shook his head. "I'm in too deep."

"Whatever it is, I can help." They were closer to the pub now. But then he surprised her by driving past it. "I promise I'll help. You know Trevor's brother-in-law is Griff Flannery with the FBI, right? We'll ask him to grant you immunity if you stop this right now."

He didn't respond. Did that mean he was considering her proposal?

"If you go through with this, you'll be an accessory to murder." She closed her eyes for a moment, then added, "A double murder. Me and my unborn child. There isn't a jury on earth that will find you innocent."

His gaze flicked to hers. But rather than seeing guilt or second thoughts, she saw a grim resolve.

"I would if I could. Like I said, I'm in too deep." Riley turned the squad onto a winding road. It took her a moment to realize he was taking her to her home. The one he'd trashed looking for whatever money they were trying to find.

Obviously, Clark had done this to her. He'd stolen money from Riley's boss, leaving her vulnerable and alone. How could he have done such a thing? Clark had to know they'd come after her.

Her stomach clenched painfully as Riley pulled up in front of her house. There were no lights on inside, and from the back seat of the cruiser, she didn't see anyone moving around inside. The cloudy sky cast a dreary backdrop to the property.

Was this it? Her last moments on earth? She wanted to believe Trevor would find her, but she feared it would be too late.

Riley pushed out from behind the wheel. He held his weapon in hand as he opened her rear passenger door. "Get out."

"Please don't do this." Tears filled her eyes. "Please don't kill me and my baby."

He looked away for a split second, then brought the gun up. "Get out."

Bailey swiped at her face, forcing herself to slide out of the seat. She glanced behind the cop at her empty driveway behind the police car but didn't bother to make a run for it. Riley stepped back as if to keep a safe distance between them. Averting her gaze from the gun, she focused on moving carefully on the snow-packed ground. As if slipping and falling were the biggest threat she faced.

Too bad she didn't have close neighbors. Someone she could flag down for help. Every step forward felt like a step toward her execution.

It wasn't until she was halfway to the front door that she remembered the mystery key she and Trevor had found on her keyring.

Knowing the key was likely what the boss wanted didn't help her feel any better. The moment she handed it over, she'd be dead.

Stall. She lifted her chin, deciding she would have to draw this out for as long as possible. Maybe Trevor would find her in time.

And if he didn't? She lifted her gaze to the over-cast sky. If God was watching over her, she prayed He would send Trevor and the Cody police to find her in time.

If not, she prayed the end would be quick and painless.

The door opened as she approached. Seeing the man standing there, she froze. Black Hat. Memories tumbled through her mind. She knew him. His name was Todd White. He was her friend Stacy White's brother. The man who'd asked her out several times after Clark's death.

"You." She pushed the word out through her tight throat. "I never expected this from you."

"Yeah, well, if you'd have just gone out with me, none of this would have had to happen." Todd glared at her as if the circumstances were her fault. "Where's the money, Bailey? I know you have it."

She slowly shook her head. Now that she'd recognized Todd, she remembered how unhappy she'd been in her marriage to Clark. How she'd planned to file for divorce two weeks before he was killed. Something she'd confided in Stacy about, which was why her friend tried to set her up with Todd. She was glad now that she hadn't gone out with him. "I don't have your money. Clark kept everything related to his business a secret. I didn't get a dime of the pub after he died."

"You better have it." Todd opened the door and grabbed her arm, pulling her inside. "If you don't know where it is, it won't end well for you."

It wasn't going to end well for her anyway, but

she didn't voice the thought. She had to play along. "I can try to search for it. But you must know Clark didn't live here with me. I bought the place after his death."

"We already searched the house you shared, earlier when it was on the market." Todd pushed her into a kitchen chair. She sat, the strap of her purse sliding off her shoulder. Todd's eyes narrowed on it. Then he reached out to snatch the handbag from her. "Are you carrying it around with you? Is that why we haven't found it?"

"I told you I don't have your money!" She didn't have to fake her desperation. She'd never been so terrified in her entire life. "If I did, I'd give it to you. I would have given it to you a long time ago. I would have done anything for you to just leave me alone."

Todd rummaged through the handbag. Then he turned and upended it onto the kitchen table. Items tumbled out, scattering around the surface. To her eye, the ring of keys looked huge and noticeable. She averted her gaze, praying Todd wouldn't notice her staring.

"What's this?" Todd snatched the keyring up. Then a terrible smile crossed his features. "Well, well. This must be the key to the safe."

She glanced up at him. "What safe?"

He sneered. "The one we found at the storage unit Clark rented. The only problem is that it's empty. We drilled holes in the safe to crack it open. Only to find it empty." His gaze narrowed. "So where is the money?"

Her heart sank to the soles of her feet. If the key was worthless, she had nothing to barter with. Nothing to use as a distraction to buy time for Trevor and the non-crooked cops on the Cody police force to find her.

Now what?

She thought about her life with Clark. The way he'd worked long hours. The way he'd been non-committal about how much money the pub was earning.

His friend Max who'd been killed in a trucking accident.

Then it hit her. The safe must have been a ruse. Or maybe it had been a temporary hiding spot. Because she knew where the money was hidden. It was something she probably would have remembered earlier if not for the crash.

"He buried it." She pushed the words past her tight throat.

"What do you mean?" Todd demanded. "Buried it where?"

"At the base of the large oak tree in our backyard." She forced herself to meet his gaze. "I remember seeing him outside late one night, digging a hole in the ground. It was late, like two in the morning. When I asked him about it, he claimed he found a dead cat at the side of the road on his way home and thought it would be more humane to bury it rather than leave it on the street." She couldn't believe now that she'd fallen for his story. Clark hadn't been much of an animal lover. She hadn't pushed the issue of getting a pet as Clark worked long hours at the pub. She knew she'd have all the responsibility and had decided it was too much work. Especially since she'd regretted marrying Clark in the first place.

She knew better now. Pets were amazing. Archie was incredible. Tears pricked her eyes when she thought of Archie and Trevor. It hurt to know she may not see them again.

"I guess we'll find out, won't we?" Todd grabbed her arm, wrenching her up from the chair. "You better not be sending me on a wild-goose chase." His grip tightened painfully. "I'll make you regret it."

"I didn't see the money," she said, between clenched teeth. "I just remember Clark burying something at the base of the tree."

"Let's go." Todd pulled her toward the front door. "My boss's truck is outside."

Bailey didn't want to leave, hoping Trevor may have had a chance to find her there if he'd sent Archie on her scent.

Riley was standing outside near his cruiser. He

looked up as she and Todd emerged from the house. "We need to get back to Clark's old place," Todd said. "And we're going to need a shovel."

"I have one." Riley frowned. "You think the money was buried in the yard?"

"That's what she claims." Todd jerked his thumb toward her. "And she'd better be right, or else."

"The ground is going to be frozen," Riley protested. "A shovel may not work."

"It has to. Because if we don't get this cash back, we're all dead. The boss has been on edge for months now. He wants the money back ASAP." Todd shoved her toward a black truck. She hadn't noticed it earlier, parked along the side of her garage. He'd been the one following her. He'd been the one hiding behind the black cowboy hat.

And he'd been the one to run her off the road.

Riley grabbed the shovel out of his trunk. "I've gotta get back on the road. I need to cover my tracks so nobody suspects I'm involved. I'm already late as it is."

"You do that." Todd snatched the shovel from his hands. "Keep them away from the house. Give them false intel to follow up somewhere far away from there." Todd steered her toward the front passenger seat. "Let's go."

Bailey thought again about Trevor and his K9, Archie. She didn't think the dog could follow her scent while driving in a car. All she could do now was pray that Todd would let her go once he had the money.

And if not? That he'd make her death as painless as possible.

~

"It's Jeff Riley. I'm sure of it." Trevor was seated beside Tom Howell as they drove through the town of Cody, following the GPS tracker on Riley's car. Archie was stretched out on the back seat. According to the tracker, Riley was at Bailey's home. The one that had been trashed by someone looking for something of value. Had the house been the target the whole time? Trevor wished he knew what they wanted. Other than Bailey. He glanced at Howell. "Where is he now?"

"Still on Windmill Lane." Howell arched a brow. "Any idea why he'd take Bailey to her house?"

"No." Trevor leaned forward, peering through the gloom. "But I'm angry he has her. This shouldn't have happened. Of all places on the planet, Bailey should have been safe inside the Cody police station."

"I don't like it either." Tom's tone was testy. "It's not like I enjoy having a dirty cop on the payroll. Especially not for the second time in a year."

Trevor glanced at him, then sighed. "I know it's not your fault. I'm just frustrated. I should have realized Riley was involved when we saw Heath at the hospital. He told Riley we were there. It wasn't much later when I saw the black truck driving past."

"I'm sorry. I feel responsible," Howell admitted.

Trevor shook his head. He was angry with himself for leaving Bailey alone. He could have taken her outside with him while Archie got busy. His concern about her needing to sit and stay on bed rest was almost laughable now that she was in the hands of a brutal murderer.

If anything happened to her or the baby, he'd never forgive himself.

Before leaving the police station, Trevor had called Griff to fill him in on the recent kidnapping. Griff had told him the FBI in New Jersey had informed him that they'd had their suspicions about Plymouth Properties, believing they were a front for a money laundering scheme. Gambling money was being funneled through the pubs they owned because they happened to be cash-heavy establishments. Trevor had wondered if Bailey's husband, Clark, had stumbled upon the operation and had been killed so he couldn't blow the whistle.

Then again, that wouldn't give anyone from Plymouth Properties a reason to go after Bailey. There had to be something more going on here. Some piece of the puzzle that was still missing.

All he cared about was getting Bailey back safely.

Griff was on his way to Cody, but the ranch was a forty-minute ride from here. Unwilling to wait, Trevor and Howell had headed out to find Riley. There was no way Trevor was sitting around while Bailey's life was at stake.

His attention was abruptly averted by the squad coming down the street toward them. He grabbed Howell's arm. "There he is!"

Howell reacted quickly, flipping on the red and blue lights, then turning crossways in the road to block Riley's path. Trevor tensed, half expecting the oncoming car to ram into them, but it stopped. For a long moment, Riley sat behind the wheel, staring at them. Then he slowly pushed out of the squad.

"Keep your hands where I can see them!" Howell snapped, using the radio to communicate with his subordinate officer. "I mean it, Riley. One wrong move and I'll take you down."

"What's going on?" Riley lifted his hands, palms facing forward, his expression full of concern. Yet Trevor wasn't buying his *I'm innocent* act.

Trevor pushed out of the car. "Where is she?"

"Who?" Again, Riley flashed a feigned look of

confusion. "I don't understand. What's going on, Sarg?"

"So help me, if you don't tell me where she is . . ." Trevor paused, struck by an idea. Without a word, he abruptly turned to open the back door of the squad. "Archie, search! Search Bailey!"

Archie jumped down, his tail wagging with excitement. Trevor hadn't taken the time to give his dog water or to rev him up for the search game. But that didn't stop his K9 from lowering his nose to the ground and sniffing with interest.

"Search," he repeated. "Search for Bailey!"

It was as if the two officers were mesmerized by his K9. Archie sniffed at Riley's shoes, then up his trouser leg. But he didn't alert. The K9 turned and trotted past the cop to his squad.

A flash of resignation filled Riley's eyes as he watched the K9 work. Trevor knew this wasn't the first time the cop had seen their K9s in action. All the Cody cops had watched the K9s in action at some point in time.

Something Riley should have considered before getting involved in something illegal. Like kidnapping Bailey from the police station.

The driver's side door of the police cruiser was still open from when Riley had gotten out to approach them. Without hesitation, Archie jumped inside. The cage would prevent Archie from getting into the back seat, but Trevor had faith in his K9. He didn't have to wait long. A minute later, Archie let out a sharp bark.

His alert!

"Bailey was in there. Probably in the back seat, right?" He narrowed his gaze on the young police officer. "It's over. We know you took Bailey from the police station and transported her here in your squad. Archie just proved it. Now tell us where she is! Did you leave her at the house? Huh? Tell us!"

Riley dropped his gaze to the ground. Then he slowly shook his head. "I know my rights. If you're going to accuse me of kidnapping, I want a lawyer."

No! Trevor ran forward grabbed the officer's jacket and shook him. To his surprise, Riley didn't resist. "Tell me where Bailey is!"

"Easy," Howell warned. The sergeant approached warily, reaching out to tug Trevor away from the cop. He reluctantly released him, doing his best to rein in his temper. "He's right, Riley. You'd better start talking," Howell advised. "If you're involved, you're in way over your head. We already know about the money laundering scheme involving the pub. Trust me, this won't end well for you."

Riley barked out a laugh. It was all Trevor could do not to step forward to grab him again. They didn't have time for this. They needed to move. He wondered how quickly Griff would get there.

Probably not soon enough.

"Fine," Riley said. "I'll talk, but only if I'm granted full immunity."

Trevor forced himself to remain calm, allowing his anger to cool. He needed Riley to cooperate. "Great. Start talking."

"Hold on a minute." Howell raised a hand. "I need the DA's approval to make a deal."

Trevor whirled on the guy. "We don't have any time to waste! We need to find Bailey before it's too late!"

"I don't have the authority to grant him a deal!" Howell gave him an exasperated look. "It won't take long. I'll call now and . . ."

"No! There's no time!" He didn't want to hear platitudes. "I'll ask Griff to support it. He'll be here any minute. Just work with me, please." Trevor wasn't above groveling. Archie jumped down from the squad, his tail wagging. Trevor belatedly bent to lavish praise on his K9. "Good boy. Good boy, Archie." Then he turned back toward Howell. "Don't you understand? Bailey is supposed to be on bed rest. Her baby could die if we don't find her soon. Two lives are at stake here, Tom."

Howell sighed. "Okay, I'll make the deal and hope the DA goes along."

"No, I think I'll wait for the DA," Riley said. He continued standing near his cruiser, his hands up. "I'm not going to risk being tossed in jail. Do you have any idea what it's like for cops in the joint? It ain't pretty."

Trevor took a step toward him. "If she dies or her baby dies, you'll be charged as an accessory to murder. That's life without parole. Understand? You'd better start talking, right now. Before it's too late for a deal."

The young cop seemed to consider that. Then he glanced at Howell. "Make the call to the DA. But you'd better hurry. Bailey was alive a few minutes ago, but once they have what they want, I can't guarantee her safety."

"Who?" Trevor demanded. "Who has her?"

Riley didn't answer, his gaze centered on his boss. Or his soon-to-be-former boss. Riley's career as a cop was over.

How he spent the rest of his life was up to him. Trevor prayed he'd cooperate.

"If Trevor is right about Bailey's condition, we have exigent circumstances," Howell said. "I promise I'll convince the DA to go along with the deal. He'll understand time was of the essence." When the cop didn't look convinced, Howell pressed again. "Come on, work with us, Riley. Don't throw your entire life away. There's a chance you can walk away from this without jail time. But only if we find Bailey within the next few minutes."

After what felt like an eternity, Riley nodded. "Fine. I expect you to hold up your end the bargain. If they find out I talked, they'll kill me."

"Understood. We'll make sure you get protection too," Howell promised.

Riley sighed. "She's with Todd White. He works with Duncan Durango, one of the owners of Plymouth Properties. They're in Durango's truck. Todd is taking her to the house she shared with Clark."

"Why?" Howell asked. "What's at the house?"

Trevor didn't care about why, he only cared about getting there as quickly as humanly possible. "I know where they lived; it's not far from the pub. Four blocks down on Robin Street. Let's go!"

"Put your hands around your back," Howell said to Riley, pulling his handcuffs from his utility belt.

Trevor didn't want to wait for Howell to take Riley into custody. He turned toward Archie. "Let's go, boy."

"Wait," Howell protested, but Trevor ignored him.

Robin Street wasn't that far from their current location. He took off running with Archie galloping along at his side. He briefly heard Howell speaking into his radio, requesting backup to Robin Street. He found himself hoping Riley was the only bad apple in the group, but even that thought didn't make him back down.

Trevor ran with all his strength, knowing Archie would be able to keep up. Without hesitation, he cut through backyards, ignoring stares and shouts as one neighbor protested. He was determined to take the most direct route to Robin Street as possible. He was beyond desperate to reach Bailey.

Silently praying he wasn't too late.

15

Bailey stood in the backyard of the house she'd once shared with Clark, shivering in the cold. The new owners were apparently not home. Or if they were, they didn't notice or object to Todd White digging in the hard dirt under the oak tree.

White cursed under his breath as he used all his weight to dig into the partially frozen ground. The cloudy sky cast a gloom over the area. While Todd was preoccupied with his task, she took one small step backward. Then another. She didn't move too much, as she didn't want to draw his attention.

He'd stuck the gun in his pocket in order to free up his hands to dig. She could try to make a run for it, but being seven months pregnant, she wasn't sure she'd get far enough to avoid being shot in the back.

Standing there doing nothing, though, wasn't working for her either. There had to be a way to escape. Glancing around, she didn't see anyone watching them. It was as if a man digging in the yard happened every day.

She eased back another step, angling her path so she was behind him more than beside him.

"If I had known he'd buried the cash weeks ago, I'd already have the money," Todd muttered harshly as he jabbed the tip of the spade shovel into the earth. "Stupid jerk should have kept his greedy paws to himself."

Wasn't Todd just as greedy? It didn't matter because she was unable to force words through her frozen throat. He had kept her alive this long only to make sure the money was where she'd said it was.

The moment he'd unearthed whatever Clark had buried in the ground, her usefulness was over.

Another shiver coursed through her. Fear or cold or something else, she didn't know. Taking another small step backward, she cast a quick glance over her shoulder, gauging the distance.

Maybe if she managed to reach the front of the house, she would be able to flag someone down for help. Before getting shot? Swallowing hard, she tried not to envision being struck by a bullet. Worse, her baby dying in her womb.

Lord Jesus, help me! Save me and my baby!

The tip of Todd's shovel hit something metallic. She froze in the act of taking another step back. Until that moment, she'd been worried her husband had found a dead cat. Now she knew otherwise. Yet Todd didn't so much as glance at her. All his attention was focused on the buried cash.

He dropped to his knees, using the shovel to dig around the metallic box with fervor. This was it. She'd have to make her move now or never.

Moving slow, she turned. Hearing nothing from Todd, she broke into a run. *So much for bed rest*, she thought, sprinting around to the front of the house. Waving her arms wildly, she glanced around for help.

But she saw no one.

It was too late to turn back. She continued pushing forward, listening for the sound of Todd following her. Then she noticed someone running toward her from between two houses across the street.

"Help!" She waved her arms. "Help me!"

Then she saw Archie's reddish coat and realized the man was Trevor. Relief washed over her, yet she knew they weren't out of the woods yet.

"He—has a—gun!" The words came out between gasping breaths. She'd never been one to go jogging even before she'd gotten pregnant. Running at this point in her pregnancy was no easy task. She felt and probably looked like an elephant swaying from side to side as she put on a burst of speed to close the gap.

"Get down!" Trevor reached out to grab her arm, pulling her to the ground just as a crack of gunfire rang out. She ducked, her breath heaving in and out of her lungs as she glanced over her shoulder.

Todd stood there with a box tucked under his arm. He fired again, then ran toward the black truck.

"Archie, stay! Guard!" Trevor darted forward, clearly intending to reach the truck before Todd did. "Stop!"

Todd didn't stop. He turned and brought his weapon up. Trevor leaped forward, knocking his arm upward just as he pulled the trigger.

Bailey's heart practically stopped in her chest, but then blue and red lights lit up the sky. The police were on the way. Or at least, she hoped they were the real police and not Officer Riley. She fumbled in her purse for the disposable phone, watching in horror as Todd and Trevor fell against the side of the pickup, struggling for control over the weapon. The box Todd had carried hit the ground with a distinct thud.

Before she found her phone, the squad pulled up. She held her breath until she saw the officer was an older guy, not Riley. He joined the fray, grabbing the weapon from Todd's hand and tossing it away.

When Todd realized he was busted, he let out a scream of frustration.

"I'm only taking back what's ours!" he shouted.

"Todd White, you're under arrest for kidnapping and attempted murder, and that's just for starters." The burly cop slapped handcuffs around Todd's wrists. Trevor took a few steps backward, glaring at Todd.

She bowed her head, looping her arm over Archie. It was over. Then a wave of nausea hit hard.

Nope, it wasn't over. Not completely. She closed her eyes, willing the nausea to go away. But it only got worse. Along with the intense pounding in her temples.

Her blood pressure was likely sky high. She pressed her face against Archie's soft fur, fighting to relax.

"Bailey? What's wrong?" Trevor rested his hand on her shoulder. "Are you hurt?"

"Sick," she whispered. "My blood pressure . . ."

"Burt!" Trevor called. "We need to get Bailey to the hospital ASAP!"

"I can't. I have White tucked in the back seat. Hold on, I'll call for assistance."

Taking a slow, deep breath, she lifted her head to see the burly officer speaking into his radio, requesting an ambulance.

Trevor knelt beside her, his expression etched with concern. "What can I do?"

"Nothing." Tears pricked her eyes as she imagined needing to deliver her baby early. Her tiny daughter maybe even needing to be put on a ventilator. "Maybe you could pray for me? For us?"

"Lord Jesus, please hold Bailey and her baby in Your loving arms," Trevor whispered. "Continue to keep them safe in Your care. Amen."

"Amen." She swallowed against the need to throw up, wondering how long it would take the ambulance to get there.

Red flashing lights raced toward them. Grateful, she stayed put, sitting on the cold hard earth next to Archie. The dog licked her cheek, making her smile.

The burly cop gestured the EMTs toward her. They hauled a gurney out of the back of the ambulance and ran toward her.

"Hey, Trevor," the male EMT greeted him by name. "What's going on?"

"This is Bailey Adams. She's seven months pregnant and has been diagnosed with preeclampsia," Trevor informed them. "We believe her blood pressure has spiked and would like her transported to the hospital right away."

"Understood," the female EMT said. "Ms. Adams, can you get up on the gurney? Or would you like us to carry you?"

"I can do it." Standing and walking wasn't going to make her condition any worse. Bailey was determined to get to the gurney, but Trevor slid his arm around her waist, helping her to her feet. Then he swung her up into his arms and carried her to the gurney, gently easing her down. She managed a grateful smile. "Thanks."

"Archie and I are riding along," Trevor's voice was firm. "We know how to stay out of the way."

She noticed the two EMTs glanced at each other. The female looked as if she wanted to argue, but the tall man nodded. "Trevor is an EMT. He'll be fine."

"Okay, then I'll drive." The woman didn't look happy but didn't argue. "Let's get her inside."

Bailey allowed them to strap her onto the gurney, staring up at the cloudy sky as they wheeled her across the snow-covered ground to the ambulance. Turning her head, she caught a glimpse of Todd White scowling at her from the back of the squad.

The threat of being shot was over. She couldn't deny being relieved Todd had been caught and arrested. She rested her hand on her belly.

Too bad the worst danger wasn't over. Her mad dash for safety had brought another threat.

And all she could do now was try to relax and pray.

TREVOR CLIMBED into the back of the ambulance. "Come, Archie."

His K9 didn't hesitate to jump up. He drew Archie out of the way, watching with a sense of doom as his former EMT colleague, Jimmy Knapp, took Bailey's blood pressure. Up front, the female EMT he didn't know slid in behind the wheel, started the engine, and pulled away from the side of the road. The hospital wasn't too far, but it was clear Bailey's blood pressure was sky high. So much for the new medication helping to keep her under control.

Granted, being kidnapped at gunpoint wasn't exactly helpful. He'd failed to keep Bailey safe, much less on bed rest. He swallowed hard as he reviewed the high numbers on the screen. If her pressures remained this high, he felt certain they'd induce labor. Even if her baby was only a little over thirty weeks gestation.

If only he could have gotten there sooner. Maybe she wouldn't have had to run for her life, putting her baby in jeopardy.

Curling his fingers into fists, he strove to remain calm. He reminded himself that Bailey would soon be in good hands back at the emergency department. And that those jerks Todd White and Jeff Riley would never hurt her again.

Disheartening to realize the danger was related to money. He and his siblings were blessed to have the trust their parents had set up for them, but they didn't use it for anything beyond their regular living expenses. That and running the ranch, which was no small task caring for eleven dogs and four horses. Their last veterinary bill had been two thousand dollars.

Yet even back when he'd thought they were broke, Trevor had never been tempted to go for easy money. Part of that was his faith. The other part was his older siblings would have slapped him upside the head if he'd gone down that path.

"Still high," Jimmy murmured. "Slightly better, but still too high."

"I'm sure it will come down soon," Bailey said.

Trevor forced a reassuring smile. "Of course it will. Especially now that you're safe."

She held his gaze for a long moment. "If anything happens to me, I want your family to raise my daughter."

Her plea knocked him off balance. Why not her brother, Miles? Because he was currently in Alaska? Maybe she didn't think her brother was capable of raising a child on his own, especially a newborn.

"Of course. Don't worry about that. You're going

to be fine." He didn't even want to imagine a world that didn't have Bailey in it. Not that he was in control. All he could do was to lift Bailey and her baby in prayer.

"Promise me . . ." She closed her eyes and turned away. He glanced at the portable monitor above her head, noting her blood pressure had dropped about ten points.

Not enough. He couldn't tear his gaze away. Her blood pressure hadn't dropped low enough to get her out of the danger zone.

The rig slowed and swayed slightly as they pulled into the hospital ambulance bay. Within seconds, Jimmy had pushed the doors open and was getting Bailey disconnected from the monitors. Trevor would have helped, but the female EMT had already joined them. He held on to Archie, staying out of the way until they had pulled Bailey from the rig.

When he jumped down, giving Archie the hand gesture for come, he heard his name. "Trevor? How is she?"

Turning, he saw his brother-in-law Griff striding toward him. He wasn't sure how Griff had known where to find him, but having family there brought a sense of relief. "Not great. Her blood pressure is too high."

"Hey, she's going to get through this." Griff gave him a one-armed brotherly hug.

"I pray you're right." He glanced over to where the EMTs had disappeared with Bailey. She was in God's hands and those of the talented medical staff now. "Todd White is the one who tried to shoot Bailey and likely the one who ran her off the road." He winced. "I should have had Archie search for shell casings. We could match them to the ones you sent to the lab."

"Funny you mention that; Kendra is at the scene with her K9, Smoky, now." At his arched look, Griff sighed. "Hey, I tried to get her to stay at the ranch, but she insisted. I wanted to interview you and Bailey before heading the police station."

"You may have to wait on Bailey's statement, but I'll tell you what little I know." Trevor quickly filled Griff in on his taking shortcuts through town to reach Bailey. "She managed to get away from White. I couldn't believe it when she ran toward me. He fired at us but thankfully missed."

"Attempted murder for sure," Griff muttered darkly. "Has she told you anything more?"

"Not yet." He hadn't even thought of questioning her. "She was already in distress by the time I was finished disarming White."

"Okay, then, I'll hold off for now." Griff clapped him on the shoulder. "You did good getting there so fast. Next time, you might want to wait for backup. Sounds to me like the guys at Plymouth Properties don't mess around. The FBI is officially taking over this case."

Waiting for backup wasn't an option, but he kept his thoughts to himself. Risking his life hadn't mattered as much as getting to Bailey's side. "I'd like to check on her. Tell Kendra I'll see her later."

"Will do." Griff stepped back. "I'll pray for Bailey."

He nodded, giving him a look of gratitude. "Thanks. Come, Archie."

When he entered the emergency department, he found Bailey's room without difficulty. There were three staff members around her bed, new faces as the night shift had left hours ago. He hovered in the doorway, not wanting to interrupt but listening in.

"Okay, her blood pressure seems to be coming down." The man who spoke stood off to the side, clearly the doctor in charge. His name tag identified him as Dr. Swanson. "The OB will be here soon."

The news was somewhat reassuring. Trevor stepped out of the way so the doctor could leave. Then he slid into the room, Archie at his heel.

He raked a gaze over Bailey, deciding she looked better. Calmer and more relaxed. Maybe the news of her improved blood pressure gave her a sense of peace.

"Excuse me." One of the nurses moved past him. He approached the empty side of the bed and reached for Bailey's hand.

"Trevor." She smiled. "Thanks for everything."

"Of course." He leaned over to brush a kiss on her forehead. "I'm glad to see your blood pressure has improved since the ambulance ride over here."

"That was stressful," she admitted. "My OB doctor, Dr. Collins, will be here soon."

"I'm glad." He used his foot to hook the chair closer. Then when he caught her gaze on Archie, he bent and lifted the seventy-five-pound dog and placed him on the cot beside her. Having Archie nearby had helped earlier. Why not give him a chance to work his magic again?

"You're a good boy, Archie." She buried her fingers in his fur. "I wouldn't be here if not for you. Both of you," she added. "The moment I saw Todd White, some of my memories returned." She frowned. "Not everything, but some things."

He tensed. "So you remember our friendship?"

"Yes. But even more so I remember how I was planning to divorce Clark before he died." Her gaze held reproach. "You said I was happily married, but that wasn't true."

The news shocked him. "I had no idea things weren't good between you."

She grimaced. "Probably because I didn't tell

you. Or my brother. I knew something was going on with him, but I never expected all of this." She sighed. "He wasn't the man I thought he was. He didn't even seem to notice me half the time; everything was about the stupid pub. Then Clark was killed. And I discovered I was pregnant."

He cradled her hand in his. "I shouldn't say this, but I never liked Clark."

A smile tugged at the corner of her mouth. "I could tell. He wasn't terrible, though. He didn't hit me or anything. Although he did steal from his employer, putting me in danger."

"He wasn't good enough for you." Trevor hesitated, then added, "I've always cared about you, Bailey. Despite the fact that Miles told me you were off-limits."

Her eyes flashed. "Miles had no right to say that."

He shrugged. "He was wrong to say that. Because these past few days have only made me care about you more." He didn't want to press; she'd been through a lot and didn't even have her full memory back. "I plan to stick around for as long as you'll have me."

"You don't need to do that," she protested.

"I want to stay." He searched her gaze, trying to gauge her reaction. "Unless my being here makes you uncomfortable."

"No, of course not. It's just . . ." She flushed and looked away. "I'm pregnant. You couldn't possibly be interested in me."

"You're wrong, Bailey. I've always been interested in you." He flashed a crooked smile. "You're beautiful, smart, and amazing. But I understand you have bigger problems on your mind right now. Your baby must come first."

"Oh, Trevor." Her eyes were bright with unshed tears. "You have no idea how long I had a crush on you. But you always kept your distance, as if you weren't interested."

He was glad Miles was in Alaska and couldn't interfere. "I kept my distance because of your brother. And then because you got engaged to Clark."

"Miles needs to mind his own business." She scowled. "He liked Clark, said he'd have enough money to take care of me, and look how that worked out?"

"Easy, don't get upset." He eyed the monitor over her head. "We can talk this through later. For now, let's just make sure your blood pressure stays low."

"I care about you, Trevor." She tightened her grip on his hand. "Will you please kiss me?"

"Uh, sure." He bent to kiss her cheek, but she turned so that his lips landed on hers. Tiny sparks of desire flashed in his eyes as he deepened their kiss. When the overhead monitor beeped, he broke away, the tips of his ears turning red when the nurse ran into the room.

"What's going on?" The nurse eyed them suspiciously. "Your pulse jumped up."

"My fault." He hoped she hadn't seen their kiss. "I, uh, it won't happen again."

"I hope that's not true," Bailey murmured after the nurse left. "Because I want nothing more than to kiss you again."

"Bailey." He sighed, shaking his head. "We need to keep your pulse and blood pressure under control."

"Okay, but, Trevor? If we had kissed before I met Clark, I can promise you I'd never have married him." Her solemn gaze held his. "I hate to admit I didn't love him the way I should have. If I'd have known . . ."

Her admission touched a chord deep in his heart. He smiled gently. "It's okay, Bailey. There's nothing to be ashamed of. You are going to have a beautiful baby girl that we will both lavish with love. This was God's plan for you, so don't look backward. Let's just focus on the future."

"God's plan." She nodded thoughtfully. "I learned a lot about faith and prayer from you, Trevor. I remember now I didn't pray regularly before this. I hope you continue to teach me how to be a good Christian like you and your family."

"Absolutely." He bent to brush a chaste kiss on her cheek.

"I have a favor to ask," she said after a moment.

"Of course. What do you need?"

She gnawed on her lower lip for a moment, then asked, "If I get discharged from the hospital again, is it okay if we head to your ranch? I don't want to go home just yet."

He couldn't help but grin. "I'd love nothing more than to take you home with me. Like I said, we have plenty of room. And lots of people to help keep an eye on you."

A knock at the door had him turning to see a female doctor entering Bailey's room. "Hi, Bailey." She greeted her warmly. "I heard you've been having some blood pressure problems."

"Dr. Collins, I'm glad to see you." Bailey didn't release his hand, causing the doctor to eye him curiously. "This is Trevor Sullivan and his K9, Archie. I—we . . ." Her voice trailed off.

"We're together," he quickly interjected. "I love her, and I want to be there for her throughout the rest of her pregnancy."

"I love him too," Bailey said. "And I want him to be my partner through this."

"That sounds great." Dr. Collins didn't seem the

least bit fazed by their announcement. "I'm glad you have someone to support you through this, Bailey. Now, let's check your blood pressure again and then listen to your baby's heartbeat."

Trevor stayed at Bailey's side while the OB doctor performed her exam. When Dr. Collins finished, she nodded thoughtfully. "I think your blood pressure is under control for now, but I'm concerned that this is your second visit in a matter of hours."

"I was in danger and had to run away from a bad guy." Bailey glanced at him. "Trevor and Archie saved me. I'm sure that's the reason my blood pressure went crazy high."

"Danger?" Dr. Collins's gaze narrowed on him. "Will she have protection moving forward?"

"We caught the gunman, so there's no need to worry on that front. If you think she's stable enough to be on bed rest at home, then I'll take her to my family's ranch where we can ensure her safety. We'll make sure she stays on bed rest." He paused, then added, "If you think Bailey needs to stay here, that's fine too. Whatever you deem best."

"Hmm." Dr. Collins looked reassured at the thought of Bailey being safe from harm. "We'll watch her here for a few more hours. If all goes well, she can be discharged. But I want to see her twice a week moving forward. If her blood pressure continues to go up and down, then we'll need to induce labor."

Bailey's brow furrowed, but her fingers clung to his. "That's fine with me. As long as we do everything possible to protect my daughter."

"That's the plan." Dr. Collins patted her arm. Archie lifted his head and thumped his tail on the mattress of the gurney. "Sounds like you have a lot of protection around you now."

"I do." Bailey's smile warmed Trevor's heart. "The best protection ever."

When the doctor left the room, he sank into the chair at her side. "Rest now," he said softly. "Archie and I will be here when you wake up."

"I love you, Trevor," Bailey whispered.

"I love you too." He stayed until her eyes slid closed, succumbing to exhaustion. He raised his head to look up at the ceiling, silently thanking God for bringing him into Bailey's life when she needed him the most.

EPILOGUE

F*our weeks later...*

Bailey shifted in the uncomfortable hospital bed. After spending an amazing Thanksgiving with Trevor and his family, she'd followed up with Dr. Collins for her semiweekly visit. Her blood pressure had started to rise again, despite being on bed rest, so Dr. Collins had insisted she be admitted to the hospital.

Her baby girl would be born six weeks early at thirty-four weeks gestation.

It wasn't easy not to panic at knowing she'd be delivering a preemie. The truth was that despite the loving attention she'd received from Trevor and his family, especially Kendra, she hadn't felt great. She was so in tune to her body that she'd been able to figure out when her blood pressure was rising. Even while sitting in bed doing nothing, it would sometimes spike too high.

If delivering a preemie was the best course of action, then she would place Naomi's future into God's capable hands.

Griff had kept her and Trevor up to date on the investigation into the Plymouth Properties organization. Todd White had agreed to testify against his boss for a lighter sentence after Jeff Riley had given up as much information as he knew. Riley wouldn't do jail time, but he was stripped of his badge and had been relocated to Florida under a different name. She didn't begrudge Jeff the chance to start over, even though she would have preferred he hadn't kidnapped her in the first place.

Griff and his FBI colleagues had raided the Sweet Water Pub and Grill, grabbing the books and the cash stored on the premises. A similar raid had taken place at the other restaurants owned by Plymouth Properties too. The Sweet Water Pub was closed now, likely permanently.

"Hey, there're my girls." Trevor beamed when he entered the hospital room. He kissed her, then kissed her belly. "I got here as fast as I could."

"Where's Archie?" She had gotten used to having the K9 at her side. In her opinion, he was a better therapy dog than a tracking K9.

"Kendra has him." He arched a brow. "Dr.

Collins mentioned you might need a C-section as they don't want you enduring a long labor with your blood pressure so unpredictable. I doubt they'll let him come into the operating room with us."

"Yeah, I know." She tried to hide her nervousness. "It's fine. I'm going to be fine. Everything is going to be fine."

"Bailey." He clasped her hands in his and kissed her again. "Please don't worry. You've got this. Naomi is going to do great. She's four and a half pounds now. Remember what Dr. Collins said? The same thing the ER doc told you the first time you were diagnosed. Babies under stress develop faster. Especially their lungs."

"I remember." Her memories had returned over the past few weeks. Probably because she'd gotten plenty of rest, and there had been no reason to press the issue. Being with Trevor was a blessing. She couldn't imagine how she'd have managed without him.

"I love you." The words came easily now that they'd spent the past four weeks together. "I'm glad you're here with me."

"I love you too." He glanced at the clock. "What time did Dr. Collins say she'd be in?"

"An hour or so." She shifted on the bed again. "Why?"

"That means there's time for this." He pulled out

a ring box. "I spoke with Miles. He was not happy at first, but I told him nobody would love you more than I do. He finally agreed and gave us his blessing." He held her gaze. "Bailey, will you marry me?"

"Oh, Trevor." Her eyes pricked with tears. Not just because of her hormones. She was still mad at her brother, even though Miles had explained he'd thought Clark would provide financial stability for her. She didn't appreciate his influence. But life was short, and she wasn't going to waste another second of it on regrets. "Yes, Trevor. I'd be honored to marry you."

He grinned and slid the ring onto her finger. Then he kissed her again. "I wish we could have been married before Naomi's birth, but bed rest and weddings don't exactly go together."

"We can get married whenever you like." She blew out a slow breath when she felt her blood pressure rising. "Naomi will know she's loved by her parents. By us, Trevor. And her new extended family."

"She will," he agreed. Then he grinned again. "Maya said it's not fair that you get to deliver Naomi before she has her baby."

That made her laugh. "I wish it wasn't necessary, but our baby girl is in God's hands now."

"Good afternoon." Dr. Collins breezed into the room. "Are you ready to get started?"

She clung to Trevor's hand. "Yes."

The next few hours were difficult. After a failed attempt at labor, Dr. Collins prepped her for a C-section. Bailey was given a spinal anesthetic so she could be awake, and when Naomi was born, the baby wailed loud enough to make Bailey cry too.

Naomi's lungs sounded fairly well developed, and she was humbly grateful.

"Four pounds six ounces and eighteen inches long," Dr. Collins announced after an all too brief skin-to-skin contact. "She's going to do just fine."

Watching as Trevor gazed at Naomi with love, she knew that was true. They were now a family in every way that mattered.

I HOPE you enjoyed Trevor and Bailey's story. I hope you'll stick with me for the last book in the series. If you're ready to read Kendra and Dominic's story in *Scent of Murder*, click here!

DEAR READER

Thanks for reading *Scent of Terror*! I hope you enjoyed Trevor and Bailey's story. I'm having so much fun writing about the Sullivan family, and I'm sad that I only have one more book to write in the series. I hope you stick with me through the end of the series!

Don't forget, you can purchase ebooks or audiobooks directly from my website and will receive a 15% discount by using the code **LauraScott15**.

I adore hearing from my readers! I can be found through my website at https://www.laurascottbook s.com, via Facebook at https://www.facebook.com/ LauraScottBooks, Instagram at https://www.insta gram.com/laurascottbooks/, and Twitter https://twit ter.com/laurascottbooks. Please take a moment to subscribe to my YouTube channel at youtube.-

com/@LauraScottBooks-wr1xl?sub_confirmation=1. Also take a moment to sign up for my monthly newsletter to learn about my new book releases! All subscribers receive a free novella not available for purchase on any platform.

Until next time,

Laura Scott

PS. Keep reading for a sneak peek of *Scent of Murder* . . .

SCENT OF MURDER

Prologue

Helen Gingrass took her dying patient's hand in hers. Stuart Ramsey was about the same age as her son, which made his imminent demise from stage four cancer difficult to bear.

"I need the chaplain." Stuart's voice was raspy. He stared up at her with eyes that weren't quite focused. "I need to confess my sins."

"The chaplain is on his way." Helen offered a reassuring smile. As a nurse for forty years, she'd heard a few confessions in her time. Mostly about infidelity.

"He needs to hurry." Stuart's eyes slid closed,

then popped open again. "I don't have much time. I can't die with this crime on my conscience."

Crime? Helen frowned. This was a first. "He's with another patient. He'll be here as soon as he can get away."

"I need to confess!" Stuart's voice held urgency. His fingers tightened on hers, and he let out a raspy cough. "I sabotaged a plane six years ago. I caused the deaths of three people. Only I didn't know there would be three people."

She was having trouble following his confession. "You didn't intend to kill anyone, right?"

He grimaced. "I was paid to kill the pilot. That's all. I took care of the plane, I used to be a mechanic, and I took care of the plane." He swallowed hard. "But I didn't know there would two other people on board." His breathing grew agitated. "I didn't know!"

"Easy, Stuart, try to relax." Helen did her best to reassure him, despite the shocking statement he'd just made. He'd purposefully sabotaged a plane to kill the pilot! She needed to call the police. Maybe even the FBI.

"I didn't know the pilot had a son. Dominic Lakeland. I ruined so many lives." He lifted his tortured gaze to hers. "I need . . . God to forgive me . . ." His voice trailed off. Then he let out another wet cough as his eyes closed. Helen frowned. She wasn't a chaplain; she wasn't sure that simply confessing his sins was good enough.

"Do you regret what you did? Do you repent your sins?" She wished the chaplain would hurry up and get there. Despite working hospice for the past year, she wasn't accustomed to taking deathbed confessions of this magnitude. And she had no idea how to guide this man spiritually. In her mind, murder was a pretty big sin.

"Yes. I needed the money . . . but I know that's not an excuse." He abruptly pulled away to rummage in the pocket of his hoodie. In hospice, patients could wear whatever made them comfortable. He pulled out something that was small and round. "Take this." He pushed it into her hand. "I don't have any family, and it's all I have left. Take it."

"Oh, I can't." Nurses weren't allowed to take money or gifts from their patients. That was against their code of ethics.

"Please, take it. Worth . . ." His voice trailed off as his breath rattled in his throat. His eyes closed.

Then he stopped breathing all together. His hand went limp, and his head lolled to the side.

Helen pulled free, staring down at the coin he'd given her. It didn't look real; it certainly wasn't any currency she recognized. It was gold in color and had the picture of a man's face on the front. Rearranging her bifocals on her nose, she could make out the words South Africa along the side. Was this a South African rand? Maybe Stuart had meant to say it was worthless. If it was worthless, it wouldn't be against the rules to take it.

Still, Helen felt uneasy as she pocketed the coin. She'd have to take it somewhere to be appraised. If it was worth money, she could take the funds and donate it to the hospice center. Satisfied with that approach, she stepped back from the bedside and made a note of the time of death.

With that task finished, she needed to call the police. And this Dominic Lakeland whose father was killed. Stuart had confessed to a crime.

Everyone, especially the man's son, needed to know the truth.

SCENT OF MURDER

Chapter One

Dominic Lakeland slowed his speed as he caught sight of the Redwood Motel. That was the place Kendra Sullivan had suggested he use while staying in Greybull. The recent news he'd learned about his father's plane crash had circled around in his brain during the long drive from Billings, Montana. What should have been a two-hour ride had turned out to be three and a half, thanks to the recent snowfall. Not only had it caused traffic to slow to a crawl, but he'd had to get out and help a stranded mother of two who'd gotten herself stuck in a high snowbank along the side of the road.

Dom wanted nothing more than to get out and

stretch his legs. Even with the large Ford, his six-foot-seven-inch frame had made him feel like a pretzel behind the wheel.

Now that he was in Wyoming, though, he was anxious to meet Kendra face-to-face. She'd reached out two months ago asking him if he knew anything about the plane crash that had killed his father, who was the pilot, and her parents, the passengers. At the time, he'd only known as much as she did. When Kendra had mentioned her sister's cadaver dog, Denali, had found skeletal remains from his father, he'd been intrigued. He and Kendra had been communicating mostly through email and text messages, along with one video computer call, when she'd encouraged him to drive down so they could discuss what might have happened. Kendra didn't believe the plane crash six years ago was an accident.

Turns out, Kendra was right. When the hospice nurse had called to let him know her patient had confessed to murdering his father, he'd been stunned. She'd called the police, too, and the very next day the Billings police had contacted him about the news. He'd asked what the plan was moving forward, but the cops had simply shrugged. The guy had confessed, and that was that. Case closed.

It wasn't case closed for him and Kendra,

though. He burned with the need to know why his dad had been killed. He and Kendra had agreed to do some digging into Stuart Ramsey to find out more. He'd agreed to drive down to Greybull, but now that he was seeing the Redwood Motel in person, he had second thoughts about the plan.

It was too late to turn back now. Glancing at the clock, he slowed and pulled into the parking lot of the motel, driving toward the back of the property. It was going on five o'clock in the afternoon. Probably too late for them to get together that evening, but they could meet for breakfast. He put the gearshift into park and sent Kendra a quick text, letting her know he'd made it to the motel. Then he killed the engine.

As he slid out from behind the wheel of his Ford truck, he caught a hint of movement from the corner of his eye. He turned to get a better look just as the sound of gunfire split the night.

What in the world? He ducked and pressed himself against the metal frame of the truck, fighting to stay calm. Fear washed over him as he crab-walked around the front of the vehicle, trying to figure out where the shooter was located. It wasn't easy to see in the dark, despite his new contact lenses. Vanity had him trading his glasses for contacts, even though he wasn't quite used to wearing them.

Another crack of gunfire had him lowering his

head even farther. His heart slammed against his sternum as adrenaline raced through his bloodstream. It didn't make any sense that someone could be gunning for him. His life was boring. Predictable. He didn't even live in Wyoming. Who was out there? A crazy hunter? Someone else? Had he interrupted some other crime in progress?

Or was this related to his father's murder? How, he wasn't sure. Even the cops had considered it case closed. He swallowed hard, realizing that staying put wasn't an option. Not if the gunman intended to keep shooting. Unless the guy had already taken off? Dom eased up to peer around the edge of his truck.

Another crack of gunfire rang out. He ducked again, blinking to clear his vision. At twenty-eight years old, he'd never once been targeted by gunfire. Would someone inside the motel call the police? Did Greybull have a police department, or would he have to wait for a sheriff's deputy to arrive?

Another bullet pinged off the hood of his truck, far too close to his head. He stifled the urge to curse. He was really starting to get ticked off. Where was this guy? And why was he shooting at him?

Since he couldn't see where the shooter was hiding, Dom quickly decided to take off. He darted into the woods, keeping his head down. The foliage provided decent cover, especially the large pine trees.

He was grateful, until he glanced back over his shoulder and realized he was leaving boot prints in the snow.

Not good. This was not good! Picking up the pace, he ran through the trees. After several yards, he made a wide circle to double back. There had to be a way to get a look at this guy who'd fired so many shots at his truck. Maybe this was a case of mistaken identity?

No, that didn't make sense. The shooter should have noticed his Montana license plates. He swallowed hard, realizing this must have been related to his father's murder. Why anyone would come after him six years after the fact, he had no idea. Especially since Stuart Ramsey had confessed to the crime.

Maybe he and Kendra were right not to consider the case closed.

Taking a quick break, he crouched behind an evergreen, straining to listen. After hearing so many gunshots, the ensuing silence was eerie. He drew in a deep breath, calming his racing heart. Had the shooter given up and left? Or had the guy headed into the woods to find him?

What if there was more than one of them? The band of fear tightened around his chest. He was about to pull out his phone to dial 911 when he heard a rustling sound.

An animal? Or human? Probably the latter. Giving up the idea of making a call, which would have given away his location, he eased farther into the woods. He glanced over his shoulder, wincing when he again saw his tracks.

They were so obvious a blind man could have followed them.

It couldn't be helped. Continuing in a half circle, he gauged where the road was located. Maybe a half mile? If he could reach the road, he knew the hardpacked snow that had been flattened by numerous tire tracks would help cover his footprints. He could take the road for a while before heading back into the woods. When he was safe, he could call 911.

Dom continued moving as swiftly as possible. Pausing near a large oak tree, he thought he saw movement. With a frown, he ducked and scanned the woods. For long moments, he didn't move, barely breathing as he watched and listened.

There! A dark shadow stepped out from behind a tree. Dom could see the guy held a handgun. Swallowing hard, he stayed put, hoping the guy would turn away.

He didn't. Instead, another crack of gunfire reverberated through the woods.

Dom spun and ran, doing a zigzag pattern from one tree to the next. His long legs worked to his advantage now, and while he'd never run for pleasure, he didn't let that slow him down.

Where were the local cops? Hadn't anyone from the motel called them?

Dom continued in the general direction of the road. After what seemed like eons, he caught a glimpse of it between a break in the trees. He slowed his pace, fearing there could be a second man out there waiting for him to emerge. Hunkering down beside a tree, he waited. Headlights indicated a car was moving down the street from the west. He waited until it had passed, then rushed out to the road.

Seeing nobody lurking nearby, he broke into a jog, running west, away from the hotel. Glancing over his shoulder, he was relieved to see his footprints weren't readily visible on the hardpacked snow. With renewed energy, he picked up his speed, putting even more distance between him and the shooter.

After traveling about a mile or so, he noticed another pair of headlights illuminating the sky behind him. The sharp curve in the road made it impossible for him to see what sort of car was approaching. Fearing the gunman had figured out his ploy, he abruptly jumped over the snowbank to get off the road, quickly diving back into the safety of the woods.

Dom kept moving, determined to stay well ahead of the gunman. When he came across a fallen log, he jumped over that, the way he'd hurdled the snowbank. Only this time, he landed at an awkward angle. His right foot slipped, and he lost his balance. Falling, the back of his head struck the fallen tree trunk.

Then there was nothing but darkness.

Kendra Sullivan frowned as she drove into the town of Greybull. Dominic Lakeland still hadn't responded to her text message. Was he ignoring her on purpose? That would be strange, since he was the one who'd texted her to say he'd arrived at the Redwood Motel.

"What do you think, Smoky?" She eyed her Alaskan malamute in the rearview mirror. "Maybe he brought his girlfriend along and is distracted by spending time alone with her?"

Smoky gave a halfhearted wag of her curved tail. Kendra grimaced and turned her attention to the road. She didn't care if Dominic brought his girlfriend along for the ride or not. She was anxious to talk to him. The news of Stuart Ramsey's confession filled her with a renewed sense of purpose. For years, she'd suspected foul play related to the deaths of her parents. Now they knew the truth. But they still didn't know why. Hopefully, she and Dominic could piece the puzzle together before Christmas.

She hadn't told her eight older siblings the recent revelation about the murder or her plan to meet Dominic. For one thing, they treated her as if she was still a kid, not a twenty-five-year-old woman. And for another, they'd take over the investigation. Maybe she was being silly, but since they hadn't taken her seriously six years ago, she was determined to uncover the truth herself.

She slowed her speed. If she remembered right, the motel was a mile past the sharp curve.

A pickup truck abruptly barreled around the hairpin curve, going much faster than the posted speed limit. Thankfully, she was hugging the right side of the street and wasn't hit. Kendra followed the dark truck with her gaze, then sighed and shook her head. Some people just didn't care about how their reckless driving impacted others.

Moments later, she saw the sign for the Redwood Motel. She slowed to pull into the parking lot, then frowned when she saw a large silver truck parked off to the side. It wasn't just the truck that drew her gaze, but the bullet hole in the rear window.

Glancing around, she didn't see any police nearby. She wasn't sure if the bullet hole had been made recently or if the owner of the truck hadn't bother to have it fixed?

That's when she noticed the Montana plates. Wait, was that Dominic's truck? She pulled up beside the vehicle, shifted into park, and killed the engine. She released the back hatch for Smoky and pushed out from behind the wheel.

"Dominic? It's Kendra. Are you out here?"

At the sound of her voice, Smoky ran over to her side. Kendra noticed there were several overlapping footprints in the snow around her feet.

"Dominic?" She scanned the area, then noticed Smoky had trotted away from her. She turned to call her K9 when the dog buried her snout in the snow, sniffing intently. Then she sat and let out a sharp bark.

Her alert! Although Kendra hadn't told her to search, the dog had found something of interest.

"What is it, girl?" Kendra hurried over. "What did you find?"

Spying the glint of brass, she bent and picked the shell casing up with her gloved hands. The Sullivan K9s mostly tracked people, but they were cross-trained to find gun powder, gun oil, and shell casings. Like this. Glancing again at the damaged truck, she wondered if the gunfire had been recent. And if so, the shell casing was evidence that would need to get to the state crime lab.

Spinning away from the truck, she dropped the shell casing into her pocket and hurried into the motel. Smoky loped at her side. A teenager sat behind the desk with AirPods in his ears, watching a movie on his phone. He didn't so much as glance up when she came inside, and she had to wave her hand in front of his screen to get his attention.

He frowned and plucked an earbud from his ear. "Yeah?"

"Did you hear gunfire?"

"No." He gave her an annoyed look. "Why?"

She barely refrained from rolling her eyes. "I'm here to see Dominic Lakeland. Is he here?"

"Nobody has checked in for the past couple of hours." The clerk glanced down at his phone, then back up at her. "Anything else?"

It was all she could do not to snatch the phone from his hands. "Will you please see if Dominic Lakeland has checked in at all today?"

Heaving a sigh, he turned and tapped keys on the computer. "Nope."

"Thanks." She turned away, her thoughts racing. Where was Dominic? The truck with the Montana plates had to be his. "Come, Smoky."

Back outside, she approached the truck. It was empty, except for an overnight case on the floor of the back seat. Seeing another bullet graze grooved into the steel of the hood, she grew more concerned.

Then she noticed the footprints heading into the woods.

Rather than following the footprints, she went back to her SUV and opened the back hatch. Filling a collapsible bowl with water, she set it down for Smoky. While the dog drank, she shouldered into her backpack. When Smoky finished with the water, she tucked the collapsible bowl into the pack, then slammed the hatch shut.

"Here, Smoky." She crossed to the truck and wrenched open the driver's side door. "This is Dominic." She patted the driver's seat. "Dominic. Are you ready to search? Huh, girl? Search Dominic!"

Smoky loved playing the search game. Her K9 pressed her nose into the seat cushion, then sniffed along the floorboard where the gas and brake pedals were located. Shoes and socks were always good scent sources. Then Smoky lifted her snout to the air. Whirling away from the truck, her K9 bounded toward the woods, her curly tail wagging from side to side.

Kendra slammed the truck door shut and quickened her pace to keep up. Smoky bounded along the deep footprints in the snow, using her nose to follow Dominic's path. At some point, another pair of tracks crossed his, making Kendra glad she'd taken the time to provide Smoky with a scent source. The last thing she wanted to do was follow the wrong set of footprints.

Her K9 continued following Dominic's scent. The prints seemed to make a wide circle, leading back to the road. When they finally reached it, Smoky turned right and headed west, still following a scent trail only the dog could find.

"Search Dominic," she called encouragingly. The malamute was at home in the wintery weather. Her thick fluffy coat kept her warm. "Search!"

Smoky trotted down the road. They walked for over a mile or so when her K9 slowed to a stop, sniffing intently at the north side of the street. Then Smoky sat and let out a sharp bark.

"Good girl!" Kendra didn't pull the stuffed hippo from her backpack. "Good girl, Smoky. Search! Search Dominic!"

The dog stared at her for a moment, as if disappointed not to be rewarded, then jumped up to continue. Rather than continuing down the road, the dog turned to head into the woods.

Once again, Kendra saw familiar boot prints in the snow. She tried to imagine why Dominic had come this way. Had the gunman pursued him through the woods? And if so, why had that person taken shots at him in the first place?

Was this related to their parents' murder? She couldn't see a connection, but then again, it seemed like a strange coincidence if the recent danger wasn't related to the past.

Troubled, she continued following Smoky through the woods. Had Dominic been followed all the way from Billings? Could Dominic be involved in something else? She had not met him in person, although their last conversation had been a face-to-face video call. Dominic was a couple of years older than she was and had short blond hair. He was tall and thin, mentioning wryly that his nickname as a kid had been bean pole.

He seemed nice enough. But now that she was tracking him through the woods, she found herself wondering if she'd made a mistake coming here. Her oldest brother, Chase, would be angry to know she'd set off to meet with a man she didn't know. Especially the son of the man who'd been murdered, taking their parents down with him.

Smoky sniffed at the base of a tree, then continued moving deeper into the forest. Kendra glanced at her compass, making a mental note of the coordinates. She'd need to make sure she could find her way out of here when she'd found Dominic.

Had he gotten lost? It was easy to get turned around in the forest, especially at night. Not that the hour was that late, only 5:45 in the evening.

Smoky put on a burst of speed, running toward a fallen tree. Her K9 gracefully leaped over the dead tree, landing nimbly on the other side. She lost sight of the dog but heard the sharp bark of her alert.

"What is it, girl? What did you find?" Kendra hurried forward, breathing heavily.

"You're a pretty dog," a low husky voice said.

She slowed her pace, approaching with caution. She had a handgun in her backpack; they were always armed on SAR missions, mostly due to the threat of wildlife. But there were times where human threats were a problem too. She should have taken the time to slip the .38 into her coat pocket. Taking a few steps closer, she frowned when she saw a man sitting on the ground, his back up against the downed tree.

"Dominic? Dominic Lakeland?" She climbed over the horizontal tree trunk, eyeing him warily. Peering through the darkness, she could tell he appeared to be the same man she'd chatted with via the computer. "What happened? Are you okay?"

"Other than being a klutz, yeah. I'm fine." He put a hand to his head, then pushed himself upward. Moving slowly, he turned to face her. "Hey, Kendra. Nice to meet you in person, although I'm sorry it's under these circumstances. Oh, and call me Dom."

"What happened?" She shrugged out of the backpack and found the stuffed hippo. She tossed it into the air for Smoky, who leaped joyously up to grab it. Her dog loved that goofy hippo, and the K9 proceeded to prance around with the toy in her mouth.

"I slipped and hit my head on the tree trunk." He looked embarrassed as he palpated the back of his head. "I don't think the skin is broken. Thankfully, I have a hard head. I was sitting there, getting ready to head back to the motel, when your dog leaped down beside me. I recognized Smoky from our screen meeting."

"I meant what happened that you're way out here?" Kendra tipped her head to the side, regarding him thoughtfully. Seeing him on the computer screen hadn't prepared her for just how tall he was. Easily six and a half feet, maybe more. Taller than any of her six older brothers, which was saying something. "I went to the motel and found your bullet-ridden truck. I checked with the kid behind the desk, he was watching some movie on his phone with earbuds in, but he said you hadn't checked in. I sent Smoky out to follow your scent trail. You're fortunate she was able to find you."

"I know you mentioned your K9s do search and rescue, but seeing her in action is amazing." He grimaced. "Sorry to cause trouble. When the bullets started flying, I headed into the woods. When the gunman followed, I decided to double back to the road to avoid leaving footprints in the snow. I feared that was making it too easy for him to find me."

"Okay, but why is someone shooting at you in the first place?" She gave him a stern look. "What's going on?"

"How should I know?" He frowned. "I was heading into the motel when I saw movement. Suddenly gunfire rings out, forcing me into ducking and running for cover. I'm not a criminal, if that's what you're asking. I assume this is related to our parents in some way."

Kendra hesitated, wondering how much she should trust him. Just because they'd texted and emailed and even met on a computer call didn't mean she knew Dom on a personal level. Granted, she was the one who'd reached out to him the moment she'd realized his father, Gary Lakeland, was the pilot of the charter plane her parents were in when it crashed six years ago.

Then he'd called her with the news of Stuart Ramsey's confession. From there, they'd agreed to this meeting.

"If you're in some kind of trouble, Dom, you may as well tell me. I have family members in law enforcement, and I'm sure they could work something out to help you."

"Me? I didn't do anything other than head here to talk to you." Annoyance flashed in his eyes. "You're the one who suggested I stay at the Redwood Motel, remember? You're the one who wanted to meet in person to dig into why Stuart Ramsey had been paid to kill my father."

She sighed. He was right. She had been the one to recommend Greybull, the Redwood Motel, and meeting in person to dig into the six-year-old crime. Her last SAR mission had been in Greybull, involving a lost woman so it seemed appropriate to meet there. "Were you followed from Billings?"

"Not that I noticed." He sighed. "I helped a young mother with two small kids get her SUV out of a snowbank about ten miles outside of Billings. I think I'd have noticed if someone had pulled over and waited for me to hit the road again to follow me here."

The nice gesture on his part, helping a young mother of two kids made her feel a little better about him. Yet the gunfire at the motel was unnerving. So much so that she knew they couldn't stay there moving forward.

With a sigh, she turned to Smoky. "Here, girl. Hand."

Her K9 trotted forward and dropped the stuffed hippo into the palm of her hand.

"Good girl." She tucked it away, then turned to Dominic. "Let's get out of here."

"I'm in agreement with that plan." He brushed the snow from his clothes, then carefully stepped over the fallen log. She did the same, giving Smoky the hand signal to come. He glanced at her as they retraced their steps. "Thanks for coming out to find me."

"That's what we do." She waved a gloved hand at their surroundings. "I've done searches like this dozens of times over the past few years."

Dom hunched his shoulders. "I feel like an idiot you had to find me. I don't suppose you saw anyone hanging around the motel? Anyone who might be the shooter?"

She thought about the dark truck that had careened around the hairpin curve in the road, nearly striking her SUV. Was the man driving the truck the same gunman who'd tracked Dominic through woods?

And if so, why? Why would anyone want Dominic dead six years after his father's murder?